"I want you more than I've ever wanted a woman in my life,"

Chase whispered, his voice husky, his breath warm and moist against her lips. "You want me, too, don't you?"

Letty longed to deny it, but she couldn't.

"Don't you?" he demanded.

Her lips parted, but something deep inside her refused to acknowledge the truth. He didn't trust her—hadn't he told her so himself? And desire shouldn't be confused with love—at least not between them.

"Don't you?" he demanded again, his hands harsh and possessive on her, his eyes sharp and insistent.

Knowing he wouldn't free her until she gave him an answer, Letty nodded once, abruptly.

The instant she did, he released her. "That's all I wanted to know."

And with that, he turned and walked away.

Dear Reader,

Welcome to the Silhouette **Special Edition** experience! With your search for consistently satisfying reading in mind, every month the authors and editors of Silhouette **Special Edition** aim to offer you a stimulating blend of deep emotions and high romance.

The name Silhouette **Special Edition** and the distinctive arch on the cover represent a commitment—a commitment to bring you six sensitive, substantial novels each month. In the pages of a Silhouette **Special Edition**, compelling true-to-life characters face riveting emotional issues—and come out winners. Both celebrated authors and newcomers to the series strive for depth and dimension, vividness and warmth, in writing these stories of living and loving in today's world.

The result, we hope, is romance you can believe in. Deeply emotional, richly romantic, infinitely rewarding—that's the Silhouette **Special Edition** experience. Come share it with us—six times a month!

From all the authors and editors of Silhouette **Special Edition**,

Best wishes,

Leslie Kazanjian
Senior Editor

DEBBIE MACOMBER

Denim and Diamonds

Published by Silhouette Books New York

America's Publisher of Contemporary Romance

To Karen Macomber,
sister, dear friend and downtown Seattle explorer

SILHOUETTE BOOKS
300 East 42nd St., New York, N.Y. 10017

ISBN: 0-373-09570-8

First Silhouette Books printing December 1989

Printed in the U.S.A.

Books by Debbie Macomber

Silhouette Romance

That Wintry Feeling #316
Promise Me Forever #341
Adam's Image #349
The Trouble with Caasi #379
A Friend or Two #392
Christmas Masquerade #405
Shadow Chasing #415
Yesterday's Hero #426
Laughter in the Rain #437
Jury of His Peers #449
Yesterday Once More #461
Friends—And Then Some #474
Sugar and Spice #494
No Competition #512
Love 'n' Marriage #522
Mail-Order Bride #539
**Cindy and the Prince* #555
**Some Kind of Wonderful* #567
**Almost Paradise* #579
Any Sunday #603
Almost an Angel #629
The Way to a Man's Heart #671

*Legendary Lovers trilogy

Silhouette Special Edition

Starlight #128
Borrowed Dreams #241
Reflections of Yesterday #284
White Lace and Promises #322
All Things Considered #392
The Playboy and the Widow #482
Navy Wife #494
Navy Blues #518
For All My Tomorrows #530
Denim and Diamonds #570

Silhouette Christmas Stories 1986

"Let It Snow"

DEBBIE MACOMBER

hails from the state of Washington. As a busy wife and mother of four, she strives to keep her family healthy and happy. As the prolific author of dozens of best-selling romance novels, she strives to keep her readers happy with each new book she writes.

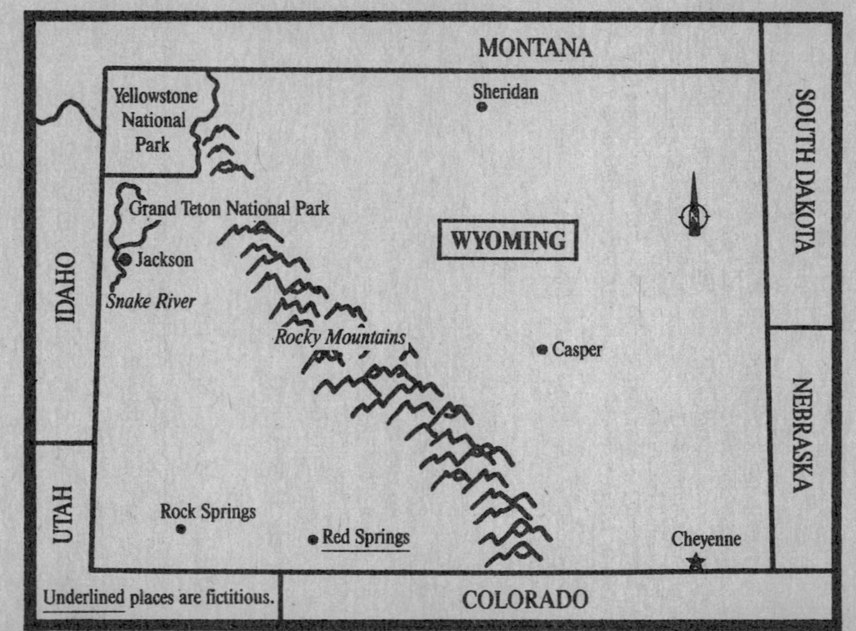
MONTANA
SOUTH DAKOTA
NEBRASKA
COLORADO
UTAH
IDAHO
Yellowstone National Park
Sheridan
Grand Teton National Park
WYOMING
Jackson
Snake River
Rocky Mountains
Casper
Rock Springs
Red Springs
Cheyenne
Underlined places are fictitious.

Prologue

Dusk had settled over the cold, harsh winter day in Red Springs, Wyoming. Chase Brown felt the chill of the north wind all the way through his bones as he rode atop Firepower, his chestnut gelding. He'd spent the better part of the afternoon searching for three heifers who had separated from the main part of his herd. Close to dusk, he'd found the trio and bullied them back to where they belonged.

That tactic might work with a few head of witless cattle, but from experience, Chase knew it wouldn't work with Letty. Damn it all, she belonged in Wyoming. More important, she belonged with him. Four years had passed since she'd taken off for Hollywood on some fool dream of becoming a recording star. Four years! As far as Chase was concerned, that was three years too long.

Chase had loved Letty from the time she was a teenager. And she'd loved him. He couldn't have spent those lazy afternoons with her on the hillside, chewing on a blade of grass and soaking up the warmth of the sun, and not know she felt something deep and abiding for him. Letty had been innocent and Chase had sworn she would stay that way until they were married. Although God knows it had been damn difficult not to love her the way he'd dreamed. But Chase was a patient man, and he was convinced a lifetime with Letty was worth the wait.

When she'd graduated from high school, Chase had come to her with a diamond ring. He'd wanted her to share his vision of Spring Valley, bear his children to fill the emptiness that had been such a large part of his life since his father had passed away. Letty had looked up at him, tears glistening in her deep blue eyes, and whispered that she loved him more than she thought she would ever love anyone. She'd begged him to come with her to California. But Chase couldn't leave his ranch and Red Springs any more than Letty could stay. And so she'd gone after her dreams.

Letting her go had cut Chase to the quick. Everyone in Sweetwater County knew Letty Ellison was a gifted singer. Chase couldn't deny she had talent, lots of it. She'd often talked of becoming a professional singer and Chase had listened to her, but he hadn't believed she would choose that path over the one he was offering. She'd kissed him before she left, with all the sweet innocence of her youth, and pleaded with him one more time to come with her. She had some fool idea of him becoming her manager. The only thing Chase had ever wanted to manage was a few head of cattle. With ambition clouding her eyes, she'd turned away from him and headed for the city lights.

That scene had played back in Chase's mind a thousand times in the past few years. He'd known when he slipped the diamond back inside his pocket four years earlier that it would be impossible to forget her. Someday, Chase knew, she would return, and when she did, he would be waiting for her. She hadn't asked him to, but there was only one woman for him, and that was Letty Ellison.

Chase wouldn't have been able to set her free if he hadn't believed she would return to him someday. The way he figured, she would be back within a year. All he had to do was show a little patience and wait. If she hadn't found those glittering diamonds she was searching for within that time, then surely she would come home.

But four long years had slipped away and still Letty hadn't returned.

The wind picked up as Chase approached the barnyard. He paused atop the hill and noticed Letty's brother's late-model truck parked outside the barn. A rush of adrenaline shot through Chase's system, accelerating his heartbeat. Involuntarily his hands tightened on Firepower's reins. Lonny had news, news that couldn't be relayed over the telephone. Quickening Firepower's pace, Chase hurried into the yard.

"'Evening, Chase," Lonny grumbled as he climbed out of the truck.

"Lonny." He touched the brim of his hat with gloved fingers. "What brings you out?"

"It's about Letty."

The chill that had nipped at Chase earlier couldn't be compared to the biting cold that sliced through him now. He eased himself out of the saddle, anxiety making the inside of his mouth dry.

"I thought you should know," Lonny continued, looking uneasy. He picked up a bit of dirt with the pointed toe of his boot. "She phoned a couple of hours ago."

Lonny wouldn't look him in the eye, and that bothered Chase. Letty's brother had always shot from the hip.

"The best way to say this is straight out," Lonny muttered, his jaw clenched. "Letty's pregnant and the man isn't going to marry her. Apparently he's already married, and he never bothered to let her know."

A fist slammed into Chase's gut wouldn't have produced the reaction Lonny's words did. He reeled back two steps before he caught himself. The pain that seared his chest was unlike anything he'd ever known.

"What's she going to do?"

Lonny shrugged. "From what she said, she plans on keeping the baby."

"Is she coming home?"

"No."

Chase's narrowed gaze accused Lonny.

"I tried to talk some sense into her, believe me, but it didn't do a damn bit of good. She seems more determined than ever to stay in California." Lonny opened the door to his truck, looking guilty and angry all in one. "Mom and Dad raised her better than this. I thank God they're both gone. I swear it would have killed Mom."

"I appreciate you letting me know," Chase said after a lengthy pause. It took him that long to gain a grip on his swirling emotions.

"I figured you had a right to know."

Chase nodded. He stood where he was, his boots planted in the frozen dirt until Lonny drove off into the fading sunlight. Firepower craned his neck toward the barn, looking toward warmth and a well-deserved dinner of oats and alfalfa. The gelding's action unsettled

Chase. He turned, reached for the saddle horn and in one smooth movement remounted the bay.

Firepower knew Chase well, and sensing his mood, the gelding galloped in a dead run until he was foaming at the mouth. Still Chase pushed him, farther and farther for what seemed like hours, until both man and horse were panting and exhausted. When the animal stopped, Chase wasn't surprised the unplanned route had led him to the hillside where he'd spent so many pleasant afternoons with Letty. Every spare inch of his land was familiar to him, but none more than those few acres.

His chest heaving from exertion, Chase climbed off Firepower and stood at the crest of the hill, letting the wind gust against him full force. His lungs hurt and he dragged in several deep breaths, struggling to gain control of himself. Pain ribboned its way around him, choking off his breath, dominating his thoughts. But nothing helped ease the terrible ache inside him.

At last a groan worked its way through his throat, nearly strangling him. He threw back his head with an anguish so intense it couldn't be held inside any longer. The sound of his piercing shout filled the night before he buckled, fell to his knees and covered his face with both hands.

Then Chase Brown did something he hadn't done in fifteen years.

He wept.

Chapter One

Five years later

Letty Ellison felt a lot like the character E.T. with his burning desire to return home. Swallowing her pride and going back to Red Springs without having achieved her big dream was one thing. But to arrive on her brother's doorstep, gleefully throw her arms around him and then casually announce she could be dying was another.

As a matter of fact, Letty had gotten pretty philosophical about the matter of death. The hole in her heart had been small enough to go undetected most of her life, but it was there, and unless she had the necessary surgery, it was lights out, belly up, buy the farm, or whatever else people said when they were about to kick the bucket.

The physicians had made her lack of options abundantly clear years before when she was pregnant with Cricket, her daughter. If her heart defect hadn't been discovered then, and had remained undetected, her doctor had assured her she would be dead before she reached thirty.

It was downright comical when she stopped to think about their dire predictions. The medical community wouldn't guarantee her a thing when she was considering having her tonsils out several years earlier. But when it came to her heart, they were full of depressing promises.

And so Letty had come home. Home to Wyoming. Home to the Bar E Ranch. Home to face whatever lay before her. Life or death.

In her dreams, Letty had often envisioned her triumphant return to Red Springs. She saw herself riding through the center of town sitting in the back seat of a red convertible, dressed in a strapless gown, holding several bouquets of red roses. The high school band would lead the procession, playing something appropriate. Naturally the good people of Red Springs, Wyoming, would be lining Main Street, hoping to get a good look at her. Being the amiable soul she was, Letty would give out autographs and speak kindly to people she hardly remembered.

Her actual return had been quite different from what she'd always envisioned. Lonny had met her at the Rock Springs Airport when she'd arrived with Cricket on the red-eye special. It really had been good to see her elder brother. Unexpected tears had filled her eyes as they'd hugged each other. Lonny might be little more than a crusty rancher, but he was the only living relative she and Cricket had. And if anything dire were to happen to her, she hoped her brother would love and care for Cricket with the same dedication as Letty herself had.

Sunlight filtered in through the curtain, and drawing in a deep breath to calm herself, Letty sat up in bed and examined her old bedroom. So little had changed in the past nine years. The lace doily decorating the old bureau was the same one that had been there when she was growing up. The photograph of her and her pony hung on the wall. How Letty had loved old Nellie. Even her bed was covered with the same quilted spread that had been there when she was eighteen.

Nothing had changed and yet everything was different.

The innocent girl who had once slept in this room was forever gone. In her stead was one who had become disenchanted with dreams, and slightly dented by life. Letty could never go back to the guileless teen she'd once been, but she wouldn't give up the woman she had become, either.

With that thought in mind, she folded back the covers and climbed out of bed. Her first night home and she had slept like an infant. She might not be the same, but the sense of welcome she felt in this old house was a balm.

Checking in the smallest bedroom across the hall, Letty found her daughter sound asleep, her faded yellow "blankey" clutched protectively against her chest. Letty and Cricket had arrived exhausted. With little more than a hug from Lonny, she and her daughter had fallen into bed. Letty had promised Lonny they would talk later.

Dressing quickly, she walked down the stairs and was surprised to discover her brother sitting at the kitchen table, waiting for her.

"I was beginning to wonder if you'd ever wake up," he said, grinning at her. The years had been good to Lonny. He'd always been a handsome cuss, and the gray hairs that streaked his temple only added to his attractiveness. Letty couldn't understand why he'd stayed single all this time. Then again she could. Lonny, like Chase Brown, their neighbor, lived for his land and his precious herd of cattle. Their whole lives revolved around the two. Lonny hadn't married because he hadn't found a woman who would be an asset to the Bar E.

"I'm surprised you aren't out rounding up cattle or repairing fences or whatever it is you do in the mornings," she teased, smiling at him.

"I wanted to properly welcome you home first."

After pouring herself a cup of coffee, Letty walked over to the table, leaned over and kissed his sun-bronzed cheek. "It's good to be back."

Surprisingly Letty meant that. Her pride had kept her away all these years. How silly that seemed now, how pointless and stubborn of her not to admit her name wasn't going to light up any marquee, when she'd lived and breathed that knowledge each and every day in California. Letty had talent; she'd known that when she left the Bar E nine years ago. It was the blind ambition and ruthless drive she'd lacked. Oh, there had been brief periods of promise and limited successes. She'd sung radio commercials and done some backup work for a couple of rising hopefuls, but she'd long ago given up the belief of ever making it big herself. At one time becoming a recording star had meant the world to her. Now it meant practically nothing.

Lonny reached for her fingers and squeezed tightly. "It's good to have you home, Sis. You've been away too long."

She sat across from him, cupping the coffee mug with both hands, and cast her gaze on the old Formica tabletop. Grinning, she noted that in nine years, Lonny hadn't replaced a single piece of furniture.

It wasn't easy to admit, but Letty needed to say it. "I should have come back long before now." She figured it was best to let him know this before she hit him with the whammy about her heart.

"Far too long," Lonny said evenly. "I wanted you back when Mom died."

"It was too soon then. I'd been in California less than a year."

It pained Letty every time she thought about losing her mother. Maren Ellison's death had been sudden. Although her mother had begged her not to leave Red Springs, Maren was a large part of the reason Letty had gone. Her mother had had talent, too. She'd been an artist whose skill had lain dormant while she wasted away on a ranch, unappreciated and unfulfilled. All her life, Letty had heard her mother talk about painting in oils someday. But the day had never come. Then, when everyone had least expected it, Maren had died. Letty had flown in for the funeral, then returned to California the following morning.

"What are your plans now?" Lonny asked, watching her closely.

Letty's immediate future meant dealing with social workers, filling out volumes of forms and having a dozen doctors examine her to tell her what she already knew. It seemed heart surgery didn't come cheap. "The first thing I thought I'd do was clean house," she said, deliberately misunderstanding him.

A guilty look crowded her brother's face and Letty chuckled softly.

"I suppose the place is a real mess," Lonny admitted, glancing around. "I've let things go around here the past few years, I know. When you phoned and said you were coming, I picked up what I could. You've probably guessed I'm not much of a housekeeper."

"I don't expect you to be when you're rearing several hundred head of cattle."

Lonny seemed surprised by her understanding. He stood and reached for his hat, adjusting it on his head as though uncertain it would fit properly. "How long do you plan to stay?"

Letty shrugged. "I'm not sure yet. Is my being here any problem?"

"Not in the least," Lonny rushed to assure her. "Stay as long as you like. I welcome the company...and decent meals for a change. If you want, I can see about finding you a job in town."

"I don't think there's much call for a ne'er-do-well singer in Red Springs, is there?"

"I thought you said you'd worked as a secretary most of the time."

"I did, part-time." In order to have flexible hours, she'd done temporary work to survive, but in following her dream she'd missed out on collecting health insurance benefits.

"There ought to be something for you then. I'll ask around."

"Don't," Letty said eagerly, perhaps a bit too eagerly. "Not yet, anyway." After the surgery would be soon enough to locate employment. For the time being she had to concentrate on making arrangements with the proper authorities. She probably should tell Lonny about her heart problem, she decided reluctantly, but it was too much to hit him with so soon. There would be plenty of time later, after the arrangements had been made. It wouldn't do any good to upset him now. Besides, she wanted him to become acquainted with Cricket before he found out that she'd be listing him as her daughter's guardian.

"Relax for a while," Lonny said, eyeing her closely, "take a vacation. There isn't any need for you to work if you don't want to."

"Thanks, I appreciate that."

"What are brothers for?" he joked, and drained his coffee cup. "I'd best get busy," he muttered, rinsing out his cup and setting it on the kitchen counter. "I should have gotten started hours ago, but I wanted to talk to you first."

"What time will you be back?"

Lonny's eyes rounded with the question, as though he didn't understand. "Five or later, I suppose. Why?"

She shrugged. "No reason. I just wanted to know when to plan dinner."

"Six or so should be fine."

Letty stood and wrapped her arms protectively around her waist. One question had been burning in her mind from the minute she'd pulled into the yard. One she needed to ask, but whose answer she feared. She hedged a little, then tentatively broached the subject. "Will you be seeing Chase?"

"I do most days."

"Does he know I'm back?"

Lonny's fingers gripped the handle to the back door. "He knows," he said without looking at her, his face tightening.

Letty nodded and she curled her hands into fists at her sides. "Is he married?"

Lonny shook his head, appearing uncomfortable. "Nope, and I don't imagine he ever will be, either." He hesitated before adding, "Chase is a lot different from the man you used to know. I hope you're not expecting anything from him, because you're headed for a big disappointment if you are. You'll know what I mean once you see him."

A short silence followed while Letty digested her brother's words. "You needn't worry that I've come home expecting things to go back to the way they were between Chase and me. If he's different...that's just fine. We've all changed over the years."

Lonny nodded and was gone.

The house was quiet after her brother left. His warning about Chase seemed to echo around the kitchen in discordant tones, bouncing off the walls, taunting her. The Chase Brown Letty knew was gentle, kind, good. When Letty was seventeen he'd been the only one to really understand her dreams. Although it had broken his heart, he'd loved her enough to encourage her to seek her destiny. Chase had loved her more than anyone before or since she'd left Wyoming.

And she'd thrown his love away.

"Mommy, you were gone when I woke up." Looking forlorn, five-year-old Cricket stood in the doorway of the kitchen, her yellow knit blanket clenched in her hand and dragging on the faded red linoleum floor.

"I was just downstairs," Letty said, holding out her arms to the youngster, who eagerly ran to her mother, climbing into Letty's lap.

"I'm hungry."

"I'll bet you are." Letty brushed the thick strands of dark hair away from her daughter's face and kissed her forehead. "I was talking to Uncle Lonny this morning."

Cricket stared up at her with deep blue eyes that were a reflection of her own. The preschooler had inherited little in the way of looks from her father. The dark hair and blue eyes were traits of the Ellison family. On rare occasions, Letty would see traces of Jason in their child, but not often. She tried not to think about him or their disastrous affair. He was out of her life and she wanted no part of him, except the very best he had to give her, and that had been Christina Maren, her Cricket.

"You know what I thought we'd do today?" Letty said.

"After breakfast?"

"After breakfast," she assured her.

"I thought we'd clean house and bake a pie for Uncle Lonny."

"Apple pie," Cricket announced with a firm shake of her head.

"I'm sure apple pie is his very favorite."

"Mine, too."

Together they cooked oatmeal. Cricket insisted on helping by setting the table and getting the milk from the refrigerator.

As soon as they'd finished, Letty mopped the floor and washed down the cupboards. Lonny's declaration about not being much of a housekeeper had been a gross understatement. He'd done a bare minimum for several years and the house was badly in need of a thorough cleaning. Usually any hard physical activity quickly wore Letty out and she became breathless and light-headed. But this morning she was filled with an enthusiasm that gifted her with a strong energy supply.

By noon, however, she was exhausted. At nap time, Letty lay down with Cricket, and didn't wake until early afternoon when the sound of male voices in the kitchen drifted up the stairway. It didn't take her a minute to realize Chase Brown was with her brother.

Running a brush through her short curly hair, Letty composed herself for the coming confrontation with Chase and calmly walked down the stairs.

Both her brother and Chase were sitting at the table, drinking coffee.

Lonny looked up when she entered the room, but Chase kept his gaze determined and focused away from her. Her brother had made a point of telling her that Chase was different. One look told the truth of his words. Like Lonny's, Chase's dark hair had streaked with gray in her absence. Deep crevices marked his forehead and grooved the sides of his mouth and eyes. In nine years he'd aged twenty, Letty thought with a stab of regret. Part of her longed to wrap her arms around him the way she had so many years before. She yearned to bury her head in his shoulder and weep for the pain she'd caused him.

But she knew she couldn't.

"Hello, Chase," she said softly, walking over to the stove and reaching for the coffeepot.

"Letty." He dipped his head in greeting, but kept his eyes averted.

"It's good to see you again."

He didn't answer that; instead he returned his attention to her brother. "I was thinking about separating part of the herd, driving them a mile or so south. Of course, that would mean hauling the feed a lot farther, but I tend to believe the benefits will outweigh that inconvenience."

"I think you're going to a lot of effort for nothing," Lonny said, frowning.

Letty pulled out a chair and sat across from Chase. He could only ignore her for so long. Still his gaze skirted hers, and he did his utmost to escape looking at her.

"Who are you?"

Letty's attention swiveled to the doorway, where Cricket was standing, her blanket gripped in her hand.

"Cricket, this is Uncle Lonny's neighbor, Mr. Brown."

"I'm Cricket," the five-year-old announced, grinning cheerfully.

"Hello," Chase returned in a gruff unfriendly tone, doing his best to disregard the little girl in the same manner he chose to overlook her mother.

A small cry of protest rose in Letty's breast. Chase could be as angry with her as he wanted. The way she figured it, that was his right, but he shouldn't take out his bitterness on an innocent child.

"Your hair's a funny color like Uncle Lonny's," Cricket commented, fascinated. "I think it's pretty like that." Her yellow blanket in tow, she marched up to Chase and raised her hand in an effort to touch the salt-and-pepper-colored strands that were more pronounced at his temple.

Chase frowned and moved back so there wasn't any chance of her succeeding.

"My mommy and I are going to bake a pie for Uncle Lonny. Do you want some?"

Letty held her breath, waiting for Chase to reply. Something about him appeared to intrigue Cricket. The youngster couldn't stop staring at him. Her actions seemed to unnerve Chase. He made it obvious that he'd like nothing better than to forget her existence.

"I don't think Mr. Brown is interested in apple pie, sweetheart," Letty said in an effort to fill the uncomfortable silence.

"Then let's make something he does like," Cricket insisted. She reached for Chase's hand and tugged, demanding his attention. "Do you like chocolate chip cookies? I do. And Mommy makes ones that are to die for—at least that's what she says."

For a moment Chase stared at Cricket, and the pain that flashed through his dark eyes went straight through Letty's. Within a split second he glanced away as though he couldn't bear to continue looking at the child.

"Do you?" Cricket persisted.

Chase nodded, although it was clearly an effort to do so.

"Come on, Mommy," Cricket cried. "I want to make them now."

"What about my apple pie?" Lonny protested, his eyes twinkling.

Cricket ignored the question, intent on the cookie-making task. She dragged her blanket after her as she started opening and closing the bottom cupboards, searching for the utensils she was going to need. She dutifully brought out two pots and rummaged through the drawers until she located a wooden spoon. Then, as though suddenly finding the blanket cumbersome, the youngster paused, lifted it from the floor and promptly planted it in Chase's lap.

Letty could hardly believe her eyes. She'd brought Cricket home from the hospital in that yellow blanket and the little girl had slept with it every night of her life since. Rarely would she entrust it to anyone, let alone a stranger.

Chase looked down on the much-loved blanket as if the youngster had deposited a dirty diaper in his lap.

"I'll take it," Letty said, holding out her hands.

Chase gave it to her, and when he did, his cold gaze locked with hers. Letty felt the chill in his eyes all the way through her bones. His bitterness toward her was evident with every breath he drew.

"It would have been better if you'd never come back," he said so softly she had to strain to hear.

She opened her mouth to argue the point. Lonny didn't know the real reason she'd returned to Wyoming. No one did, except her doctor in California. She hadn't meant to come back and disrupt Chase's life—or anyone else's for that matter. Chase didn't need to spell out to her that he didn't want anything to do with her. He'd made that much clear the minute she'd walked into the kitchen.

"Mommy, hurry," Cricket cried. "We have to bake cookies."

"Just a minute, sweetheart." Letty was uncertain how to handle this new problem. She sincerely doubted Lonny kept chocolate chips around and a trip into town was more than she wanted to tackle that afternoon—especially for a single bag of chips.

"Cricket..."

Lonny and Chase both stood. "I'm driving on over to Chase's for the rest of the afternoon," Lonny told her flatly. He obviously wasn't accustomed to letting anyone know his whereabouts and did so now only as an afterthought.

"Can I go, too?" Cricket piped up, so eager her deep blue eyes sparkled with the idea.

Letty wanted her daughter to be comfortable with Lonny, and Letty would have liked to encourage the two of them becoming friends, but from the frown that darkened Chase's brow, Letty realized now wasn't the time.

"Not today," Letty murmured, looking away from the pair of men.

Cricket pouted for a couple of minutes, but didn't argue. It wouldn't have mattered if she had, because both Lonny and Chase left without another word.

Dinner was ready and waiting by the time Lonny returned to the house that evening. Cricket ran to greet him, her pigtails bouncing. "Mommy and me cooked dinner for you."

Lonny smiled down on her and absently patted her head before heading for the bathroom to wash his hands. Letty watched him and felt a tugging sense of discontent. After years of living alone, Lonny tended not to be as communicative as Letty would have liked. This was understandable, but it made her realize how lonely he must be out here on the ranch night after night without anyone to share his life. Ranchers had to be more stubborn than any other breed of male, Letty thought.

To complicate matters slightly, there was the problem of Cricket staying with Lonny while Letty went in for the surgery. The little girl had never been away from her for more than a few hours. And never overnight.

Letty's prognosis for a complete recovery was good, but there was always the possibility that she wouldn't be coming home from the hospital. Any number of risks had to be considered with this type of operation, and if anything were to happen, then Lonny would be left to raise Cricket on his own. Letty didn't doubt he would do so with the greatest of care, but he simply wasn't accustomed to dealing with children.

By the time her brother had finished washing up, dinner was on the table. He looked down at the ample amount of food and grinned appreciatively. "I can't tell you how long it's been since I've had a good home-cooked meal like this. I've missed it."

"What have you been eating?"

He shrugged. "I'd come up with something, but nothing as appetizing as this." He sat down and eagerly filled his plate, hardly waiting for Cricket and Letty to join him.

He was buttering his biscuit, when he paused and looked at Letty. Slowly he placed his knife next to his plate. "Are you feeling all right?" he asked.

"Sure," she answered, smiling weakly. Actually, she wasn't—the day had been exhausting. She'd tried to do too much, testing her limitations, and she was paying the price now, feeling weak and shaky. "What makes you ask?"

"You're terribly pale."

That could be attributed to seeing Chase again, but Letty didn't say so. Their brief meeting had left her feeling melancholy all afternoon. She'd been so young and so foolish, seeking bright lights, utterly convinced she would never be satisfied with the lot of a rancher's wife. She'd wanted diamonds, not denim.

"Mommy couldn't find any chocolate chips," Cricket said, frowning, "so we had to bake the apple pie."

Lonny grinned and nodded, far more interested in the gravy and biscuits than in conversing with a child.

"I took Cricket out to the barn and showed her the horses," Letty said, picking up the sagging conversation.

Lonny nodded, then helped himself to seconds on the freshly baked biscuits. He spread a thick layer of butter over the halves and reached across the table for the jam.

"I thought maybe later you could let Cricket give them their oats," Letty prompted.

"The barn isn't any place for a little girl," Lonny countered with a frown, dismissing the idea with a quick shake of his head.

Cricket looked disappointed and Letty mentally chastised herself for mentioning the outing in front of her daughter. She should have known better.

"Maybe Uncle Lonny will let me ride his horsey?" Cricket asked, her eyes wide and hopeful. "Mommy had a horsey when she was a little girl—I saw the picture in her room. I want one, too."

"You have to grow up first," Lonny said brusquely, terminating the subject.

It was on the tip of Letty's tongue to suggest that Lonny at least let Cricket sit in a saddle, but he showed no inclination toward forming a relationship with her daughter. Nor wanting to.

Letty was encouraged somewhat when Cricket went in to watch television with Lonny later while she finished the dishes. But no more than ten minutes had passed before Letty heard Cricket burst into tears. In a moment she came running into the kitchen. She buried her face in Letty's stomach and wrapped her arms around her mother's thighs, sobbing so hard her shoulders shook.

Looking completely unnerved, Lonny followed the child into the room. His face was a study in guilt and frustration.

"What happened?" Letty asked, running her hand down the back of Cricket's head.

Lonny tossed his hands into the air. "Hell, I don't know. I turned on the television and was watching the news, when Cricket said something about wanting to see cartoons."

"There aren't any on at this time of night."

Cricket sobbed louder, then lifted her head. Tears ran unrestrained down her cheeks. "He said *no*, real mean."

"She started talking to me right in the middle of John Chancellor's commentary, for pete's sake," Lonny cried, and stabbed his fingers through his hair.

"Cricket, Uncle Lonny didn't mean to upset you," Letty explained softly. "He was watching his program and you interrupted him, that's all."

"But he said it mean."

"I hardly raised my voice," Lonny came back, obviously perplexed. "Are kids always this sensitive?"

"Not usually," Letty assured him. Cricket was normally a good-natured child. Fits of crying were rare and usually the result of being overly tired. "It was probably a combination of the flight and an extrabusy day."

Lonny nodded and returned to the living room without making an effort to talk to Cricket directly. Letty watched him go with a growing sense of uneasiness. Lonny hadn't been around children in years and didn't have the foggiest notion of how to deal with a five-year-old. Cricket had felt more of a rapport with Chase than she did her own uncle, and Chase had done everything he could to ignore the little girl.

Letty spent the next few minutes comforting her daughter, her mind in a whirl of doubts and confusion.

After giving Cricket a bath, Letty read her a story and tucked her in for the night. With her hand on the light switch, she acted out a game they'd played since Cricket had been two.

"Blow out the light, Cricket," she whispered.

The child grinned and blew with all her might. At that precise moment, Letty flipped the switch.

"Good night, Mommy."

"'Night, sweetheart."

Lonny was waiting for her in the living room, still frowning over the incident between him and his niece. "I don't know, Letty," he said, apparently still troubled. "I don't seem to be worth much in the uncle department."

"Don't worry about it," she said, trying to smile, but her heart was troubled and her thoughts heavy. She couldn't schedule the surgery if she wasn't certain Cricket was going to be comfortable with Lonny.

"I'll try not to upset her again," Lonny said, looking doubtful, "but I don't think I relate well to kids. I've been a bachelor for too long."

The word *bachelor* seemed to circle the living room and then settle on top of Letty's breast.

That was it. The solution to all her worries. All evening she'd been thinking how lonely her brother was and how he needed someone to share his life. The timing was perfect.

Her gaze flew to her brother and she nearly sighed aloud with relief. What Lonny needed was a wife.

And Letty was determined to find him one.

Fast.

Chapter Two

It wasn't exactly the welcoming parade Letty had dreamed about all these years, with the bright red convertible and the high school marching band, but Red Springs's reception was characteristically warm.

"Letty, it's good to see you again."

"Why, Letty Ellison, I swear I thought you were your dear mother. I never realized how much you resembled Maren. I still miss her, you know."

"Glad you're back, Letty. Hope you plan to stay a spell."

Letty smiled and shook hands and received hugs for so long she was late for the opening hymn at the Methodist church the following Sunday morning.

With Cricket at her side, she silently slipped into a pew and reached for a hymnal. The song was a familiar one from her childhood and Letty knew the lyrics well. But even before she opened her mouth to join the others, tears filled her eyes. The organ music swirled around her like the mist from a cool rain, filling what seemed to be an unending void in her life. It felt so good to be back. So right to be standing in church with her childhood friends and the people she loved.

Attending Sunday services was somehow part of the magnetic pull that had brought her back to Wyoming—what she jokingly referred to as "the E.T. phenomenon." As much as she liked to kid about this heart condition, the issue was a serious one. Attending church services helped to remind her that problems were like mountains. There wasn't a one she couldn't handle with God's help. Either she would climb it, forge a pass around or carve a tunnel through it. If that didn't work, she would plant herself at the base of that mountain and dig for gold.

The music continued and Letty reached for a tissue, dabbing at the tears that sprang to her eyes. Singing was impossible the way her throat had closed up, so she stood silently with her eyes shut, soaking up the words of the age-old hymn.

On the surface, Letty was as serene as a duck swimming across a pond, but like that duck, she was paddling below the water line for all she was worth. Facing a mountain, especially one this steep, demanded something extra. It was for this reason that Letty had come back to Red Springs, back to the Bar E and the small Methodist church on the outskirts of town. Led by instinct, she was wrapping everything that was important and familiar around her like a warm homemade quilt on a December night.

The organ music faded and Pastor Taylor stepped forward to offer a short prayer. As Letty bowed her head, she could feel someone's bold stare. The uneasy feeling grew in severity until hot pin prickles migrated down her spine. It was a sensation her mother had often referred to as someone walking over her grave. An involuntary smile tugged at Letty's mouth. That analogy certainly hit close to home. Much too close.

When the prayer was finished, it was all Letty could do not to turn around and find out who was glaring at her so intently.

"Mommy," Cricket whispered, loud enough for half the congregation to hear. "The man who likes chocolate chip cookies is here. He's two rows behind us."

Chase. Letty released an inward sigh. Naturally he would be the one challenging her appearance in church, as if her presence would corrupt the good people of this godly gathering. If it were up to him, Letty mused, he would probably prefer it if she wore a giant "A" on her chest so everyone would know she was a sinner.

Lonny had gone out of his way to warn her that Chase was different. And he was. The Chase Brown Letty remembered wasn't the least bit judgmental or unkind. He used to be fond of children. Years ago, Letty recalled that when they walked through town, the kids would automatically come running to Chase. He usually had a few pennies for the gum-ball machine tucked away in his pocket, which he would dole out judiciously. As far as Letty could tell, Chase had never asked to be favored, but something about him automatically attracted children. That Cricket had instantly taken to him was proof of his appeal.

An icy knot closed around Letty's heart at the memory. Chase was the type of man who should have married and fathered a houseful of youngsters. Over the years, she'd hoped that he had done exactly that.

But he hadn't. Instead Chase had turned bitter and hard. Letty didn't need anyone to tell her she'd hurt Chase terribly. How she regretted that. Chase had loved her, but all he felt for her now was disdain. He couldn't even look at her without her feeling his annoyance. In years past, he hadn't been able to disguise his love; now, sadly, he had difficulty hiding his dislike.

Letty had been witness to that wounded look in his eyes when she'd walked into the kitchen the day before. She'd known then that she had been the one to put it there. If she hadn't been so familiar with him, he might have been able to fool her. If only she could go back and alter the past. But that would be impossible.

"Mommy, what's his name?" Cricket demanded.

"Mr. Brown."

"Can I wave to him?"

"Not now."

"I want to talk to him."

Growing exasperated, Letty placed her hand on her daughter's shoulders and leaned down to whisper, "Why?"

"Because I bet he has a horse. Uncle Lonny won't let me ride his. Maybe Mr. Brown will."

"Oh, Cricket, I don't think asking him is a good idea."

"Why not?" the little girl pressed.

"We'll talk about this later."

"But I can ask, can't I? Pretty please?"

By this time, the elderly couple in the pew in front of them had turned around to find out what all the commotion was about.

"Mommy?" Cricket persisted, clearly running out of patience.

"Yes," Letty agreed, against her better judgment.

From that moment on Cricket started to fidget. Letty had to speak to her twice about squirming during the fifteen-minute sermon, and during the closing hymn, Cricket turned around twice to wave at Chase. The five-year-old could barely wait for the end of the service so she could rush over and ask him about his horse.

Letty could feel the dread mounting inside her. Chase didn't want anything to do with Cricket and Letty hated the thought of him wounding the little girl's gentle spirit. When the final prayer was being offered, Letty added a small request of her own.

"Can we leave now?" Cricket said, reaching for her mother's hand and tugging at it as the concluding burst of organ music filled the church.

Letty nodded. Cricket dropped her hand and was off like a race horse from the starting gate. Letty groaned inwardly and hurried after her.

Standing on the church steps, Letty noted that Chase was walking toward the parking lot when Cricket caught up with him. She must have called his name, because Chase turned around abruptly. Even from that distance, Letty could see a dark frown crowd his features. Quickening her step, Letty hurried toward the pair.

"Good morning, Chase," she greeted him, forcing a smile as she stood at Cricket's side and placed a protective hand around her daughter's shoulders.

"Letty." His hat was in his hand and he rotated the brim as though he were eager to make his escape, which Letty was sure he was.

"I asked him already," Cricket blurted out enthusiastically, glancing up at her mother.

From the look Chase was giving Letty, he seemed to think she had put Cricket up to this. As if she spent precious time thinking up ways to irritate him!

"I'm sure Mr. Brown is much too busy, sweetheart," Letty said, struggling to keep her voice even and controlled. "Perhaps you can ride his horse another time."

Cricket nodded and grinned. "That's what he said, too."

Surprised, Letty's gaze lifted to meet Chase's. She was grateful he hadn't been overly harsh with her daughter. From somewhere deep inside she dredged up a smile to thank him. But he didn't answer her with one of his own. A fresh sadness settled over Letty. The past would always stand between them in the form of an invisible wedge and there was nothing Letty could do to remove it. She wasn't even sure she should try.

"If you'll excuse me," she said, reaching for Cricket's hand, "there are some people we wanted to see."

"More people?" Cricket whined. "I didn't know there were so many people in the whole world."

"It was good to see you again, Chase," Letty said, turning away. Not until several minutes later did she realize that he hadn't echoed her greeting.

Chase couldn't get away from the church fast enough. He didn't know why he'd decided to attend services this particular morning. It wasn't as if he made a regular practice of it, although he'd been raised in the church. He supposed that something perverse deep inside him was interested in knowing if Letty had the guts to show up.

Damn, that woman had nerve. Another word that bounced against the far corner of his mind was *courage*, but he refused to believe that. It wouldn't be easy to face all those people with an illegitimate daughter holding on to her hand. Outwardly folks would smile, but the gossip would start up soon enough. Once it did, Letty would pack up her bags and leave again.

He wished to hell she would. One look at her the day she'd arrived and he knew he'd been lying to himself all these years. She was paler than he remembered, but her face was still a perfect oval, her skin creamy and smooth. Her blue eyes were round and her mouth a lush curve. How he'd loved the taste of her mouth. For years he'd battled the memory of her sweet lips moving under his. There was no way he could continue lying to himself. He was still in love with her—and he always would be.

He climbed inside his pickup and started the engine viciously, as if to punish it for his feelings. He gripped the steering wheel hard enough to make indentations in his flesh, until he gained control of his emotions. Who the hell was he trying to kid? He'd been waiting for years for Letty to come back. Lying to himself about hating her was nothing more than a futile effort to bolster his pride. He wished there could be someone else for him, but there wasn't; there never would be. Letty was the only woman he'd ever loved heart and soul. If she couldn't be the one to fill his arms during the long nights, then they would remain empty. But there was no reason for Letty ever to know that. The fact was, he would prefer it if she never found out. Chase Brown might be fool enough to fall in love with the wrong woman, but he knew better than to hand her the weapon that would shred what remained of his pride.

"You must be Lonny's sister," a feminine voice drawled from behind Letty in a faint Southern accent.

Letty finished greeting one of her mother's friends before turning. When she did, she met a statuesque blonde, whom she guessed to be close to thirty. "Yes, I'm Lonny's sister," she said, smiling.

"I'm so happy to meet you. I'm Mary Brandon," the woman continued. "I hope you'll forgive me for being so direct, but I heard someone mention your name and I thought I'd introduce myself."

"I'm pleased to meet you, Mary." The two exchanged quick handshakes as Letty quickly sized up the other woman. Single and eager. "How do you know Lonny?"

"I work at the hardware store and your brother comes in every now and then. He might have mentioned me?" she asked hopefully. When Letty shook her head, Mary shrugged and gave a nervous laugh. "He stops in and gets whatever he needs and is quickly on his way. I find your brother to be such an attractive man. He must be lonely living out on that ranch all by himself."

"Lonny always was good-looking," Letty murmured. Already she could feel the excitement bubbling up inside her. Mary Brandon definitely looked like wife material to her, and it was obvious the woman was more than casually interested in Lonny. As far as Letty was concerned there wasn't any better place to find a prospective mate for her elder brother than in church.

The night before she'd lain in bed wondering where she would ever meet someone suitable for Lonny. If he hadn't found anyone in the past several years, there was nothing to guarantee that she could locate him the perfect mate within the next few months. The problem, Letty had decided, was that Lonny had stopped looking. The responsibility of the ranch had fallen heavily upon his shoulders after their father's death, when Lonny was in his early twenties, and there hadn't been the time for him to pursue a relationship since then.

Another obstacle was that her brother was so single-minded and dedicated to the ranch that he'd developed tunnel vision. The Bar E demanded the majority of his energy and his time and consequently his personal life had suffered. His whole world had narrowed to his commitment to the ranch, and he didn't seem to notice that he was missing out on other aspects of life.

Letty hadn't a clue what it was about cattle and land that men found so intriguing. Lonny had become so leathery that he wouldn't know what was good for him if someone slapped him in the face with it. Which was something Letty had every intention of doing. Only it would be a very polite slap.

"Your brother certainly seems nice."

And eligible, Letty added silently. "He's wonderful, but he works so hard it's difficult for anyone to get to know him."

Mary gave her a look that said she understood that fact all too well. "He's not seeing anyone regularly, is he?"

"No." But Letty sincerely wished that he were.

Mary's eyes virtually snapped with excitement. "He hides himself away on the Bar E and rarely socializes. I firmly believe that he needs a little fun in his life."

Letty's own eyes were gleaming. "I think you may be right. Listen, Mary, perhaps we should get to know each other better."

Chase was working inside the barn, when he heard the familiar sound of Lonny's truck. He removed his hat and wiped the perspiration off his brow with his forearm.

It didn't take Chase two seconds to recognize that Lonny was upset. Chase shoved the pitchfork into the hay and leaned against it. "Problems?"

Lonny didn't answer him right away. He couldn't seem to stand in one place. "It's that fool sister of mine."

Automatically Chase's hand closed around the pitchfork. Letty had been on his mind all morning and she was the last person he wanted to discuss. Lonny appeared to be waiting for a response, so Chase gave him one. "I knew she'd be nothing but trouble from the moment you told me she was coming home."

Lonny removed his hat and slapped it against his thigh. "She went to church this morning." He paused and turned to glance in Chase's direction. "Said she saw you there. Actually, it was that kid of hers who mentioned your name. She calls you 'the guy who likes chocolate chip cookies.'" He grinned slightly at that, amused.

"I was there," Chase said tersely.

"At any rate, Letty talked to Mary Brandon afterward."

A smile sprang to Chase's lips. Mary had set her sights on Lonny three months earlier and she wasn't about to let up until she got her man.

"Wipe that smug look off your face, Chase Brown. You're supposed to be my friend."

"I am." He lifted a forkful of hay and tossed it behind him. Lonny had been complaining about the Brandon woman for weeks. Mary had done everything but stand on her head to garner his attention. And a wedding ring.

Lonny stalked aggressively to the other end of the barn, then returned. "Letty's overstepped the bounds of good taste this time," he muttered disparagingly.

"Oh? What did she do?"

"She invited Mary to dinner tomorrow night."

Despite himself, Chase burst out laughing. He turned around to discover his friend glaring at him, and stopped abruptly. "You're kidding, I hope?"

"Would I be this upset if I was? She invited that... woman right into my house without so much as asking me how I felt about it. I told her I had other plans for dinner tomorrow, but she claimed she needs me there to cut the meat. Nine years in California and she didn't learn how to cut meat?"

"If that's the case, then it seems to me you're stuck eating dinner with Mary Brandon." Chase realized he couldn't find the situation so funny. But the truth was, it was downright comical. Chase wasn't keen on Mary himself. There was something faintly irritating about the woman, something about her that rubbed him the wrong way. Lonny had the same reaction, although they'd never discussed what it was that annoyed them so much. Chase supposed it was the fact that Mary came on so strong. She was a tad too desperate to find herself a husband.

Brooding, Lonny silently paced the length of the barn a couple of more times. "I told Letty the only way I was staying for dinner was if you were there, too."

Chase stabbed the pitchfork into the ground. "You did what?"

"If I'm going to suffer through an entire dinner with that she-devil, I need another man around to run interference. You can't honestly expect me to sit across the dinner table from those two women."

"Three," Chase corrected absently. Lonny hadn't included Cricket in his tabulations.

"Oh, God, that's right. Three against one. It's more than any man can handle on his own." He rubbed a hand over his face as though to dispel the image that had formed in his mind. "I love my sister, don't get me wrong. I'm even glad she'd decided to come home. She should have come back years ago...but I'm telling you right now, I like my life exactly the way it is. Every time I turn around that kid of hers is underfoot, asking questions. Hell, I can't even listen to the evening news without her wanting to know if she can watch cartoons."

"If I were you, I'd ask Letty to leave." A part of Chase prayed that Lonny would. He hadn't had a decent night's sleep since he'd found out she was returning to Red Springs. He'd worked himself until he was ready to drop, and still his mind refused to give him the rest he craved. Instead he'd been tormented by resurrected memories he'd thought he'd buried years before. Like his friend, Chase had found a comfortable niche in life and he didn't like the invasion to his peace of mind Letty Ellison being close wrought. As far as he was concerned, everyone would be much better off if she turned around and went back to where she'd come from.

"I can't ask Letty to leave," Lonny said in a burst of impatience. "She's my sister, for God's sake."

Chase shrugged. "Then tell her to uninvite Mary."

"I tried that. Hell, before I knew it, she was talking to me ever so nice, reminding me how much Mom enjoyed company. Then she claimed that since she was moving back into the community, it was only right for her to get to know the new folks from town. At the time it made perfect sense to me, and before I knew what I was doing, I'd agreed to be there for that stupid dinner. But there's only one way I'll go through with this and that's if you come, as well."

"Cancel the dinner, then."

"Chase! How often do I ask a favor of you?"

He paused and glared at his neighbor.

"All right, that kind of favor!"

"I'm sorry, Lonny, but I won't have anything to do with Mary Brandon."

Lonny was quiet for so long that Chase finally turned to meet his friend's narrowed gaze. "Is it Mary or Letty who troubles you so much?"

Chase tightened his fingers around the pitchfork. "Doesn't matter which one, because I won't be there."

Letty took an afternoon nap with Cricket, hoping her explanation to Lonny wouldn't raise his suspicions. She'd told him she was suffering from the lingering effects of jet lag.

The first thing Monday morning, she planned to contact the state social services office. It wasn't something she could put off any longer. Each day it seemed she grew weaker and tired more easily. The thought of dealing with the state agency filled her with apprehension. Accepting charity went against the very fabric of her being, but the cost of the surgery was prohibitive. Letty, who'd once been so proud, was being forced to accept the generosity of the taxpayers of the state of Wyoming.

Cricket stirred beside her in the bed as Letty drifted into an uneasy sleep. When she awoke, the first thing she noticed was Cricket's yellow blanket was haphazardly draped over her shoulders. Her daughter was gone.

Yawning, she went down the stairs to discover Cricket sitting in front of the television. "Uncle Lonny says he doesn't want dinner tonight."

"That's tomorrow night," Lonny shouted from the kitchen. "Chase and I won't be there."

Letty's shoulders sagged with defeat. She didn't know how one man could be so stubborn. "Why not?"

"Chase refuses to come flat out and I have no intention of sticking around to cut up a piece of meat for you three women."

Letty poured herself a cup of coffee. The fact that Chase wouldn't be there shouldn't come as any big shock, but it was, accompanied by a curious pain.

Scowling, she sat down at the square table, bracing her elbows against the edge. Disappointment came at her like a fist. Until that moment, she hadn't realized how much she would like to settle the past with Chase. It was something she needed to do before the surgery.

"I said Chase wasn't coming," Lonny told her a second time.

"I heard you—it's all right," she replied, doing her best to reassure her brother with an easy smile that belied the emotion churning inside her. It had been a mistake to invite Mary Brandon to dinner without consulting Lonny first. In her enthusiasm, Letty had seen the other woman as a gift from God that had practically fallen into her lap. How was she to know her brother disliked Mary so passionately?

Lonny tensed. "What do you mean, 'all right'? I don't like the look you've got in your eye."

Letty dropped her gaze. "I mean it's perfectly fine if you prefer not to be here tomorrow night for dinner. I thought it might be a way of getting to know some new people in town, but I should have cleared the evening with you first."

"Yes, you should have."

"Mary seems nice enough," Letty commented, trying once more.

"So did the snake in the Garden of Eden."

Letty chuckled. "Honestly, Lonny, one would think you're afraid of the woman."

"This one's got moves that would make the heavyweight champion of the world envious."

"Obviously she hasn't used them, because she's single."

"Oh, no, she's too smart for that," Lonny countered, gesturing with his hands. "She's been saving them up, just waiting to sink her claws into me."

"Oh, Lonny, honestly, you're beginning to sound paranoid, but don't worry, I understand. What kind of sister would I be if I insisted you eat Mama's prime rib dinner with the likes of Mary Brandon?"

Lonny's head shot up and his Adam's apple worked its way up and down his throat. "You're planning on cooking Mom's recipe for prime rib?"

She hated to be so manipulative, but if Lonny were to give Mary half a chance, he might change his mind. "You don't mind if I use some of the meat in the freezer, do you?"

"No," he said, and swallowed once more. "I suppose there'll be plenty of leftovers?"

Letty shrugged. "I can't say, since I'm thawing out a small roast. I hope you understand."

"Sure," Lonny muttered, frowning.

Apparently he understood all too well, because an hour later, her brother announced he probably would be around for dinner the following night, after all.

Monday morning Letty rose early. The coffee had perked and bacon was sizzling in the skillet when Lonny wandered into the kitchen.

"'Morning," he said.

"'Morning," she returned cheerfully.

Lonny poured himself a cup of coffee and headed for the door, pausing just before he opened it. "I'll be back in a few minutes."

At the sound of a pickup pulling into the yard, Letty glanced out the kitchen window. Her heart sped up at the sight of Chase climbing out of the cab. It was as if those nine years had been wiped away and he'd come for her the way he had when she was a teenager. His muscular, tall form was clad in jeans and shirt with a well-worn leather vest. His dark hair curled crisply at his sun-bronzed nape and he needed a haircut, but in him, Letty recognized strength and rich masculinity.

He walked in the back door without knocking and stopped short when he found her. "Letty," he said, as though her name was dragged out of him by force.

"Good morning, Chase," she greeted him simply. Unwilling to see the bitterness in his gaze, she didn't look up from the stove. "Lonny's stepped outside for a moment. Pour yourself a cup of coffee."

"No, thanks." Already he'd turned back to the door.

"Chase." She stopped him, her heart pounding so hard it felt as if it was about to storm into her throat. The sooner she cleared the air between them the better. "Do you have a minute?"

"Not really."

Ignoring his words, she removed the pan from the burner. "There comes a time in everyone's life when—"

"I said I didn't have the time, Letty."

"But—"

"If you're figuring to give me some line about how life has done you wrong and how sorry you are about the past, then save your breath, because I don't need it."

"Maybe you don't need to hear it," she said gently, "but I have to say it."

"Then do it in front of a mirror."

"Chase, honestly, you're my brother's best friend. It isn't as if we can simply ignore each other. It's too uncomfortable to pretend nothing's wrong."

"As far as I'm concerned nothing *is* wrong."

"But—"

"Save your breath, Letty."

Chapter Three

Mr. Chase," Cricket called excitedly from the foot of the stairs. "You're here!"

Letty turned back to the stove, fighting down anger and indignation. Chase wouldn't so much as listen to her. Fine. If he wanted to pretend there was nothing wrong, then she would give award winning performances herself. He wasn't the only one who could play childish games.

The back door opened with a swish and Lonny blithely stepped into the kitchen. "You're early, aren't you?" he asked Chase as he refilled his coffee cup.

"No," Chase snapped impatiently. The look he shot Letty said he wouldn't have come in the house at all if he'd known she was up.

Lonny apparently chose to ignore the censure in his neighbor's voice. He pulled out a chair at the table and sat down. "I'm not ready to leave yet. Letty's cooking breakfast."

"Mr. Chase, Mr. Chase, did you bring over your horsey?"

"It's Mr. 'Brown,'" Letty corrected gently as she delivered two plates to the table. Lonny immediately dug into the bacon-and-egg breakfast, but Chase ignored the meal, as though eating anything Letty cooked would contaminate him.

"You'd better answer the kid," Lonny muttered between bites. "Otherwise she'll drive you nuts."

"I drove my truck over," Chase told Cricket.

"Do you ever bring your horsey to Uncle Lonny's?"

"Sometimes."

"Are you a cowboy?"

"I suppose."

"Wyoming's the Cowboy State," Letty told her daughter.

"Does that mean everyone who lives here has to be a cowboy?"

"Not exactly."

"But close," Lonny said with a grin.

Cricket climbed onto the chair next to Chase and dragged her yellow blanket with her, gathering it on her lap. She plopped her elbows on the table and cupped her face with her hands. "Aren't you going to eat?" she asked, studying him intently.

"I had breakfast," he said without looking at her, and scooted the plate in her direction.

Cricket didn't need to be asked twice. Kneeling on the chair, she stretched across Chase and reached for his fork. She smiled up at him, her eyes sparkling.

Letty joined the others at the table. Lately her appetite hadn't been good, but she was forcing herself to eat a piece of toast.

The atmosphere at the table was strained at best. Letty tried to avoid looking in Chase's direction, but it was impossible to ignore the man. He turned toward her unexpectedly, catching her look and holding it. His eyes were dark and intense. Caught off guard, Letty blushed.

Chase's gaze darted from her eyes to her mouth and stayed there. She longed to turn primly away from him with a haughty shrug of indifference, but she couldn't. Years ago, Letty had loved looking into Chase's eyes. He had the most soulful eyes of any man she'd ever known. She was trapped in the memory of how it used to be for them. At one time, she'd been able to read whole libraries in Chase's dark look and had cherished every word. His gaze was cold now, and filled with angry sparks that flared briefly before he glanced away.

What little appetite Letty had was gone, and she put her toast back on the plate and pushed it aside. "Would it be all right if I took the truck this morning?" she asked her brother, surprised by the slight quiver in her voice. She wished she could ignore Chase altogether, but that had proved impossible. He refused to deal with the past and clear the air between them, and she couldn't force him into talking to her. From everything Letty could tell, he preferred to simply overlook her presence. Only he seemed to find that as difficult as she found ignoring him. The small piece of information went a long ways toward raising her spirits.

"Where are you going?"

Letty's gaze fell to her coffee mug. "I thought I'd do a little shopping for dinner tonight." That was only a half-truth. She needed to drive to Rock Springs, which was fifty miles west of Red Springs, and talk to the social services people there about her eligibility for medicaid.

"That's right...Mary Brandon's coming to dinner tonight, isn't she?" Lonny asked, looking disturbed by the mere thought.

It was a mistake to have mentioned the evening meal, because her brother's face tightened the instant he said Mary's name. "I suppose I won't be needing the truck," he said, scowling.

"I'd appreciate it. Thanks," Letty said brightly.

Her brother shrugged. "It isn't any skin off my nose."

"Are you coming to dinner with Mommy's friend?" Cricket asked Chase.

"No," he said brusquely.

"How come?"

"Because he's smart, that's why," Lonny answered, and stood abruptly. He reached for his hat, settled it on his head and didn't look back.

Within a minute both men were gone.

"You'll need to fill out these forms," the woman behind the desk told Letty, handing her several sheets.

The social worker looked frazzled and overburdened. It was well past noon, and Letty guessed that the woman hadn't had a coffee break all morning and was probably late for her lunch. The woman briefly read over the letter from the physician Letty had been seeing in California, and made a copy of it to attach to Letty's file.

"Once you're done with those forms, please bring them back to me," the woman requested.

"Of course," Letty said.

Bored, Cricket had circled her arms around her mother's waist and was pressing her head against Letty's stomach.

"If you have any questions, feel free to ask," her social worker said.

"None right now. Thank you for all your help," Letty said, standing.

For the first time since Letty had entered the government office, the young woman smiled.

Letty took the sheets with her and sat at a table in a large vestibule area. One by one, she started answering the myriad questions, doing her best to be as thorough as possible. Before she would be eligible for Wyoming's medical assistance program, she would have to be accepted into the Supplemental Security Income program offered through the federal government. It was a humiliating fact of life, but the proud, independent Letty Ellison was about to go on welfare.

Tears blurred her eyes as she filled in the first sheet. She stopped long enough to wipe away the moisture before it spilled onto the papers. God only knows what she would tell Lonny once the government checks started arriving. Especially when he seemed so confident he could find her some kind of employment in town.

"When can we leave here?" Cricket said, close to her mother's ear.

"Soon." Letty was writing as fast as she could, eager to escape herself.

"I don't like it here," Cricket whispered.

"I don't, either," Letty whispered back. But she was grateful the service existed; otherwise she didn't know what would have happened to her.

Cricket fell asleep in the truck during the hour drive home. Letty was thankful for the silence because it gave her a chance to think through a few of the immediate problems that faced her. She couldn't delay seeing a physician much longer, and eventually she would need to tell Lonny about her heart condition. She hadn't intended to keep it a deep, dark secret, but there wasn't any need to worry him until everything was settled with the medicaid people. Once she'd completed all the paperwork, been examined by a variety of knowledgeable doctors so they could tell her what she already knew, then she would be free to explain to Lonny what was happening.

Until then she would keep this problem her own.

"Letty," Lonny cried from the top of the stairs. "Honest to God, do I have to dress for dinner?"

"Please," she answered sweetly, basting the rib roast once more before sliding it back into the oven for a few more minutes.

"A tie, too?"

He didn't sound the least bit enthusiastic about that.

"A nice sweater would do."

"I don't own a 'nice' sweater," he shouted back.

A couple of muffled curses followed, but Letty chose to ignore them. At least she knew what to get her brother next Christmas.

Lonny had been in a bad temper from the minute he'd walked in the door an hour earlier. Already Letty could see that this evening was headed toward disaster.

"Mommy," Cricket cried, her pigtails flying as she raced into the kitchen. "Your friend is here."

"Oh." Letty quickly removed the oven mitt and glanced at her watch. Marry was a good ten minutes early and Letty needed every second of that extra time. The table had yet to be set, and the roast was still in the oven.

"Mary, it's good to see you," Letty greeted her with a bright smile as she rushed into the living room.

Mary walked into the Ellison home, her gaze wide and curious as she examined the living-room furniture. "It's good to be here. I brought along some freshly baked rolls for Lonny."

"How thoughtful." Letty moved into the center of the table. "I'm running just a little behind schedule, so if you'll excuse me for a minute?"

"Of course."

"Make yourself comfortable," Letty called over her shoulder as she returned to the kitchen. She stood in the middle of the floor and looked around, wondering which task to complete first. After she'd returned from Rock Springs that afternoon and done the marketing, she'd taken a nap with Cricket. Now she regretted having wasted that time. The whole meal felt so disorganized, and with Lonny's attitude, well—

"This is a lovely watercolor in here," Mary called in to her.

"My mother was an artist," Letty answered, taking the salad out of the refrigerator. She grabbed the silverware and napkins on her way into the dining room. "Cricket, would you set the table for me?"

"Okay," the youngster agreed willingly.

Mary stood in the room, hands behind her back as she studied the painting of a lush field of wildflowers. "Your mother certainly had an eye for color, didn't she?"

"Mom was very talented," Letty replied wistfully.

"Did she paint any of the others?" Mary asked, glancing around the living room.

"No...actually, this is the only painting we have of hers."

"She gave the others away?"

"Not exactly," Letty admitted with a flash of resentment. With all her mother's obligations on the ranch, plus helping Dad when she could the last few years of his life, there hadn't been time for her to work on the thing she'd loved most, which was her art. Letty's mother had lived a hard life. The land had sucked the energy out of her, like water through a straw, crippling her for anything creative or fun. Letty had been a silent witness to what had happened to her mother and swore it wouldn't be repeated in her own life. Yet here she was back in Wyoming. Back on the Bar E, and grateful she had a home.

"How come we're eating in the dining room?" Lonny muttered when he came downstairs, appearing irritated and bored. He buried his hands in his pants pockets and did his best to ignore Mary, who stood no more than five feet away.

"You remember Mary, don't you?" Letty asked pointedly.

Lonny nodded in the other woman's direction, but he managed to do so without actually looking at her.

"Hello, Lonny," Mary cooed. "It's a real pleasure to see you again. I brought you some rolls—they're still hot from the oven."

"Mary brought over some homemade dinner rolls," Letty reiterated, resisting the urge to kick her brother in the shin. It was obvious he was going to be only borderline polite.

"Looks like those rolls came from the Red Springs Bakery to me," he muttered, pulling out the chair and sitting down.

Letty half expected him to grab hold of his knife and fork, pound the table with them and chant, Dinner, dinner, dinner. If he couldn't disinterest Mary by being rude, he would probably try the more advanced "caveman" approach.

"Well, yes, I did pick up the rolls there," Mary said, obviously flustered. "I didn't have time after work to bake myself."

"Naturally, you wouldn't have," Letty responded mildly, shooting her brother a heated glare.

Cricket scooted past the two women and handed her uncle a clean plate. "Anything else, Mommy?"

Letty quickly checked the table to see what else was needed. "Glasses," she mumbled, rushing back into the kitchen. While she was there, she took the peas off the burner. The vegetable had been an expensive addition to the meal, but Letty had picked them up at the market in town after remembering how much Lonny loved fresh peas. He deserved some reward for being such a good sport, or so she'd thought earlier.

Cricket finished setting the table and Letty brought out the rest of their dinner. She smiled as she joined the others. Her brother had made a small tactical error when he'd chosen to sit down first. Mary had immediately opted for the chair closest to him. She planted her elbows on the table and gazed at him with wide adoring eyes while Lonny did his best to ignore her.

As Letty had predicted earlier, the meal was a disaster. The tension in the air was as thick as a London fog in March. Letty made a couple of attempts at conversation, which Mary leaped upon, but the minute she attempted to include Lonny, the subject died. It was all Letty could do to keep from kicking her brother under the table. Mary didn't linger long after the meal and everyone was grateful.

"Don't ever do that to me again," Lonny grumbled as soon as Letty was back from escorting Mary to the front door.

She plopped herself in the chair beside him and closed her eyes, exhausted. She didn't have the energy to argue with her brother. If he was looking for an apology, she would give him one. "I'm sorry, Lonny. I was only trying to help."

"Help what? Ruin my life?"

"No," Letty cried, her eyes flying open. "You need someone."

"Who says?"

"I do."

"Did you ever stop to think that's a bit presumptuous on your part? You're gone nine years and then you waltz home, look around and decide what you can change?"

"Lonny, I said I was sorry."

He was silent for a lengthy moment, then he sighed expressively. "I didn't mean to shout."

"I know you didn't." Letty was so tired she didn't know how she was going to manage to wash all the dishes. One meal and she'd used every pan in the house. Cricket was clearing the table for her and she was so grateful she stopped her daughter long enough to kiss her forehead.

Lonny dawdled over his coffee, his gaze downcast. "What makes you think I need someone?" he asked quietly.

"It seems so lonely out here. I assumed—incorrectly, it appears—that you'd be more content if there was someone to share your life with. You're a handsome man, Lonny, and there are plenty of women who would enjoy being your wife."

One corner of his mouth edged up with that. "I fully intend to marry someday. I just haven't gotten around to it, that's all."

"Well, for heaven's sake, what are you waiting for?" Letty teased. "You're thirty-four now and you're not getting any younger."

"I'm not exactly ready for social security."

Letty smiled. "Mary's nice—"

"Ah, come off it, Letty, would you? I don't like that woman. How many times do I have to tell you that?"

"—but I understand why she isn't your type," Letty finished, undaunted.

"You do?"

She nodded. "Mary needs a man who's willing to spend a good deal of time and money keeping her entertained. She'd make a poor rancher's wife."

"I knew that the minute I met her," Lonny grumbled, his smile slightly off-center. "I just didn't know how to put it in words." He mulled over his thoughts a moment, then added, "Look at the way she let you and Cricket do all the fiddling with dinner. She didn't once help. That wouldn't set well with most folks."

"She was company." Letty felt an obligation to defend Mary. After all, she hadn't *asked* the other woman to help with the meal, although she would have been grateful if she had. Besides, Lonny didn't have a lot of room to talk; he'd sat back and waited to be served the same way Mary had.

"Company, my foot," Lonny countered. "Could you see Mom or any other woman you know, sitting around making idle chatter while everyone else is working around her?"

Letty was forced to admit that was true enough.

"Did you notice the way she wanted everyone to think she'd made those rolls herself?"

Letty had noticed, but she didn't consider that such a terrible thing.

Lonny reached in the middle of the table for a carrot stick, chewing on it with a thoughtful frown. "A wife," he murmured. "A woman would certainly take more interest in the house than I have the past few years, that's true enough." He took another bite, munching on the vegetable. "I have to admit it's been rather nice having my meals cooked and my laundry folded. Those are a couple of hassles I can live without."

Letty practically swallowed her tongue to keep from commenting.

"I think you might be right, Letty. A wife would come in handy."

"You could always hire a housekeeper," Letty said sarcastically, irritated by his attitude.

"What are you so irked about? You're the one who suggested I think about getting married in the first place."

"From the way you're talking, you seem to think of a wife as a hired hand who'll clean house and cook your meals. You don't want a wife. You're looking for a servant. A woman's got to have more out of a relationship than knowing she's around for a few basic essentials."

Lonny gave a short disgruntled snort. "I thought you females need to be needed. For crying out loud, what else is there to a marriage but cooking and cleaning and regular sex?"

Letty glared at her brother, stood and reached for their coffee cups. "Lonny, I was wrong. Do some woman the ultimate favor and stay single."

With that she walked out of the dining room.

* * *

"So how did dinner go?" Chase asked his friend the following morning.

Lonny's response was little more than a grunt.

"That bad?"

"Worse."

Although his friend wouldn't appreciate it, Chase had gotten a good laugh over this hot dinner date of Lonny's with the gal from the hardware store. "Is Letty going to set you up with that Brandon woman again?"

"Not while I'm breathing, she won't."

Chase chuckled and loosened the reins on Firepower. Mary Brandon was about as subtle as a jackhammer. She'd done everything but throw herself at Lonny's feet, and she would probably have done that if she'd thought it would do any good. Chase would like to blame Letty for getting Lonny into this mess, but the Brandon woman was wily and had probably manipulated the invitation out of Letty. Unfortunately Lonny was the one who'd suffered the consequences.

Chase smiled, content. Riding the range in May, looking for newborn calves, was one of his favorite duties as a rancher. All creation seemed to be bursting out, fresh and alive on a lush green carpet. The trees were budding and the wind was warm and carried the sweet scent of wildflowers with it. He liked it best after it rained; everything felt so pure then and the land seemed to glisten.

"That sister of yours is bound and determined to find you a wife, isn't she?" Chase teased, still smiling. "She isn't back two weeks and she's matchmaking to beat the band. Before you know it, Lonny Ellison, she'll have you married off. I only hope you get some say in whom Letty chooses."

"Letty doesn't mean any harm."

"Neither did Lizzy Borden."

When Lonny didn't respond with the appropriate chuckle, Chase glanced in his friend's direction. "You're frowning. What's wrong?"

"It's Letty."

Chase noted how Lonny's eyes had darkened with worry. "What about her?"

"Does she seem any different to you?"

Chase shrugged, hating the sudden concern that surged through his blood. The only thing he wanted to experience for Letty was apathy, or at best the faint stirring of remembrance that one had for a casual acquaintance. As it was, his heart, his head, every part of him went into overdrive whenever Lonny brought his sister into the conversation.

"How do you mean—different?" Chase asked.

"I don't know for sure." He hesitated and tipped his hat farther back on his head, as if the action would aid his thought process. "It's the craziest thing, but she takes naps every afternoon. And I mean *every* afternoon. At first she claimed it was jet lag."

"So she sleeps a lot. Big deal," Chase responded, struggling to sound disinterested.

"Hell, Chase, you know my sister as well as I do. Can you figure Letty, who was always a fireball of energy, taking naps in the middle of the day?"

Chase couldn't, but he didn't say so.

"Another thing," Lonny said as he held his gelding's reins loose in his fingers. "Letty's always been a neatness freak. Remember how she used to drive me crazy with the way everything had to be just so?"

Chase nodded.

"She left the dinner dishes in the sink all night. I found her washing them this morning, claiming she'd been too tired to bother after Mary left. Good Lord, Mary was gone before seven."

"So she's a little tired," Chase muttered. "Let her sleep if it makes her happy."

"It's more than that," Lonny continued. "She doesn't sing anymore—not a note. For nine years she struggled to make it in the entertainment business, and now it's as if she never had a voice. She hasn't so much as touched the piano since she's been home—at least not when I was there to hear her." Lonny hesitated and frowned. "It's like the song's gone out of her life."

Chase didn't want to talk about Letty; he didn't even want to think about her. In an effort to turn the subject he said, "Old man Wilber was by the other day?"

Slowly Lonny shook his head. "I suppose he was after those same acres again."

"Every year he asks me if I'm willing to sell that strip of land." Some people knew it was spring when flowers started to bloom. Chase could tell the season had changed when Henry Wilber approached him about a narrow strip of land that bordered their two property lines. It wasn't the land that interested Wilber as much as the water. Nothing on this earth would convince Chase to sell that land. Spring Valley had been in his family for nearly eighty years and each generation had managed to hold on to those acres through the most difficult times. Ranching wasn't exactly making Chase a millionaire, but he would die before he sold off a single inch of his inheritance.

"You'd be a fool to let it go," Lonny added.

No one needed to tell Chase that. "I wonder when he'll give up asking."

"Knowing old man Wilber," Lonny said with a chuckle, "I'd say never."

"Are you going to plant any avocados?" Cricket asked as Letty stabbed the spading fork into the rich soil that had once been her mother's garden space. Lonny had protested, but he'd tilled a large section close to the house for her and Cricket to plant. Now Letty was eager to get her hands in the earth.

"Avocados won't grow in Wyoming, Cricket. The climate isn't mild enough."

"What about oranges?"

"Not those, either."

"What *does* grow in Wyoming?" she asked indignantly. "Cowboys?"

Letty chuckled as she used the sturdy fork to turn the lush soil.

"Mommy, look! Chase is here...on his horsey." Cricket took off, running as fast as her stubby legs would carry her. Her reaction was the same whenever Chase appeared.

Letty planted the spading fork in the soft ground and reluctantly followed her daughter. By the time she arrived in the yard, Chase had climbed down from the saddle and had dropped the reins. Cricket stood awestruck on the steps leading up to the back porch, her mouth agape, her eyes wide.

"Hello, Chase," Letty said softly.

He looked down at her and frowned. "Didn't that old straw hat used to belong to your mother?"

Letty nodded and bounced her hand on the top of it. "She wore it when she worked in the garden. I found it the other day." Other than mentioning the wide-brimmed hat, Chase made no comment, although Letty was certain he'd wanted to say something more.

Eagerly Cricket bounded down the stairs to stand beside her mother. Her small hand crept into Letty's, holding on tightly. "I didn't know horsies were so big and pretty."

"Firepower's special," Letty explained. Chase had raised him from a yearling, and had broken in the bay himself, working long, patient hours.

"You said you wanted to see Firepower," Chase said, a bit gruffly. "I haven't got all day, so if you want to ride it's got to be now."

"I can ride him? Oh, Mommy, can I really?"

Letty's blood became a deafening roar in her ears. She opened her mouth to tell Chase she wasn't about to set her daughter alone atop Firepower.

Before she could voice her objection, however, Chase quieted her fears. "She'll be riding with me." With that he swung his weight atop the chestnut-colored horse and reached down to hoist Cricket into the saddle with him.

As if she'd been born to ride, Cricket sat in front of Chase on the huge animal without revealing the least bit of fear. Her grin was so wide it split her face in two. "Look at me," the youngster shouted. "I'm riding a horsey. I'm riding a horsey."

Even Chase was smiling at such unabashed enthusiasm. "I'll take her around the yard a couple of times," he told Letty before gently kicking at Firepower's sides. The bay obediently trotted around in a short circle.

"Can we go over there?" Cricket cried, pointing to some undistinguishable location in the distance.

"Cricket," Letty said, holding the straw hat on her head and looking up. "Chase is a busy man. He hasn't got time to run you all over the countryside."

"Hold on, partner," Chase responded, taking the reins in both hands and heading in the direction Cricket had indicated.

"Chase," Letty cried, running after him. "She's just a little girl. Please be careful."

He didn't answer her, and not knowing what to expect, Letty followed the pair to the end of the long driveway. By the time she arrived there, she was breathless and light-headed. It took her several minutes to walk back to the house. She was certain anyone watching her would assume she was drunk. Stopping in the kitchen, Letty reached for her prescription bottle and took a couple of capsules without water.

Not wanting to raise unnecessary alarm, she returned to the garden, but was forced to sit on an old stump until her breathing returned to normal. Apparently her heart had gotten worse since she'd returned home. Much worse.

"Mommy, look, no hands," Cricket called out, her arms raised high in the air as Firepower trotted back into the yard and Chase directed toward the animal to the garden.

Smiling, Letty stood and reached for the spading fork, using it to help her keep her balance.

"Don't try to pretend you were working," Chase muttered, frowning down on her. "We saw you sitting in the sun. What's the matter, Letty? Did the easy life in California make you lazy?"

Once more Chase was baiting her. And once more Letty let the comment slide. "It must have," she said, and looked away.

Chapter Four

Chase awoke just before dawn. He lay on his back, listening to the sounds of birds chirping outside his half-opened window. Normally their singing would have amused and entertained him, but this morning his thoughts were heavy. He'd slept poorly, his mind preoccupied with Letty. Everything Lonny had said the week before about her not being herself had bounced around his brain for most of the night.

Something *was* different about Letty, but not in the way Chase would have assumed the years she'd spent in California had transformed her. To his surprise, he discovered that in several cases she was very much like the naive young woman who'd left nine years earlier to follow a dream. But the changes were there, lots of them, complex and subtle, when he'd expected them to be simple and glaring. Perhaps what troubled Chase was his deep inner feeling that something was unmistakably wrong with her. But try as he might, he couldn't pinpoint what it was. That was what disturbed him most.

Sitting on the edge of the mattress, Chase rubbed his callused hands over his face and glanced outside. The cloudless dawn sky was a luminous shade of gray. The air smelled crisp and clean as Wyoming went about producing another perfect spring morning.

Chase stood and dressed in his jeans and a simple Western shirt. Downstairs, he didn't bother to fix himself a cup of coffee; instead he walked directly outside, climbed into his pickup and headed over to the Bar E.

Only it wasn't Lonny who drew him there.

The lights were on in the kitchen when Chase pulled into the yard. He didn't bother to knock, but stepped directly into the large family kitchen. Letty was at the stove, the way he knew she would be. She turned when he walked in the door and smiled softly.

"'Morning, Chase."

"'Morning." Without another word, he moved over to the cupboard and took himself down a mug. Standing next to her, he poured his own coffee.

"Lonny's taking care of the horses," she said, as if she needed to explain where her brother was.

Briefly Chase wondered how she would have responded if he'd claimed it wasn't Lonny he'd come to speak to.

"Cricket talked nonstop for hours about riding Firepower. It was the thrill of her life. Thank you for being kind to her, Chase."

Chase held back a short derisive laugh. He hadn't planned to let Cricket anywhere near his gelding. His intentions all along had been to avoid Letty's daughter entirely. To Chase's way of thinking, the less he had to do with the child the better.

Ignoring Cricket was the only thing he could do, because every time he looked at the sweet little girl, he felt nothing but pain. Not a faint flicker of discomfort, but a deep wrenching distress that struck him in the solar plexus like nothing he'd ever experienced. Cricket represented everything about Letty that he wanted to forget. He couldn't glance at the child without remembering that Letty had given herself to another man, and the sense of betrayal cut him to the bone.

Naturally Cricket was innocent of the circumstances surrounding her birth, and Chase would never do anything to deliberately hurt the little girl, but he couldn't help feeling the things he did. Yet he'd given her a ride atop Firepower the day before, and despite everything, he'd enjoyed himself.

If the truth be known, the ride had been an accident. Chase had been working on the ridge above the Bar E fence line, when he saw two faint dots silhouetted against the landscape, far in the distance. Almost immediately he'd realized those images were Letty and her daughter, working outside. From that moment on, Chase hadn't been able to stay away. Without a thought in his head, he'd hurried down the hill. But once he was in the yard, he had to come up with some logical reason for showing up in the middle of the day. Giving Cricket a chance to see Firepower had sounded solid enough at the time.

"Would you like a waffle?" Letty asked, breaking into his musings.

"No, thanks."

Letty nodded and turned around. "I don't know why Cricket has taken to you he way she has. She gets excited every time someone even mentions your name. I'm afraid you've made a friend for life, whether you like it or not."

Chase made a noise that sounded appropriate.

"I can't thank you enough for bringing Firepower over," Letty continued. "It meant a good deal to me."

"I didn't do it for you," he said bluntly, watching her, almost wanting her to come back with some snappy retort. The calm way in which Letty swallowed his barbs troubled him more than anything else.

As he suspected, Letty didn't respond. Instead she delivered butter and syrup to the table, avoiding his gaze.

The Letty Ellison Chase remembered had been feisty and fearless. She wouldn't have tolerated impatience or tactlessness from anyone, least of all him.

"This coffee tastes like it came out of a sewer," he claimed, setting his cup down hard on the tabletop. The action made a sharp noise that echoed through the kitchen like a rifle shot in the dark.

The coffee was fine, but he wanted to test Letty's reactions. In years past, she would have flared right back at him, giving as well as she took. Nine years ago, Letty would have told him exactly what he could do with that cup of coffee if he didn't like the taste of it.

She looked up and smiled faintly, her face expressionless. "I'll make another pot."

Chase was stunned. "Forget it," he said quickly, not knowing how else to respond. She glanced at him, her eyes large and soulful.

"But you just said there's something wrong with the coffee."

Chase was left speechless. He watched her, his thoughts twisted and confused.

Dear God, he mused, what had happened to his dauntless Letty?

Letty was working in the garden, carefully planting even rows of corn, when her brother's pickup truck came barreling down the driveway, leaving a thick plume of dust in its wake. When he slammed on the brakes, jumped out of the cab and kicked the side of his truck, Letty paused and left the seed bag behind. She had a sinking suspicion her brother was angry about something.

"Lonny?" she asked quietly. "What's wrong?"

"Of all the stupid, idiotic, crazy women in the world, why did I have to run into this one?"

"What woman?" Letty pried gently.

Lonny pumped his index finger under Letty's nose several times while he struggled to find the words to explain. "She's going to pay for this. There's no way in hell I'm going to let her get away with what she did."

"Lonny, settle down and tell me what happened."

"Look," he shouted, his voice so filled with indignation it shook.

His hand was directed toward the front of the pickup. Letty scanned the area, but she didn't see anything amiss. "What?"

"Here," he said, steering her attention to a nearly indistinguishable dent in the bumper of his ten-year-old vehicle.

The entire truck was full of nicks and dents. A rancher didn't drive a vehicle for as many years as Lonny had without it collecting its share of battle scars. It needed a new left fender, and a new paint job all the way around wouldn't have hurt, either. As far as Letty could tell, Lonny's truck was on its last legs as it was—or tires, as the case might be.

"Oh, you mean that tiny dent," she said, satisfied she'd found the one he was referring to.

"Tiny dent!" he shouted. "That...woman nearly cost me ten years of my life."

"Settle down and just tell me what happened," Letty demanded a second time. She couldn't remember ever seeing her brother this agitated.

"She ran a stop sign. Claimed she didn't see it. What kind of idiot misses a stop sign, for pete's sake?"

"Did she slam into you?"

"Not exactly. I was able to avoid a collision, but in the process I hit the pole."

"What pole?"

"The one holding up the stop sign."

"Oh." Letty didn't mean to appear dense, but Lonny was so angry, he was hardly explaining himself clearly.

He jerked his hat off his head, threading his fingers through his hair hard enough to pull out several strands. "Then ever so sweetly she climbs out of her car, tells me how sorry she is and asks if there's any damage."

"I hope to God you slugged her for that," Letty murmured, rolling her eyes. She didn't know what her brother expected, but as far as Letty could see, Lonny was being completely unreasonable.

"Right away I could see what had happened and I pointed it out to her. But that's not the worst of it," he cried. "She took one look at my truck and said there were so many dents in it, she couldn't possibly know which one our minor altercation had caused." His voice wavered, getting higher in pitch as his agitation grew.

In Letty's opinion the other driver was absolutely right, but it was clear that saying as much could prove dangerous.

"We exchanged a few words," he admitted, kicking the dirt, and avoiding Letty's gaze. "Then she said my truck was nothing more than a pile a junk." Lonny walked all the way around his Ford before he continued, his eyes flashing fire. "There's no way in hell I'm going to let some blind battle ax insult me that way."

"I'm sure her insurance will take care of it," Letty reminded him calmly.

"You're damn straight it will." He slapped his hat back on his head. "You know what else she did? She tried to buy me off!" he declared righteously. "Right there in the middle of the street, in broad daylight, in front of God and man. Now I ask you, do I look like the kind of guy who can easily be bribed?"

At Letty's questioning look, her irate brother continued. "She offered me fifty bucks."

"I take it you refused."

"You're damn right I refused," he shouted. "There's two or three hundred dollars' damage here."

Letty bent over to examine the bumper once more. It looked more like a fifty-dollar dent to her, but she wasn't about to say so. It did seem, however, that Lonny was protesting much too loud and long over a silly dent. Whoever this woman was had certainly managed to gain his attention.

"I got her name and license number right here." Lonny yanked a small piece of paper from his shirt pocket and gingerly unfolded it. "This Joy Fuller is damn lucky I'm not going to report her to the police."

"Joy Fuller," Letty cried, taking the paper away from him. "I know her."

That stopped Lonny short. "Big woman with eyes that spit nails. There's an evil look about her, too—I suspect she normally travels by broom."

"Joy's tall, but not big, and from what I remember, she has pretty eyes. She plays the organ for church on Sundays."

"It's not the same woman," he announced flatly.

"Lonny, honestly, how many women in Red Springs are going to have the same name?"

"What does she do when she isn't playing the church organ? Shrink heads?"

"No," Letty assured him, doing her best not to laugh outright. "I believe she teaches school."

"Dear God," Lonny whispered, shooting a look toward the cloudless sky. "Do the good people of Red Springs realize the kind of woman they're exposing their children to? By all rights, someone should tell the school board."

"I think you've been standing too long in the sun myself. Come inside and have some lunch," Letty offered.

"I'm too damn mad to think about eating. You go ahead without me." With that he stalked off toward the barn.

Letty went into the house, and after pouring herself a glass of iced tea, she reached for the church directory and dialed Joy Fuller's number.

Joy answered brusquely on the first ring. "Yes," she snapped.

"Joy, it's Letty Ellison."

"Letty, I'm sorry, but your brother is the rudest... most arrogant, unreasonable man I've ever encountered."

"I can't tell you how sorry I am about what happened," Letty said, but she had the feeling Joy hadn't even heard her.

"I made a simple mistake and he wouldn't be satisfied with anything less than blood."

"Can you tell me what happened?" She was hoping Joy would be a little more composed than Lonny, but she was beginning to have her doubts.

"I'm sure my version is nothing like your brother's," Joy said, but her voice was raised and filled with agitation. "It's simple, really. I ran the stop sign between Oak and Spruce. Frankly, I don't go that way often and I simply forgot it was there."

Letty knew the intersection. A huge weeping willow partially obscured the stop sign. There had been a short piece in the weekly paper about having the tree trimmed before a collision occurred.

"I was more than willing to admit the entire incident was my fault," Joy continued. "But I couldn't even tell which dent I'd caused, and when I said as much, your brother started acting like a crazy man."

"I don't know what's wrong with Lonny," Letty confessed. "I've never seen him like this."

"I told him I'd contact my insurance company, but to hear him tell it, he figures it'll take two or three thousand dollars to repair all the damage I caused."

That was ridiculous. "I'm sure he didn't mean that... he was just upset—"

"Oh, he meant it all right," Joy interrupted. "Personally, I'd rather have the insurance people deal with him, anyway. As far as I'm concerned, I never want to see your ill-tempered brother again."

Letty didn't blame her, but she had the feeling that for the first time in his life her brother had met his match.

At four o'clock, Lonny came into the house, and it seemed his mood had vastly improved, because he offered Letty a shy smile and said, "Don't worry about cooking me any dinner tonight, I'm going into town."

"Oh?" Letty said, looking up from folding laundry.

"Chase and I are going out to eat."

She smiled and nodded. "Have a good time. You deserve a break."

"I just hope to God that Fuller woman isn't on the streets."

"Honestly, Lonny, are you still mad about that?"

"You're damn right I am. It isn't safe for man or beast with someone like her behind a wheel. Her husband shouldn't let her out of the house without an escort."

"I don't believe she's married."

Lonny snickered. "Trust me, I know why."

"It seems to me you're protesting far too loudly over a simple accident. Could it be that you're attracted to Joy?"

"Attracted?" He stalked off, turned back around and gave a short laugh. "I'd rather tangle with a rattlesnake than with her."

Letty didn't comment, but she couldn't help smiling.

The bath water was running when Lonny returned several minutes later, his shirt unbuttoned and the tails out. "What about you, Letty?"

"What about me?" she responded absently, lifting the laundry basket onto the table. The fresh, clean scent of sun-dried towels made the extra effort of hanging them on the line worth it.

"What are you doing tonight?"

"Nothing much." She planned to do what she did every Saturday night. Sit and watch a little television, polish her nails and read. This Saturday wasn't any different from the rest.

Her brother pulled out a chair, twisted it around and straddled it. "From the minute you arrived home, you've talked about marrying me off. That was the reason you invited that Brandon woman over for dinner. You admitted it yourself."

"A mistake that won't be repeated," she assured him, fluffing up a thick towel.

"But you seemed to think I need a woman."

"A wife, Lonny. There's a difference."

"I've been thinking about what you said, and you might even be right. But what about you?"

Letty found the process of an even crease in the bath towels vitally important. "I don't understand."

"When are you going to get married?"

Never, her mind flashed spontaneously.

"Letty?"

She shrugged, wishing to avoid the issue and knowing it was impossible. "Someday... maybe."

"You're not getting any younger."

Letty supposed she deserved this. Lonny's words were an echo of her own earlier ones to him. Now she was paying the penalty for her one miserable attempt at matchmaking. However, giving Lonny a couple of pat answers wasn't going to work any more than it had worked with her. "Frankly, I don't know that I'll ever marry," she murmured, keeping her gaze lowered.

"Did... Cricket's father hurt you that much?"

Purposely she looked over her shoulder and asked stiffly. "Isn't your bathwater going to overrun?"

"I doubt it. Answer me, Letty."

"I have no intention of discussing what happened with Jason. It's in the past and best forgotten."

Lonny was silent for several moments. "You're so different now. I'm your brother—I care about you—and it hurts me to see you like this. A man isn't worth this kind of pain."

"Lonny, please." She held the towels to her stomach, pressing them hard against her midsection. "If I'm different it isn't because of what happened between me and Jason. It's... other things."

"What other things?" Lonny asked, his eyes filled with gentle concern.

That was one question Letty couldn't answer. At least not yet. So she did her best to sidestep it. "Jason didn't really hurt me, but he taught me an extremely valuable lesson. Oh, it was painful at the time, don't misunderstand me, but he gave me Cricket, and she's my joy. I can only be grateful to Jason for my daughter."

"But don't you hate him for the way he deceived you and then deserted you?"

"No," she admitted reluctantly, uncertain that her brother would understand. "What possible good would that do?"

Apparently absorbed in thought, Lonny rubbed his hand along the back of his neck. After a moment he said, "I don't know, I suppose something deep inside me wants him to suffer for what he put you through. Some guy I've never seen got you pregnant and walked away from you when you needed him most. I guess it hurts my brotherly pride to allow him to get off scot-free for something that underhanded."

Unexpected tears pooled in Letty's eyes at the tenderness she saw in her brother. She blinked them away, and when she was confident her voice was strong enough to speak evenly, she murmured, "If there's anything I learned all those years away from home, it's that there's an order to life. Eventually everything rights itself. I don't need revenge, because sooner or later, as the old adage claims, what goes around, comes around."

"How can you be so calm about it, though?"

"Take your bath, Lonny," she teased with a short laugh. She shoved a freshly folded towel in the direction of his abdomen. "You're driving me nuts. And you say Cricket asks a lot of questions."

* * *

Chase arrived a couple of hours later, gingerly stepping into the kitchen. He completely avoided looking at or speaking to Letty, who was busy getting her and Cricket's dinner ready. He walked past Letty, but was waylaid by Cricket, who was coloring in her book at the dining room table.

Chase seemed somewhat short with the child, Letty noted, but Cricket had a minimum of ten important questions Chase needed to answer regarding Firepower. The five-year-old didn't seem to mind or care when Chase was a little abrupt. Apparently her hero could do no wrong.

Soon enough Lonny appeared. He opened a can of beer, and Letty sat back and listened to her brother relate his hair-raising encounter with the Fuller woman at the stop sign in town as if he were lucky to have escaped with his life.

Letty stayed in the kitchen. It was obvious Chase wanted to avoid her, and that was just as well. He'd gone out of his way to irritate her lately and she'd stood about all she could. Doing battle with Chase now would only deplete her energy. She'd tried to square things with him, once, and he'd made his feelings crystal clear. For now Letty could do nothing but accept the situation.

Her brother continued talking about the car accident, exaggerating the details even more. Letty was astonished that Chase managed to keep from bursting into laughter through the lengthy story. Even more amazing was the fact their neighbor was completely sympathetic to her brother's part in this tale of woe. "Where do you figure we'll eat?" Lonny asked, coming into the kitchen for a second can of beer.

"Billy's Steak House?" Chase called out from the living room. "I'm in the mood for a thick sirloin. A rare one."

Letty remembered Chase had always liked his meat bloody. "You know what else I'm in the mood for?" Lonny asked, and his voice dipped in a suggestive murmur.

Letty didn't hear the response, but whatever it was caused the two men to laugh like a couple of rambunctious teenagers. Amused, Letty smiled faintly and placed the cookie sheet with frozen French fries inside the oven.

It wasn't until later, while Letty was washing up the dinner dishes, that she understood exactly what Chase and Lonny had been mumbling about. They were going out to eat all right, but it wasn't the church bazaar they were headed for afterward.

Following their meal, Lonny and Chase were going to a well-known house on the outskirts of town. One with a red light bulb on the front porch.

Rinsing off the cookie sheet, Letty dropped it against the countertop as if it had burned her. Next she jerked the hand towel off the holder so hard it nearly took the wire rack off the wall.

Tight-lipped, she stormed into the living room and plopped herself down in the overstuffed chair, crossing her arms hard enough to slice her in two. Cricket was playing with her dolls on the carpet and Letty pushed the buttons on the remote control for the television with a vengeance. Unable to force herself to watch the situation comedy she usually enjoyed, she turned off the set and placed a hand over her face. Closing her eyes was a mistake. A bad one.

Instantly a vision of Chase in front of a large-breasted woman lying on a bed, holding her arms open to receive him, filled her mind. Letty could see Chase as clear as a picture. He was undressing matter-of-factly, unselfconscious, until he stood completely naked in front of the woman on the bed. Letty's mind's eye was struck by the smooth-muscled, arrogant masculinity of his golden frame. Her fingers flexed, longing to touch him and experience for herself the strength and power of his body. The vision didn't dissipate, and trapped in the vivid musing, Letty was powerless to move. She noted that there wasn't a spare ounce of fat on him. He held himself with a straight-limbed grace and when he moved toward the bed, his muscles rippled. Something stopped him, however, and he turned back to discover Letty watching him. The hungry look in his eyes was quickly replaced with an angry frown.

"Oh, God," Letty cried, bolting upright out of the chair, needing an escape.

"Mommy?"

Letty was breathing so hard her pulse started to roar in her ear, drowning out reason. She looked down on Cricket, playing so contentedly, and announced, as if it were of vital importance, "It's time for bed."

"Already?"

"Yes... remember we have church in the morning," she said, forcing some enthusiasm into her voice.

"Will Chase be there?"

"I... I don't know." If he was, she would take a good deal of pleasure in staring him down. He would have one hell of a nerve showing up in church after a night... a night like the one he was planning. She recalled the way he'd glared at her the first Sunday she was back in church. Her shoulders heaved with indignation all the way up the stairs.

Several hours later, Cricket was in bed asleep and Letty stared sightlessly into the dark. There wasn't anything potent enough for her to take that would induce sleep. To her consternation, her fury multiplied with every passing minute. When she could stand it no longer, Letty marched down the stairs and sat in the dark.

As she lingered there waiting, her anger grew. She was suffering with an indescribable, unexplainable pain that cut deep and sharp into the core of her being.

Letty wasn't there long before she heard the sounds of a vehicle coming up the driveway. The back door opened and the two men stumbled into the house loudly enough to terrorize the barn animals.

"Sh-h-h," Chase whispered loudly, "you'll wake Letty."

"God forbid." Lonny's slurred words were followed by a husky laugh.

"You needn't worry, I'm already awake," Letty announced righteously, arms akimbo, as she stood in the doorway leading from the dining room into the living room. She turned on the light and took one look at her brother, who was leaning heavily against Chase, one arm draped across his neighbor's neck, and announced, "You're drunk."

Lonny circled the air with his index finger. "Nothing gets past you, does it?"

"I'll get him up the stairs for you," Chase said, half dragging Lonny across the kitchen.

Lonny's mood was jovial and he attempted to sing some ditty, off-key, the words barely recognizable. Chase shushed him a second time, reminding him that Cricket was asleep even if Letty wasn't, but his warning went unheeded.

Letty led the way, marching up the stairs with the precision an army general would have admired. She held open Lonny's bedroom door and flipped on the light with an authority that few would question.

Once inside his bedroom, Lonny stumbled and fell across the mattress, glaring up at the ceiling. Letty moved into the room and, with some effort, managed to remove his boots.

Chase brought down a quilt from inside the closet and unfolded it across his friend. "He'll sleep most of the night now."

"I'm sure he will," Letty said tightly. She left Lonny's bedroom and marched down the stairs in the same clipped gait she'd ascended with a few minutes earlier. She was pacing the kitchen when Chase joined her.

"What's the matter with you?" he asked, frowning.

"How dare you bring my brother home in that condition," she demanded, turning on him.

"You wanted me to leave him in town? Drunk?"

If he'd revealed the least amount of guilt or contrition for what he'd done, Letty might have been able to let him go without a word. But he stood in front of her, and all Letty could see was the naked woman in the bed, holding her arms open to him.

Fury surged up inside her, blocking out sanity. All week he'd been baiting her, wanting to hurt her for the pain she'd caused him. Tonight he'd succeeded.

"I hate you," she sobbed, lunging at him, wanting him to suffer the way she had.

He grabbed her wrists and held them tightly at her sides. "Letty, good God, what's gotten into you?"

She squirmed and twisted in his arms, frantically trying to free herself, but she was helplessly trapped, despite her best efforts.

"Letty?"

She glared up at him, her face streaked with tears she didn't care to explain, her shoulders heaving with emotion.

"You're angry because Lonny is drunk?" he whispered, his words gentle and disturbed.

"No," she cried, struggling once more, flinging her torso back and forth. "You went to that house...you think I don't know...but I do."

"What the hell are you talking about?"

"The house...with the red light," she cried, and swallowed a huge, wrenching sob.

Chase frowned, then slowly shook his head. "Letty, no!"

"Don't lie to me...don't, I can't bear it."

"Letty." He tightened his hold on her wrists, hauling her against him until she felt like a flower crushed between the pages of a fat dictionary. Furious, she buckled, but he held her firm within his steely embrace. When her energy was spent, she glared up at him, wanting to hate him with everything that was in her. Her eyes were wild and brimmed with hot tears.

"Oh, Letty," he murmured, and leaned down to settle his mouth over hers.

The last thing Letty wanted at that moment was his touch or his kiss. She tried to shake her head and free herself from this small intimacy, but he wouldn't allow it. The hard pressure of his mouth, burning over hers, forced her head back.

"No," she begged, sobbing.

"Yes." He released her hands and wrapped his arms around her waist, half lifting her from the floor. All the while he was kissing her with a passion that was as heated as her anger, as though he had only a few seconds to convey all that he was feeling.

Letty meant to brace her hands against his chest and use her strength to push him away. Instead her arms inched upward until she was gripping his lapels. The anger that had consumed her seconds before was dissolving into a firestorm of desire, bringing a part of her to life that had lain dormant from the moment she'd left Chase Brown's arms nine years before.

Chapter Five

Chase kissed her again and again while his hands roved up and down the curve of her spine as though he couldn't get enough of the feel of her.

Letty felt her body come alive in his arms as his touch began to strip away the pain and disappointment that had come into her life in their long years apart. She was completely vulnerable to him in that moment. Vulnerable to his hands, his mouth and, above all, his will.

And Chase wanted her.

He couldn't seem to hold still. His hands were impatiently fiddling with the sash that held together the front of her long robe. While he worked at the opening, he ground his hips into her, until the evidence of his arousal was boldly pressed against her.

"Letty..."

Whatever he'd meant to say was lost when his mouth covered hers with a hungry groan that seemed to have been painfully forced from him. Letty's lips parted in eager response. Their tongues met in a fiery duel that created the fiercest, hottest ache in her abdomen. A weakness flooded her entire being and her legs felt so rubbery she was forced to lean into him, letting him absorb the bulk of her weight.

Letty had been back in Red Springs for several weeks, but she wasn't truly home until Chase had taken her in his arms and kissed her. Now that she was with him, a peace settled over her. Whatever lay before her with her heart condition, life or death, she was ready, wrapped in the serenity his embrace offered. Returning to this small town and the Bar E were only a tiny part of what made it so important to have come home for this heart surgery. Her love for Chase had been the real draw; it was what had pulled her back, and for the first time she was willing to acknowledge it.

Once Chase had succeeded in opening her robe, he slowly eased it off her shoulders, letting it slip soundlessly onto the floor. Then his eager fingers were busy with the small buttons that held together the front of her silk gown. When he'd freed the material, he slowly, reluctantly, relinquished her mouth. Burying his face in the curve of her neck, he dragged several deep, savage breaths into his lungs in what appeared to be an effort to gain control of himself.

Letty burrowed her fingers into his hair, her eyes squeezed shut, her head tossed back. Neither she nor Chase spoke. They held on to each other as though they feared letting go would separate them for all eternity.

Chase's arms were wound around her so tightly it was nearly impossible for Letty to breathe properly. He must have sensed this, because slowly, as if against every dictate of his will, he worked his hands from her back to her front. He slid his callused fingertips first over her ribs, gently examining each finely shaped bone, then made his way upward until the undersides of her breasts amply filled his palms. His touch was like silk and satin, gentle beyond belief as he lifted each breast as though weighing it in a delicate measure.

A sigh eased from Letty at the exquisite pleasure his velvet stroke evoked within her. Chase lifted his head and tenderly kissed her lips. The thick pad of his thumb circled her hard nipples and she blinked at the soft ribbon of delight that blanketed her.

Chase brought her even closer into his arms and deepened his probing kiss, until Letty was sure her knees were about to buckle. Then his mouth abandoned hers to explore the scented hollow of her throat with a series of deliciously moist forays. Gradually he eased his mouth lower until his lips found the tips of her full breasts. Ever so gently, as if in awe, he kissed the valley between them, sliding his face back and forth, his tongue teasing and coaxing a whimpering response from her. Moving slightly, his lips traced wide imaginary circles around one peaked, trembling nipple until Letty shuddered and whimpered anew.

Chase's hungry lips silenced her soft cry of pleasure.

Tears welled in her eyes, then ran unheeded down her face. The moisture added to the excitement as Chase pressed endless kisses over her face until she forgot everything but the love she'd stored in her heart for him.

When she was certain nothing could bring her any more pleasure than his kiss, he brought his hand to the juncture between her legs, easing the silken material away until his fingers softly brushed the sensitive skin of her inner thigh.

"Mommy."

Cricket's voice, coming from the top of the stairway, penetrated the fog of Letty's desire. Chase apparently hadn't heard her, and Letty was forced to murmur a protest and gently push him aside.

"Yes, darling, what's wrong?" Her voice sounded wobbly and weak even to herself.

Chase stumbled back and raised a hand to his face, as if he'd been suddenly awakened from a dream and was still lost and disoriented. Letty longed to go to him, but she dared not.

"Uncle Lonny keeps singing and he woke me up," Cricket cried.

Letty groaned and quickly refastened her gown. She couldn't look at Chase, fearing what she would read in his eyes, although she prayed he understood that she couldn't ignore her daughter.

"Mommy!" Cricket called louder this time. "Please hurry. Uncle Lonny sings terrible!"

"I'll be right there." She bent and retrieved her robe, her fingers shaking. "Chase..."

"This isn't the time to do any talking," he said gruffly, sounding annoyed and unsettled.

"But there's so much we need to discuss." She brushed the soft curls away from her face. "Don't you think so?"

"Not now."

"But..."

"Go take care of Cricket," he said, and turned away from her.

Letty's heart was heavy as she started for the stairway. A dim light illuminated the top, where Cricket was standing, her fingers plugging her ears.

In the background, Letty heard her brother's drunken rendition of "Puff the Magic Dragon." Another sound blended with the first, as Chase opened the kitchen door and walked out of the house.

The next morning, Letty moved around the downstairs as quietly as possible in an effort not to wake her brother. From everything she'd seen of him the night before, Lonny was going to have one hell of a hangover.

The coffee was perking merrily in the kitchen as Letty worked the brush through Cricket's long hair while the five-year-old stood patiently still in the bathroom.

"Was Uncle Lonny sick last night?" Cricket asked.

"I don't think so." Letty couldn't remember hearing him get out of bed.

"He sounded sick when he was singing."

Letty smiled, amused. "I suppose he did at that." She finished tying the bright red ribbons in Cricket's hair and returned to the kitchen for a cup of coffee. To her surprise, Lonny was sitting at the table, neatly dressed in a suit and tie.

"Lonny!"

"'Morning," he greeted her.

Although his eyes appeared bloodshot, Lonny didn't look bad. In fact, it appeared he was going out of his way to act chipper.

Letty eyed him warily, unsure what to make of him. Only a few hours earlier he'd been decidedly drunk.

"How are you feeling?" she asked, carefully studying him.

"Wonderful."

He didn't look as though his escapades from his night on the town had done him any harm. Unexpectedly he stood, then reached for his Bible, doing his best to wipe the dust off the leather binding.

"Well, are you two coming to church with me or not?" he asked, staring at both of them.

Letty was so shocked it took her a moment to respond. "Yes, of course."

It wasn't until they'd pulled into the church parking lot that Letty understood her brother's newly formed desire for religion. He was attending the morning service not because of any real longing to worship. He'd come expecting to meet Joy Fuller again. The thought surprised Letty as much as it pleased her. As she'd guessed earlier, Red Springs's second-grade teacher had managed to stir some interest in her crusty bachelor brother. The thought of Lonny and Joy together produced a smile. From what little bit Letty knew of the church organist, she would never fit Lonny's definition of the dutiful wife.

The congregation had started to file through the wide double doors by the time they'd arrived. "I want to sit close to the front," Lonny told Letty, anxiously looking around.

"If you don't mind I'd prefer to sit near the back," Letty countered, feeling somewhat guilty. "Cricket is often restless."

"She'll be good today, won't you, cupcake?"

In an effort to please her uncle, the child nodded eagerly. Lonny took her small hand in his and, disregarding Letty's wishes, led the way up the center aisle.

Groaning inwardly, Letty followed her brother. One thing his choice of seats did do was give Letty the opportunity to scan the church for any sign of Chase. Her quick survey told her he'd decided against attending services this morning, which was just as well.

Letty had been dreading encountering him again, yet at the same moment she was eager to talk to him. She felt both frightened and excited by their rekindled desire for each other. But he'd left her so brusquely the night before that she wasn't sure what to expect. So much would depend on his reaction to her at their next meeting. Then she would know what he was feeling—if he regretted kissing her or if he felt the same swirling excitement she had.

Organ music filled the church, and once they were settled in the pew, Letty reached for a hymnal. Lonny sang at the top of his voice while staring intently at Joy as she played the organ. Letty had to resist the urge to remind him his behavior bordered on the impolite.

When Joy faltered over a couple of notes, Lonny smiled with what resembled smug satisfaction. Letty moaned inwardly. So this was her brother's game!

"Mommy," Cricket whispered, standing on the pew and staring into the crowd. "Chase is here."

Letty's grip on the hymnal tightened. "That's nice, sweetheart."

"Can I go sit with him?"

"Not now."

"Later?"

"No."

"How come?"

"Cricket," Letty pleaded. "Sit down and be quiet."

"But I like Chase and I want to sit with him."

"Maybe next week," she said in a low voice in an effort to appease the squirming child.

"Can I ask him after the pastor's through talking at everybody?"

Letty nodded, willing to agree to just about anything by then. The next time her brother insisted on sitting in the front row, he would do so alone.

No worship service had ever seemed to take longer for Letty. Cricket fidgeted the entire hour, eager to run and talk to Chase. Lonny wasn't much better. He continued to stare at Joy and did everything but make funny faces at her to distract the poor woman. Before the service was half over, Letty felt like giving him a good, hard shake. Even as a teenager, she'd never seen her elder brother behave more childishly. The only reason he'd come to church was to make poor Joy as uncomfortable as he possibly could.

By the time Letty made her way outside the church, Cricket had already found Chase. Just from the stiff way in which he was standing, Letty knew he'd planned on escaping without talking to her. The last thing he'd wanted was to be confronted by Cricket. Letty's heart swelled with fresh pain. So this was how he felt.

He regretted everything.

Letty hastened to her daughter's side and took her small hand in his own. "Uncle Lonny is waiting for us by the truck," she said, her eyes avoiding Chase.

"But I haven't asked Chase if I can sit with him next week."

"I'm sure he has other friends he'd prefer beside him," Letty answered, hiding her impatience.

"I can answer for myself." Chase's voice was clipped and unfriendly. "As it happens, Cricket, I think your mother is right. It would be best if you continued to sit with her in church."

"Can't you sit in the same row with us?"

"No."

"Why not?"

Chase didn't answer her for an awkward moment, but when he did, he looked past Letty. "Because I prefer not to."

"Okay," Cricket said, accepting that explanation without a problem.

"It's time to go," Letty said tightly. A low-grade pain continued to ripple down her spine. Only a few hours earlier, Chase had held her in his arms, kissed her as if there were no tomorrow and loved her with a gentleness that had fired her senses back to life. And in the light of a fresh day, he'd told her as plainly as if he'd shouted it from the church steps that it had all been a mistake, nothing had changed and he didn't want anything to do with her.

After all the hurt she'd suffered in California, Letty thought she was immune to this kind of pain.

In the span of a few minutes Chase had taught her otherwise.

Cricket raced ahead of Letty to Lonny's truck and eagerly climbed inside. For his part, her brother seemed to be taking his own sweet time about heading back to the ranch. He talked to a couple of the men, then joined Cricket and Letty.

"We're ready anytime you are," Letty said from inside the truck.

"In a minute," he returned absently, glancing around.

It didn't take Letty long to realize Lonny was waiting for Joy to make an appearance. In minutes the parking lot was nearly deserted. There were only three other cars left, and Lonny had parked next to one of those vehicles. Letty didn't need a college degree to figure out that one belonged to Joy.

Lonny was sitting in the truck, with the window down, his elbow resting on the frame, utterly content to laze away in the sunshine while he waited.

"Lonny?" Letty pressed. "Can we please go?" After the way he'd behaved, Letty had every intention of having a serious discussion with her brother regarding his behavior in church, but she preferred to do it when Cricket wasn't around to listen.

"It'll only be a minute more."

His words were true enough. Within a few seconds, Joy came out of the church. She hesitated momentarily when she saw Lonny's pickup.

"What are you going to say to her?" Letty whispered angrily, her patience quickly evaporating.

"Nothing much," Lonny murmured back, clearly distracted. When the organist approached her car, Lonny climbed out of the pickup, leaned indolently against the side, bracing his foot against the fender.

"I wouldn't do that if I were you," Joy warned, stiffly meeting his look.

She was nearly as tall as Lonny, her dark hair softly styled so it fell in lazy curls around her face. Her cheeks were a bright rosy hue and Letty couldn't help wonder if confronting Lonny again was the cause for their being so flushed.

"Do what?" Lonny demanded.

"Put your foot on the side of that truck. You might damage that priceless antique."

"I'll have you know, this truck is only ten years old."

Joy feigned surprise, widening her eyes while she pressed her hand against her chest. "Is that so? I could have sworn you claimed otherwise only yesterday. But, then, it seems you have a good deal of trouble keeping your facts straight."

"You were impossible to talk to yesterday and I can see that today isn't going to be any better."

"Impossible?" Joy echoed. "Me? You were the one jumping up and down and acting like an idiot."

"Me?" Lonny threw back his head and forced a loud laugh. "That's priceless."

Joy ignored him and continued walking to her car.

Lonny dropped his foot and yanked open the truck door. "I thought we might be able to settle our differences, but it's clear you're in no mood to be reasonable. Well, that's perfectly fine with me. You're completely unreasonable."

"Perhaps I am, but at least I don't throw temper tantrums in the middle of the street."

"I don't run down innocent motorists."

"You're about as innocent as Adolf Hitler."

"Hitler!" Lonny cried, and slapped his hat against his thigh. "Just who the hell do you think you are talking to me like that?"

"If you don't like the way I talk, then stay away from me."

"It'll be my pleasure."

For all his patience earlier, Lonny couldn't seem to get out of the parking lot fast enough. He gripped the steering wheel as if he planned to drive in the Indy 500.

"Lonny," Letty ordered, "slow down."

When he reached the stop sign at the end of the street, he drove off as if the very fires of hell were licking at his heels.

"Lonny," cried Letty a second time. If he continued to drive in this manner, she would prefer to walk home. "You're driving like a maniac. Stop the truck this minute!"

"Didn't I tell you that woman was a living, breathing shrew?" he demanded, quickly reducing his speed. To his credit, he looked surprised by how fast he'd been traveling. "I swear she drives me over the edge."

"Then do as she suggests and stay away from her," Letty advised, shaking her head in wonder. But to be honest, she doubted that Lonny would.

"I figured you had to be wrong," her brother continued, as though he hadn't heard her. "The Joy Fuller you mentioned yesterday couldn't possibly be the same one. I decided I had to check it out personally."

Letty didn't believe him for a moment. "I think Joy got under your skin, big brother."

He ignored her comment. "Did you see the way she laid into me?"

"Lonny, to be honest, I thought you provoked her."

"Then you didn't see things the way they happened," he shouted, shooting Letty a look of indignation. "I was only trying to be friendly."

Her brother was being unreasonable, but he was too hotheaded to recognize as much. "Frankly, I like Joy and I think you were unnecessarily rude to her this morning," Letty returned primly.

"When?"

"Oh, honestly, think about it! The only reason you came to church was to intimidate her into making a mistake while she was playing the organ. When you succeeded, I thought you were going to stand up and cheer."

Lonny cast her a look that suggested Letty consider counseling for her wild imagination. "You're all wet, little sister."

Letty rolled her eyes. "Have you figured out why you feel so strongly?"

"Because she's a wildcat who needs to be put in her place, that's why!"

"And you think you're the one to do it?"

"You're damn right! I'm not about to let any woman get away with the things she said to me."

"Calling this truck an antique doesn't exactly sound like fighting words to me." Her brother had been bitten all right; he just didn't know how to deal with the itch.

Lonny turned into the long dusty driveway leading to the house. "You women really stick together, don't you? I have to say I would admire that quality if you weren't all so blame stupid."

"Stupid?"

Lonny pulled the truck into his usual parking spot and turned off the engine. "That's right! Look at you—you're the perfect example, taking off on some fool dream. Chase should have never have let you go."

"He couldn't have stopped me—no one could have. I wasn't going to end up like Mom, stuck out here in no-man's-land, working so hard... why she was little more than a slave."

Lonny's gaze widened as he turned to her. "That's the way you see Mom?"

"You mean you don't?" How could her brother be so blind? Their mother had worked herself into an early grave, sacrificing her talent and her dreams for a few head of cattle and a cruel, unforgiving land.

"Of course I don't. Mom had a good life here. She loved the ranch and everything about it."

"You're so oblivious to the facts that you can't see the truth, can you? You're too much like Dad. You even think like him! Women aren't good for anything except cooking and cleaning and an occasional tumble in bed. Mom hated it here, only she wasn't honest enough to admit it, not even to herself."

"And you hate it, too?"

"I did."

Lonny climbed out of the pickup and slammed the door shut. "No one asked you to come back, Letty. You could turn around and head right back to California for all I care." With that he stormed into the house.

Fueled by her anger, Letty continued to sit in the truck, tears running down her face. She and Lonny had both been furious and the conversation had quickly gotten out of control. She should never have said the things she did. And Lonny shouldn't have, either. Now wasn't the time or the place to deal with the past.

"Mommy?" Cricket leaned against her mother, obviously confused and a little frightened. "Why was Uncle Lonny shouting at you?"

"He was angry, honey."

"You were shouting at him, too."

"I know." She climbed out of the cab, and walked into the house. Lonny glared at her and she glared right back, surprised by how heated her response to him remained. In an effort to avoiding continuing their argument, Letty went upstairs and changed her clothes. Without another word, she marched outside and reached for the hoe. Venting her frustration in the garden was bound to help. Once they'd both cooled down, they could discuss the matter rationally.

Without a word, Lonny left soon afterward, barreling down the driveway as if he couldn't get away from her fast enough.

She was happy to see him go.

Nothing felt right to Chase. It was as if his world had been knocked off its axis and he was struggling against an unknown force to right it again.

Letty was to blame for this, but Chase was at a loss to know how to deal with her and, worse, to understand himself. A part of him yearned with everything in him to take Letty in his arms, love her, care for her and make up to her for the pain and disappointment she'd suffered. Yet something deep and powerful within him wouldn't allow him to do it. He found himself saying and doing things he'd never intended.

Telling her he preferred not to sit in church with her was a prime example. The only reason he even attended the service was to be close to Letty. It was only when he was in the house of God that the resentment and the bitterness left him. He rarely listened to the sermons. Instead he sat and pretended Letty was the one sitting next to him. He thought about what it would be like to hear her sweet voice again as she sang. He imagined how it would feel to sit and hold her hand while the pastor spoke.

Cricket had provided him with the perfect excuse to do those things. His pride need not have suffered, and he would be doing something to appease the kid. No one need know that being with Letty was what he'd wanted all along.

Yet he'd rejected Letty's offer flat out. Chase didn't know how to explain his own actions. He was behaving like an idiot and he had no one to blame but himself.

On second thought, his actions made perfect sense. He was protecting himself, and with damn good reason. The way he saw things, if Letty intended to make a life for herself in Red Springs, then she would be doing something about finding a decent job and settling down. Every piece of evidence pointed in the direction of her leaving again. It was as if she were planning an extended vacation and once she'd rested, she would be on her way again. Other than the garden she'd planted, he couldn't see any signs of permanence.

Chase couldn't allow his heart to get involved with Letty a second time. He hadn't fully healed from the first go around. It wasn't so simple, however. He loved her, and frankly, he doubted he would ever stop.

Rubbing his hand across his face, Chase drew in a deep, sobering breath. He hadn't intended to touch her the night before, but her eyes had been shooting sharp bullets of outrage at him, and it was so much like the old Letty that he'd forgotten that he'd promised himself he would never touch her again. One kiss and he'd been lost. Dear Lord, she tasted of everything that was good. A small piece of paradise in his arms, and after one sample of her honeyed lips, there had been no stopping him.

Even now, hours later, the memory of the way she'd melted in his embrace had the power to arouse him. He forcibly pushed the thought out of his mind. The best thing to do was forget it ever happened. That was the only way he could deal with it.

He went outside and climbed inside the truck, intending to go into town and do some shopping. Perhaps keeping busy would ease the ache in his loins.

Still confused, Chase wondered if he would feel differently if Letty had made more of an effort to acknowledge their lovemaking. Cricket had come running up to him after the church service and Letty wouldn't even meet his eye. Obviously the memory of their encounter served only to embarrass her.

That pleased him.

That infuriated him.

If Letty was disconcerted by their kissing and touching, then it said she didn't often let men love her like that. The thought of another man intimately touching her the way he had was enough to produce a fireball of resentment in the pit of his stomach. It was a subject he went to great lengths to avoid considering.

Her actions that morning infuriated him, too, because she so obviously regretted the things they'd done. While he'd spent the night dreaming of holding and kissing her, she'd apparently been filled with remorse. Maybe she thought he wasn't good enough to touch her.

Telephone poles whizzed past him as he considered the bleak thought.

Out of the corner of his eye a flash of red captured his attention. He looked again. By God, it was Cricket, standing alone at the end of the Bar E driveway, crying. She was wearing the same dress she'd worn at church.

Chase stepped on his brakes and quickly backed up. When he reached the little girl, she looked up and immediately started running to him.

"Chase...oh, Mr. Chase."

"Cricket," he snapped, climbing out of the truck, angry with Letty for being so irresponsible about her young daughter. "What are you doing here? Where's your mother?"

The little girl ran and hugged his waist, sobbing and trembling. "Uncle Lonny and Mommy shouted at each other. Then Uncle Lonny left and Mommy went outside. Now she's sleeping in the garden and I can't wake her up."

Chapter Six

Letty sat on the porch steps, rubbing her hand across her face. Her knees felt incredibly weak and her eyes stubbornly refused to focus. It had been through the sheer force of her will that she'd made it from the garden to the back steps. Alarm circled her like a hawk scrutinizing its prey. Although she'd called for Cricket, the little girl was nowhere to be found. Letty had to find her daughter despite the spiraling waves of nausea and weakness.

The last thing Letty remembered clearly was standing in the garden, shoveling the hoe for all she was worth, weeding because she was furious with Lonny and equally upset with herself for being drawn into such a pointless argument.

"Cricket," Letty called out once more, shocked by how incredibly rickety her voice sounded. Her daughter had been standing beside her only a minute or two before. Now she was gone.

The roar of an approaching truck was nearly deafening. Letty didn't have the strength or the energy to stand, so she sat with her back ramrod straight and waited. Whoever it was would simply have to come to her.

"Letty?"

"Mommy, Mommy."

Chase was out of the pickup so fast he looked like a jagged piece of lightning. He quickly devoured the space that separated them. Cricket was directly behind him, her face wet and streaked with tears.

Confused, Letty glanced up at the pair. She hadn't a clue how Cricket had come to be with Chase. Ever more surprising was the way he looked, as though he were ill himself. His face was gray, set and determined, but for what reason she couldn't understand.

"What the hell happened?" Chase demanded, his voice sounding like a roaring clap of thunder.

For a long moment her mind refused to function. "I . . . I think I fainted."

"Fainted?"

"I must have." Once more she wiped a hand across her face, forcing a smile, although the action depleted her of strength. By sheer resolution, she started to stand, but before she was fully on her feet, Chase had loaded her into his arms.

"Chase," she protested, her voice weak and strained. "Put me down . . . I'm perfectly all right."

"Like hell you are."

He sounded furious, as if she'd purposely fainted as a ploy to gain his sympathy. The thought added to her frustration and she arched her back and kicked a couple of times, bucking thin air, demanding that he free her.

Her efforts, however, were futile; Chase tightened his grip on her.

Cricket ran ahead of him and opened the back door. "Is Mommy sick?"

"Yes," Chase answered, his mouth a white line of impatience. He didn't so much as look at Letty as he marched through the house, his stride clipped and hasty.

"I'm perfectly fine, sweetheart," Letty countered, doing her best to reassure the little girl, who ran next to Chase, her young face intently studying her mother. Cricket looked so worried and frightened, and that only served to distress Letty all the more.

Chase gently deposited Letty on the sofa, then knelt beside her, his gaze roaming her face with narrowed eyes, inspecting her for any apparent injury. Reluctantly, as if he remained annoyed, he raised his hand and pressed it over her forehead. "You're not feverish," he announced.

"Of course I'm not," she shot back, awkwardly rising to an upright position. If everyone would only give her a few minutes alone and some breathing space, she would feel worlds better. "I'm fine, I tell you. I was weeding the garden, and the next thing I knew I was lying between rows of corn. Obviously I had too much sun."

Cricket knelt on the carpet next to Chase. "I couldn't wake you up," she murmured, her blue eyes as round as beach balls, her face shiny with tears. Her lower lip started to tremble.

Letty reached out to hug her close. "I'm sorry I frightened you, honey."

"Did you hit your head?" Chase demanded.

"I don't think so." Tentatively she touched the back of her skull. As far as she could tell, there wasn't so much as a lump to suggest she'd hit anything besides the soft dirt.

"Cricket, go get your mother a glass of water."

The child took off, running as if doing within the next five seconds as Chase had requested was a life-and-death matter.

"How in heaven's name did Cricket ever find you?" Letty asked, frowning. Her daughter wouldn't have known the way to Chase's ranch, and even if she had, it was several minutes away by car.

"I saw her on the road."

Letty's long lashes fluttered downward, darkening her face as the realization struck her. "Dear God, she got that far?"

"She was in a panic, and with Lonny gone, she didn't know what to do."

Letty opened her eyes and focused them on Chase. "I'm grateful you stopped. Thank you."

Cricket charged into the living room with the glass of water, which was only partially filled. Letty assumed the other half had spilled from one end of the house to the other. She planted a soft kiss on her daughter's cheek as a thank-you.

"I think your mother could use a blanket, too," Chase murmured. His mouth was set and obstinate, but for what reason Letty could only speculate. It was unreasonable for him to be angry with her because she'd fainted!

Once more Cricket raced out of the room.

Chase continued to stare at Letty, his forehead rutted by concern. He seemed to think that if he glared at her long enough, then he would discover the reason she'd taken ill so suddenly. She boldly met his look, and did her best to reassure him with a smile, but obviously failed.

Chase briefly closed his eyes, and when he opened them again, the concerned agony that briefly fluttered into his gaze was a shock. He turned away from her as if he couldn't bear to have her look at him, his profile as hard as rock.

"Dear God, Letty, I didn't know what to think when I found Cricket," he said, and dragged a breath between clenched teeth. "For all I knew you could have been dead."

Motivated by something other than reason, Letty raised her hand to his face, running the tips of her fingers down the side of his tensed jaw. "Would you have cared?" she whispered.

"Yes," he cried, as though the word had been tortured out of him. "I don't want to, but God help me, I do."

He reached for her, kissing her awkwardly, then hungrily, his mouth roving from one side of her face to the other as if he had to keep kissing her to know she was alive. His lips nipped at hers in a short series of kisses, then moved to brush against her eyes, her cheek, her ears and finally her throat.

They were interrupted by Cricket, who whisked into the room with enough racket for Letty to suspect she'd brought a pair of charging elephants with her.

"I brought Mommy a blankey," Cricket announced. She edged her way between Letty and Chase and draped her knit yellow blanket across Letty's lap.

"Thank you, sweetheart."

Chase rose and paced the area in front of the sofa. "I'm calling Doc Hanley."

Letty was overcome by panic. She'd purposely avoided the physician, who'd been seeing her family members for as long as she could remember. Although she trusted Doc

Hanley implicitly, if she were to be seen going in and out of his office on a regular basis there might be talk that would filter back to Lonny or Chase and cause them concern.

"Chase," she cried, "calling Doc Hanley isn't necessary. I was in the sun too long...that's all...I should have known better."

"You're in the sun every day, damn it. Something's wrong. I want you to see a doctor."

"All right," she agreed, thinking fast. "I'll make an appointment, if it'll make you feel any better, but I can't today—none of the offices are open."

"I'll drive you to the hospital," he countered, his mouth set in a tight, stubborn line.

"The nearest hospital is a good hour from here."

"I don't care."

"Chase, please, I'm a little unsettled, but basically I'm fine. What I need more than anything is a little rest. The last thing I want to do is sit in a hot, stuffy truck and ride all the way into Rock Springs so some doctor can tell me I had too much sun."

Chase paced back and forth a couple of times, clearly undecided. He resembled a thundercloud.

"I think I'll just go upstairs and lie down. It's about time for Cricket's nap, anyway," Letty said calmly, although her heart was racing. She really did feel terrible. Dizzy. Disoriented. Nauseous.

Chase wasn't pleased about Letty's proposal, but nodded. "I'll stay here in case you need me later."

"That really isn't necessary, Chase."

He turned and glared at her. "Don't argue with me, Letty, I'm not in the mood for it."

That much was obvious. With some effort, although she struggled to conceal it, Letty stood and walked up the stairs. Chase followed her as though he suspected she didn't have the strength to make it. Letty was exhausted by the time she entered her bedroom.

"I'll take a nap and feel fresh as a rosebud in a couple of hours. You wait and see."

"Right," Chase said tersely. As soon as she was lying down, he left.

Letty sat across the desk from Dr. Faraday the following Monday afternoon. He'd wanted to talk to her after the examination.

"I haven't received your records from your physician in California yet, but I'm expecting them any day," he said, frowning.

Letty nodded, doing her best to disguise her uneasiness. As she'd promised Chase, she'd contacted the doctor first thing Monday morning. The heart specialist she'd seen the week before in Rock Springs had asked that she come in right away. His brooding look troubled her now.

"Generally, how are you feeling?"

"Fine." That was a slight exaggeration, but overall, other than being excessively tired and the one fainting spell, she *had* felt generally healthy most of the time.

Dr. Faraday nodded and entered something in her file. It was all Letty could do not to stand up and read what he'd written. He was a large man, his face dominated by a bushy mustache that reminded Letty of an umbrella. His eyes were piercing, and Letty doubted that much got past him.

"The results from the tests we did last week are back from the lab, and I've had a chance to review them. The way I see it, we won't be able to delay this surgery much longer. I'll confer with my colleague, Dr. Frederickson, and make my report to the state. I'm going to ask that they put a rush on their approval."

Letty nodded and watched as he lifted his prescription pad from the corner of his desk. "I want you to start taking these tablets right away."

"Okay," Letty agreed. "How long will I be in the hospital, Doctor?" As much as she tried to appear outwardly calm, Letty was frightened. She'd never felt more alone. Her sense of humor, which had helped her earlier, seemed to have deserted her. The mountain had never loomed so steep and appeared, at that moment, unscalable.

"You should plan on being hospitalized for as long as two weeks," he replied absently, writing out a second prescription.

"Two weeks?" Letty cried. It sounded like an eternity, far longer than what she'd expected.

His gaze caught hers. "Is that a problem?"

"Not exactly." It seemed foolish now, but Letty had automatically assumed that Lonny would be able to watch Cricket for her. He would be more than happy to do exactly that, she was confident, if her hospital stay was only a few days. Even with the responsibilities of the ranch, he'd have found a way to look after the five-year-old. True, it would have been a hassle for him, but Lonny was family. Two weeks, though, was much too long for Letty even to consider asking him.

Lonny and Cricket were just beginning to find their footing with each other. Cricket had accepted him and Lonny seemed to think that as far as kids went, his niece was all right. Letty smiled to herself—she didn't want to do anything that would threaten their budding relationship.

A list of people who could possibly watch Cricket flashed through Letty's mind. There were several older women from church who had been her mother's friends, whom Letty would feel comfortable asking. Any one of them would take excellent care of her daughter. Whoever Letty found would have her hands full, though. Cricket had never spent any real length of time away from Letty.

"I'd like you to make an appointment for Thursday," Dr. Faraday said, adding a couple of notes to her file. "See my receptionist before you leave and she'll give you a time."

Letty nodded, chewing on the corner of her lower lip. She wondered what she was going to say to Lonny about needing the truck again so soon.

Cricket was waiting for her in the hallway outside Dr. Faraday's office. She sat next to the receptionist and was busy coloring in her book. The child looked up and smiled when Letty came out. Neatly she placed her crayons back in the box, folded her book and crawled down from the chair, hurrying to Letty's side.

Letty made her appointment for later in the week and she and Cricket headed for the parking lot.

It was during the long drive home that Letty decided to broach the subject of their being separated.

"Cricket, Mommy may have to go away for a few days."

"Can I go with you?"

"Not this time. Uncle Lonny will be busy with the ranch, so you won't be able to stay with him, either."

"That's all right."

Letty didn't think Cricket would mind not staying with Lonny. Her brother still hadn't come to appreciate the finer points of watching cartoons.

"Do you remember Mrs. Martin from church?" Letty asked. "She was my mommy's good friend." Dorothy Martin was a dear soul, although she'd aged considerably in the past few years since her husband had died. In her heart, Letty knew her mother's friend would take excellent care of Cricket until Letty would be able to do so herself.

Cricket shrugged. "Does Mrs. Martin have gray hair and sing as bad as Uncle Lonny?"

"That's the lady. I was thinking you could stay with her while I was away."

"Don't want to." Cricket rejected Mrs. Martin flat out.

"I see." Letty nibbled on her lower lip. There were other choices, of course, but they were all women that Cricket had only met briefly.

"What about—"

Cricket didn't allow her to finish.

"If you're going away and I can't go with you, then I'd like to stay with Chase best of all. I bet he'd let me ride Firepower again, and we could make chocolate chip cookies."

Letty should have guessed Chase would be her first choice.

"He'd read me stories the way you do and let me blow out the lights at bedtime," Cricket continued. "We'd have lots and lots of fun together and I wouldn't miss you near as much. I like Chase better than anyone." She paused, then added as extra incentive, "We could sit in church together and everything."

The tight knot that formed in Letty's throat came suddenly and unexpectedly. In making her decision to return to Red Springs, she could never have predicted that Cricket would take such a strong and instant liking to Chase.

"Mommy, could I?"

"I'm afraid that Chase has to work on his ranch the way Uncle Lonny does."

"Oh."

The lone word was filled with disappointment. Cricket sighed and her shoulders moved up and down with the action.

"Think of all the people we've met since we came to live with Uncle Lonny," Letty suggested softly. "Who do you like best other than Chase?"

Cricket seemed to need some time to mull the question over. She crossed her short legs and tugged at one pigtail, winding the dark hair around and around her index finger as she considered this important decision.

"I like the lady who plays the organ second best."

Joy Fuller was the perfect choice, although Letty was certain Lonny wouldn't take Cricket's preference sitting down. "I like Miss Fuller, too," she told her daughter. "I'll talk to her. But my going away isn't for sure yet, honey, so there's no need to say anything to anyone. Okay?"

"Is it a surprise?"

"Yes." Letty's fingers tightened against the steering wheel. She hated to mislead Cricket, but she couldn't have her daughter announce to Chase or her brother that she was going away and leaving Cricket behind.

"Oh, goody, I like surprises. I won't tell anyone." She pretended to zip her mouth closed, sealing her promise not to say a word.

"It's good to see you, Letty," Joy said as she stood in the doorway to her small one bedroom apartment. "You, too, Cricket." A soft smile lit up Joy's face. "Your phone call came as a pleasant surprise."

Cricket followed Letty into the apartment.

"I made some iced tea. Would you like some?"

"Please." Letty sat in the compact living room; as always, Cricket was at her side.

"Cricket, I've got some Play-Do in the kitchen if you'd like to play with that. My second-graders still enjoy it. I made some juice just for you."

Cricket looked to her mother and Letty nodded, granting her permission. Without another thought, the youngster followed Joy into the kitchen. Letty could hear the two of them chatting, and although it was difficult to stay where she was, Letty did so in order for the two of them to become better acquainted.

Joy returned a couple of minutes later with two frosty glasses of iced tea. She set one in front of Letty, then claimed the chair opposite her.

"Cricket certainly is a well-behaved child. You must be very proud of her."

"Thank you, I am." Letty's gaze fell to her fingers, which were clenching the glass of iced tea. "I take it you and Lonny have come to some sort of an agreement?"

Joy sighed, her shoulders rising reflectively, then sagging with defeat. "To be honest, I think it's best if the two of us don't have a thing to do with or say to each other. I don't know what it is about your brother that irritates me so much, but frankly, I can't remember anyone who's rubbed me so wrong. We can't even talk civilly to each other."

"I can't understand what's wrong with my brother."

Letty could, but she doubted that Joy would believe her if she claimed Lonny was strongly attracted to Joy. The problem was that he was fighting it so hard.

"You may find this difficult to believe," Letty continued, "but Lonny's normally a calm, in-control type of man. I swear to you, Joy, I have never seen him behave the way he has lately."

"I knew who he was before . . . the accident," Joy admitted, reluctantly, her gaze downcast. "I'd seen him around town now and again, but I had no idea he was that type of hothead."

"Trust me, he usually isn't."

"He phoned me last Sunday."

At Letty's obvious surprise, Joy continued, her eyes just managing to avoid her guests. "He started shouting at me over the phone, claiming it was my fault that you'd gotten sick. I did question him about what had happened to you, but then I got so furious I didn't stay on the line long enough to find out what he meant."

Letty could hardly believe her ears.

"What happened to you? He sounded terribly upset."

"He was, but mostly he was angry with himself. We got in an argument, and well, we both said things we didn't mean and immediately regretted. I went outside to work in the garden, and I don't know," she murmured, her eyes shifting away from Joy. "The sun must have bothered me, because the next thing I knew, I'd fainted."

"Oh, dear, Letty, are you all right?"

"I'm fine, thanks." Letty realized she was beginning to get good at exaggerating about her health.

"Did you see a doctor?"

"Yes. Everything's under control, so don't worry."

Cricket wandered in from the kitchen with a miniature cookie sheet holding several flat circles. "Mommy, I'm baking some chocolate chip cookies for Chase."

"Good, sweetheart. Will you bake me some, too?"

The child nodded eagerly. She smiled shyly up at Joy, then tossed a fleeting glance at Letty and said, "Did you ask her?"

"Not yet."

Letty's gaze followed Cricket back into the kitchen. She could feel Joy's curiosity, and wished that she'd been able to lead into the subject of Cricket staying with her just a little more naturally.

"There's a possibility I'll need to be away for a week or more in the near future," she explained, holding the narrow glass with both hands. "Unfortunately I won't be able to take Cricket with me, and I doubt Lonny could watch her for that length of time."

"I wouldn't trust your brother to properly care for Cricket's dolls," Joy said stiffly, then looked embarrassed.

"Don't worry, I don't think I'd feel any differently toward my brother if I were in your shoes," Letty said, understanding her friend's feelings.

"As you were saying?" Joy prompted, obviously disturbed by the way the subject of Lonny had crept into the conversation. She clearly wanted to talk about other things.

"Yes," Letty said, and straightened. This wasn't easy, and it was a lot to ask of someone she barely knew. "As I explained, there's a possibility I may have to go away for a couple of weeks, and since I can't leave Cricket with my brother, I'm looking for someone she could stay with while I'm gone."

Joy didn't so much as hedge. "I'd be more than happy to keep her for you. But there's one small problem. There's still three more weeks of school left. I wouldn't be able to take her until the first week of June. Would you need to leave before then?"

"No...I'd make sure of that." For the first time, Letty felt the urge to tell someone about her condition. The words to explain the necessity of this separation from her daughter burned on the tip of her tongue like acid. It would be so good to share this burden with someone she considered a friend, someone who would calm and reassure her. Someone she trusted.

But Joy was a recent friend, and it seemed almost wrong to shift the burden onto her slim shoulders. And if Lonny were to somehow discover Letty's secret, he would be justifiably irritated that she had confided her troubles in someone she barely knew and not her own flesh and blood.

"Letty..."

She looked up then and realized her thoughts had been so deep she'd missed whatever it was Joy had been saying. "I'm sorry," she said, looking absently toward Joy and feeling foolish.

"I was just suggesting that perhaps you could leave Cricket with me for an afternoon sometime soon and give us the opportunity to become better acquainted. That way Cricket won't feel so lost while you're away."

"That would be wonderful."

As if knowing the adults had been discussing her, Cricket moved into the living room. "Your chocolate chip cookies are almost cooked, Mommy."

"Thank you, sweetheart. I'm in the mood for something chocolate."

"Me, too," Joy agreed, smiling.

"Mommy will share with you," Cricket stated confidently. "After all, chocolate is her life."

All three laughed.

"Since Cricket is getting along so well now, why don't you leave her here for an hour or two."

Letty stood. "Cricket?" She looked toward her daughter, wanting to be sure the child felt comfortable enough to be left alone with Joy.

"I have to stay," Cricket said. "My cookies aren't finished cooking yet."

"I'd be more than happy for the company," Joy assured Letty so sincerely Letty couldn't doubt her words. "I haven't got anything planned for the next hour or so, and since you're here, it would save you a trip into town later."

"All right," Letty said, not knowing exactly where she would go to kill time. Of course, she could run back to the Bar E, but there was nothing for her there. She stood and reached for her purse. "I'll be back . . . soon."

"Take your time," Joy said, walking her to the door. Cricket came, too, and kissed Letty goodbye with such calm acceptance it tugged at the strings of Letty's heart.

Once inside her brother's battered pickup, she drove aimlessly through town. It was then that she thought of visiting the town's lone cemetery. No doubt her parents' graves had been neglected over the years. The thought saddened her and filled her with purpose.

She parked outside the gates and ambled over the green lawn until she reached their grave sites. To her surprise they were well maintained. Lonny had obviously been out recently.

Standing silent, feeling saddened by an overwhelming sense of loss, Letty bowed her head prayerfully. Unexpected tears gathered in the corners of her eyes. Letty wiped them aside; she hadn't come here to weep. Her visit had been an impromptu one, but the emotions were churning inside her like a boiling kettle, spitting over the edge.

"Hi, Daddy," she whispered. "Hi, Mom. I'm back...I tried...California, but it didn't work out. I never knew there were so many talented singers in the world." She paused, as though they would have some comment to make. Only silence came back to her. "Lonny welcomed me home. He didn't have to, but he did. I suppose you know about my heart...that's what finally convinced me I had to be here."

She waited, not anticipating any deep dark voice to rain down from the heaven, but needing something...only she didn't know what.

"What's it like...on the other side?" Letty realized that even asking such a question as if they could answer her was preposterous, but after her visit with Dr. Faraday, she'd entertained serious doubts that she would ever recover. "Don't worry, I don't actually expect you to tell me. I always did like to be surprised."

Despite the melancholy feeling, Letty smiled. She knelt beside the tombstones and reverently ran the tips of her fingers over deeply engraved words in the marble. Blunt facts that said so little about their lives and those who had loved them so deeply.

"I went to the doctor today," she whispered, her voice cracking. "I'm frightened, Mom. Remember how you used to comfort me when I was a little girl? How I wish I could crawl into your lap now, and press my head to your breast and have you tell me everything is going to be all right." With the back of her hand she swiped at the moisture that slid unrestrained down her cheeks.

"There's so much I want to live for now, so many things I long to experience." She remembered how she'd joked and kidded the California doctors about her condition. But the surgery was imminent, and Letty wasn't laughing any more.

"Mom. Dad." She paused and straightened, coming to her feet. "I know you loved me... never once did I doubt that... and I loved you with all my heart... damaged as it is," she said with a soft hysterical laugh. "How I wish you were here with me now... I need you both so much."

Letty waited a couple of minutes, staring down at the graves of the two people who had shaped and guided her life with such tender care. A tranquillity came to her then, a deep inner knowledge that if it had been humanly possible, her mother would have looped her arms around her, hugged her close and given her the assurance she needed.

"I need someone," Letty admitted openly. The weight of her burden was becoming almost more than she could bear. "Could you send me a friend?" she whispered. "Someone I can talk to who will understand?" Names bounced in and out of her mind. The pastor was a good choice. Dorothy Martin was another.

"Letty?"

At the sound of her name, she turned around and looked into Chase's eyes.

Chapter Seven

I saw Lonny's pickup parked on the roadway,'' Chase explained, glancing briefly over his shoulder. His hat was tipped back on his head as he studied her, his expression severe. ''What are you doing here, Letty?''

She looked down at her parents' graves as a gentle warm breeze blew over the top of her shoulders. ''I stopped off to talk to Mom and Dad.''

Her answer didn't appear to please him and he frowned. He paused and his gaze scanned the cemetery. ''Where's Cricket?''

''She's with Joy Fuller.''

''Joy Fuller,'' he repeated the name slowly, as if he should remember where he'd last heard it. When he made the connection to Lonny, his gaze widened. ''Not Lonny's Joy Fuller?''

''One and the same.''

A hesitant smile crowded his face. "Lonny certainly has taken a disliking to that woman."

"For no reason whatsoever," Letty returned heatedly. "Lonny's making an utter fool of himself."

"It's easy enough to do," Chase returned grimly. His face tightened and he met her look. "Did you make an appointment with the doctor the way you promised?"

Letty nodded. She's hoped to avoid the subject, but she should have known Chase wouldn't have allowed that.

"And?" he barked impatiently. "Did you see him?"

"First thing this afternoon." She would have thought the information would satisfy him, but it apparently didn't. If anything his frown grew darker.

"What did he say?"

"Not to vent my anger in the hot sun," she returned almost flippantly, then immediately regretted responding to Chase's concern in such a glib manner. He was a friend, perhaps the best she'd ever had, and instead of answering him in an offhanded manner, Letty should be grateful for his thoughtfulness. Only minutes before she'd been praying for someone whom she could share her burdens with, and Chase had magically appeared like something out of a dream.

He very well could be the answer to her prayer.

"Chase," she said, strolling between the headstones, unsure how to broach the difficult subject. "Have you ever thought very much about death?"

"No," he said curtly.

Strangely stung by his sharp reaction, she continued strolling, her hands linked behind her back. "I've thought a lot about it lately," she said, hoping he would pick up on the subject and ask her why.

"That's sick, Letty."

"I don't think so," she returned, carefully measuring each word. "Death, like birth, is a natural part of life. It's sunrise and sunset just the way the song says."

"Is that the reason you're wandering among the tombstones like some vampire seeking out fresh victims?"

It took several moments for her to swallow a heated response. Did she need to hit this man over the head before he realized what she was trying to tell him? "Oh, Chase, that's a mean thing to say."

"Sometimes I feel like being cruel to you."

Letty couldn't help but notice that, but she didn't want to argue with Chase—she needed him.

"Do you often stroll through graveyards like they were park grounds?" he asked, his voice still clipped and vehement. "Or is this a recent pastime?"

"Recent," she said, glancing toward him and smiling softly. She hoped he understood that no matter how much he goaded her, she wasn't going to react to his anger.

"Then may I suggest that you snap out of whatever trance you're in and join the land of the living. There's a bright world out there just waiting to be explored."

"But the world isn't always a friendly place. Bad things happen to good people every day. No one said life is fair. I wish it was, believe me, but it isn't."

"Stop talking like that. Wake up, Letty," he snapped.

He stepped toward her as if he'd experienced a sudden fierce urge to shake her, but if that was the case, he restrained the desire.

"I'm awake," she returned calmly, yearning for him to understand that she felt life in a vibrant form, but was powerless to control her own destiny. Something deep inside her found it necessary to prepare him for her vulnerability to death. Now if only he would listen.

"It's really very lovely here, don't you think?" she asked. "The air is crisp and clear and there's the faint scent of sage mingled in with the wildflowers. Can't you smell it?"

"No."

Letty ignored his obvious lack of appreciation. "The sky is lovely today. So blue—when it's this bright I sometimes think it's about to sag down so far it'll touch the earth." She paused, waiting for Chase to make some kind of response, but he remained resolutely silent. "Those huge white clouds resemble Spanish galleons sailing across the seas, don't they?"

"I suppose."

Her linked hands remained behind her back as she ambled away from their parked vehicles and down a short hill. Chase continued to walk with her, but the silence between them was an uneasy one. Just when Letty felt the courage building inside her to mention needing surgery, he spoke.

"You lied to me, Letty."

His words were stark and without emotion. Surprised, she turned to him and met his gaze. It was strangely impassive, as if her deceit didn't matter one whit to him, as though he'd come to expect such things from her.

"When?" she demanded.

"Just now. I phoned Doc Hanley's office and they claimed you hadn't so much as called. You're a liar...on top of everything else."

Letty felt the color leave her cheeks. Her breath caught painfully in her throat. The words to prove him wrong burned on her lips like acid. "I didn't lie to you. I never have. But I'm not going to argue with you, if that's what you're looking for."

"Are you saying Doc Hanley's office lied?"

"I'm not going to discuss this. Believe what you want." She quickened her steps as she turned and headed toward the wrought-iron gates at the cemetery entrance. He followed her until they stood next to the trucks.

"Letty?"

She paused and looked at him. Anger kindled in his eyes like tiny white flames that longed to reach out and scorch her, but Letty was too hurt and furious to care to appease him with an explanation. She'd wanted to share a deep part of herself with this man because she trusted and loved him. But she couldn't now. His accusation had ruined what she'd wanted to share.

He reached out and gripped her shoulders. "I need to know. Did you or did you not lie to me?"

The scorn was gone from his eyes, replaced with a pain that melted her own.

"No...I did see a doctor, I swear to you by everything I hold dear." She held her head at a proud angle, her gaze unwavering, but when she spoke, her voice broke.

His eyes drifted closed as if he didn't know what to believe anymore. Whatever he was thinking, he didn't say. Instead he pulled her firmly into his embrace and set his mouth over hers.

A small, tingling current traveled down her body at his touch. Letty whimpered—angry, hurt, excited, pleased. Emotions came flying at her, each one hitting its mark.

Chase's mouth was ruthless and plundering. His hands slid down to caress her back, tugging her against him until her breasts were crushed into his warm, sturdy chest. This was a trial by fire, Letty thought, and her body was aflame and trembling with so many needs.

Chase was both rough and tender at the same time. He held her tightly as he slipped one hand up to tangle with her short curls. His actions were slow, hesitant, as if he were desperately trying to stop himself from kissing her. If that was the case, he changed his mind, because his mouth closed over hers in a hungry demanding kiss no more than a second later.

"Letty..." he moaned, his breath a feather against her upturned face. "You make me want you..."

She bowed her head. The desire she felt for him was equally ravenous. Her appetite for Chase shook her to the very core of her being.

Chase dragged in a heavy breath and expelled it. "I don't want to feel the things I do."

"I know." It was a heady knowledge, and Letty took delight in it. She moved against him, craving the feel of his arms around her, and as she did, she unintentionally brushed against his arousal.

Chase groaned like a man lost. His mouth found hers once more and he kissed her tentatively, as if he didn't really want to be touching her again, but had been unable to help himself. This increased Letty's reckless sensation of power.

He slid his hands up her arms and gripped her shoulders as if he dared not place them anywhere else. Taking delight in her ability to make him desire her, Letty shyly moved her body against him once more. Unfortunately the loving torment wasn't his alone, and she halted abruptly at the intense heat that surged through her.

He kissed her, slanting his lips over her, his tongue roaming her mouth until she felt as if she were about to be swallowed whole. His desire for her seemed like a bottomless well as his mouth continually slid back and forth over hers.

A car zoomed past them, sounding its horn.

Letty had forgotten that they stood on the edge of the roadway. Groaning with embarrassment, she buried her face against his heaving chest. Chase's heart felt like a heavy hammer beating against her, matching her own excited pulse.

"Listen to me, Letty," he whispered, his voice husky and possessive.

He captured her head and gently lifted her face upward. His breath was warm and moist against her own.

"I want you more than I've ever wanted a woman in my life. You want me, too, don't you?"

It was in her to deny everything, but she couldn't.

"Don't you?" he demanded. His hands, which were holding her face, were now harsh and possessive. His eyes, which had so recently been clouded with passion, were now sharp and insistent.

Letty opened her mouth to reply, but some deep part of her refused to acknowledge the truth. Her fear was that Chase would find a way to use the knowledge against her. He didn't trust her; he'd told her that himself. Desire couldn't be confused with love—at least not between them.

"Don't you?" he questioned a second time, his gaze demanding a response.

Knowing he wouldn't free her until she gave him an answer, Letty nodded once, abruptly.

The instant she did, he released her. "That's all I wanted to know." With that he turned and walked away.

For the three days that followed her confrontation with Chase, Letty managed to avoid him. When she knew he would be over at the house, she made it a point to be elsewhere. Her thoughts were in chaos, her emotions so muddled and confused that she didn't know what to think or feel toward him anymore.

Apparently Chase was feeling just as perplexed as she was, because he seemed to be avoiding her with the same fervor. Normally he stopped by the house in the mornings, twice or more a week. Not once since they'd met in the cemetery had he shown up for breakfast. Letty was grateful.

She cracked three eggs in a bowl and started whipping them into a frothy mixture. Lonny was due back into the house any minute and she wanted to have his meal ready when he arrived. Since her argument with her brother, he had gone out of his way to let her know he was pleased she was home. He appeared to regret their heated exchange as much as Letty did.

The back door opened, and Lonny stepped inside and hung his hat on the peg next to the door. "Looks like we're in for some rain."

"My garden could use it," Letty returned absently as she poured the eggs into the heated frying pan, stirring them while they cooked. "Do you want one piece of toast this morning or two?"

"Two."

She put the bread in the toaster and watched as the slices slowly lowered. Her back was to her brother when she spoke. "Do you have any plans for today?"

"Nothing out of the ordinary."

She nodded. "I thought you were supposed to see the insurance adjuster about having the fender on the truck repaired."

"It isn't worth the hassle," Lonny said, stepping to the stove to refill his coffee cup.

"But I thought—"

Lonny had made such a fuss over that miniscule dent in his truck that Letty had assumed he would surely want to have it fixed, if for nothing more than to irritate Joy.

"I decided against it," he answered shortly.

"I see." Letty didn't, but that was neither here nor there. She'd given up trying to figure out what Lonny was thinking when it came to his relationship with the church organist. The man was completely irrational.

"Damn, I hate it when you say that."

"Say what?" Letty asked, puzzled.

"'I see' in that prim voice, as if you know exactly what I'm thinking."

"Oh."

"There," he cried, slamming his coffee cup against the tabletop. "You just did it again."

"I'm sorry, Lonny. I didn't mean anything by it." She dished up his eggs, buttered the toast and delivered his plate to where he was seated at the table.

He glanced at her apologetically when she set his breakfast in front of him, picked up his fork, then hesitated. "If I turn in a claim against Joy, her insurance rates will probably go up. Right?"

Letty would have thought that would be the least of her brother's concerns. "That's true enough. She'd probably be willing to pay you something. Come to think of it, didn't she offer you fifty dollars to forget the whole matter?"

Lonny's blue eyes flared briefly with the memory. "Yes, she did."

"I'm confident Joy would be more than happy to give you the money if you'd prefer to handle the situation that way. She wants to be as fair as she can be. After all, she admitted from the first that the accident was her fault."

"The fool woman couldn't do anything else."

"Perhaps not," Letty said, sitting in the chair across from her brother.

"I don't dare contact her, though," Lonny muttered, his voice low and discouraged.

Letty noted that he hadn't taken a single bite of his eggs. "Why not?"

He sighed and looked away, clearly uncomfortable. "The last time I tried to call her she hung up as soon as she knew it was me."

"You shouldn't have blamed her for our spat."

A lengthy pause followed. "I know," Lonny admitted reluctantly. "I was lashing out at her because I was furious with myself. I was feeling bad enough about saying the things I did to you. Then I learned you'd fainted soon afterward and I felt like a real heel. The truth is, I had every intention of apologizing to you when I got back to the house. But you were upstairs sleeping and Chase was sitting here, madder than I've ever seen him. I swear he nearly flayed me alive. I guess I was looking for a scapegoat, and since Joy was indirectly involved, I phoned her."

"Lonny, honestly, that was a foolish thing to do."

"I regretted it the minute we started talking, but I couldn't seem to stop myself. It's best if we don't talk to each other again."

"Chase had no right to be angry with you," Letty murmured.

"To his way of thinking, he did, and frankly, I didn't blame him once I heard you'd fainted." Lonny paused and exhaled sharply. "I sometimes wonder about you and Chase. The two of you have been avoiding each other all week. I mention your name and he gets defensive. I mention him to you and you change the subject. The fact is, I thought that once you were home and settled down the two of you might consider getting married."

The words ricocheted around the kitchen, and Letty did exactly what Lonny said she would. She changed the subject. "Since you won't be taking the truck in, someone needs to tell Joy. Would you like me to talk to her for you?"

Lonny shrugged. "I suppose."

"What do you want me to tell her?"

Lonny shrugged. "Hell, I don't know. I guess you can say that I want to drop the whole insurance thing. She doesn't need to worry about giving me that fifty dollars, either—I don't want her money."

Letty toyed with the rim of her coffee cup. "Is there anything else?"

Her brother hesitated. "I suppose it wouldn't do any harm to mention that I was willing to admit I might have overreacted just a tad the day of the accident, and being the sensitive kind of guy that I am, I feel duty bound to tell her I regret the way I behaved . . . this, of course, all depends on how receptive she is to my apology."

"Naturally," Letty said, feigning a sympathetic look. "But I'm sure Joy will be more than happy to accept your apology." Letty wasn't the least bit certain that was true, but she wanted to reassure her brother, who was making giant leaps in improving his attitude toward her friend.

Digging his fork into his scrambled eggs, Lonny snorted softly. "Now that's something I doubt. Knowing that woman the way I do, Joy Fuller will probably demand an apology written out in blood. But this is the best she's going to get. You tell her that for me, will you?"

"Be glad to," Letty said.

Lonny took a huge bite of his breakfast, as if he suddenly realized how hungry he was. He picked up a piece of toast with one hand and waved it at Letty. "You might even tell her I think she does a good job at church with the organ. But play that part by ear, if you know what I mean. Be sure you don't make it sound like I'm buttering her up for anything, though."

"Right."

"I suppose you'll want the truck today?"

"Please." Letty had another doctor's appointment and she wasn't exactly sure how else she was going to get there.

Lonny stood up and delivered his plate to the sink. "I'll talk to you this afternoon, then." He set his hat atop his head, readjusted it a couple of times, then turned to Letty and smiled. "You might follow your own advice, you know."

"About what?"

"With you and Chase. I don't know what's going on between you, but I have the feeling that a word or two from you would patch things up. Since I'm doing the honorable thing with Joy, I'd think you could do nothing less with Chase."

With that announcement he was gone.

Letty sat at the table, both hands cupping the warm coffee mug, while she mulled over Lonny's words. She didn't know what to say to Chase, or even how to talk to him anymore.

More than a week had passed since Chase had last seen Letty. Each day his mood worsened. Each day he grew more irritable and short-tempered. Even Firepower, who had always sensed his disposition and adjusted his own temperament to his master's, seemed to be losing patience with him. Chase didn't blame the gelding; he was getting to the point where he hated himself.

Something had to be done.

The day Chase had found Letty wandering through the cemetery, he'd been driving around looking for her. She'd promised him Sunday before he'd left her that she would see Doc Hanley. Somehow he hadn't believed she would do it. Chase had been furious when he'd discovered she hadn't seen Doc Hanley. It'd taken him close to an hour to locate Letty. When he had, it had required a good deal of restraint to keep him from shaking some common sense into her. She'd fainted, for God's sake! A normal healthy person didn't just up and faint. Something was wrong.

But before Chase had been able to say a word, Letty had started in on the macabre subject of death and on how life could be so unfair. His temper hadn't improved with her choice of subject matter. The old Letty had been too full of life even to contemplate the topic of death. It was only when she was in his arms that Chase discovered the vibrant woman he'd always known, only when he was kissing her that she seemed to snap out of the trance that held her emotions captive.

It was as though Letty were only half-alive. She met his taunts with a smile, refused to argue with him even when he worked hard to provoke her. He'd insulted her and accused her, but nothing had kindled a response from her, with the exception of his kisses.

Only then did she reveal some life.

Chase was through playing games with her. He was going to talk to her and find out what had happened to change her from the spirited, dauntless woman he'd always known. And he didn't plan to leave until he had his answers.

When he pulled his truck into the yard, Cricket was the only one Chase saw. The child was sitting on the porch steps, looking bored and unhappy. She brightened the minute he came into view.

"Chase," she called, and leaped to her feet.

She ran toward him with an eagerness that tugged at his heart. Chase didn't know why Cricket was so keen on him. He'd done nothing to deserve her devotion. A welcoming smile would blossom across her face like a rose in summer every time she saw him. She was so pleased, so excited, that her warm welcome couldn't help but affect him.

"I'm so glad you're here," she greeted him cheerfully.

"Hello, Cricket."

She slipped her small hand into his and smiled up at him with a cheery brightness that rivaled the sun. "It's been ages and ages since you came over to see us. I missed you a whole bunch."

"I know."

"Where have you been all this time? Mommy said I wasn't even supposed to ask Uncle Lonny about you anymore, but I was afraid I wouldn't see you again. You weren't in church on Sunday—church is food for the soul, you know."

"I've been busy."

The child sighed expressively, then added, "That's what Mommy said." Then, as though suddenly remembering something important, Cricket tore into the house, returning a moment later with a picture from a coloring book that had been filled in with the utmost care. "I made this for you," she announced proudly, and presented it to him.

"Thank you, sweetheart." He examined the picture, then carefully folded it and inserted it in his shirt pocket.

"I made it 'cause you're my friend and you let me ride Firepower."

He patted the top of her head. "Where is your mother?"

"She had to go to Rock Springs."

"Who's watching you?"

Cricket rolled her eyes and her bottom lip jutted out. "Uncle Lonny, but he doesn't do a very good job. He fell asleep in front of the television, and when I changed the channel, he got mad and told me to leave it where it was 'cause he was watching it. But he had his eyes closed. How can you watch television with your eyes closed?"

She didn't seem to expect an answer, but plopped herself down and braced her elbows against her knees, her small hands framing her face.

Almost against his will, Chase sat down next to her. "Is that the reason you're sitting out here all by yourself?"

Cricket nodded. "Mommy says I'll have lots of friends to play with when I go to kindergarten, but that's not for months and months."

"I'm sure she's right."

Cricket agreed with a nod. "You're my friend and so is Firepower. I like Firepower, even if he is a big horse and not a pony. Someday, Mommy said, I could have a horsey like she did when she was little."

He smiled at the child, fighting down an emotion he couldn't name that kept bobbing to the surface of his mind. He remembered Letty so well when she was only a few years older than Cricket. They had the same color hair, the same eyes and, more important, that same streak of stubbornness, which Chase swore was a mile wide.

"My pony's going to be the best one that ever was," Cricket prattled on, clearly content to have him sit beside her, satisfied that he was her friend.

It hit Chase then, hard and powerful, with an impact so strong he couldn't breathe. His heart constricted, trapped in a burning grip within his chest, while his Adam's apple worked up and down in his throat. The emotion was strangling. He loved this little girl. There was nothing powerful enough on this earth to stamp out his feelings. He didn't *want* to love Cricket, didn't want to experience this tenderness, but the child was Letty's daughter. He loved Letty. In the last few weeks he'd been forced to admit that nine long years hadn't altered his feelings toward her. And Cricket was a part of her.

The very best part.

"Chase—" Lonny stepped outside and joined the two on the porch. "When did you arrive?"

"A few minutes ago." He had some trouble finding his voice. "I came over to talk to Letty, but apparently she's not here."

"No, she left a couple of hours ago." He paused to check his watch, frowning as he did so. "I don't know what time to expect her back."

"Did she say where she was going?"

Lonny glanced away, his look narrowed and uncomfortable. "Hell, I don't know what's going on with that woman. I wish I did."

"What do you mean?" Chase knew his friend well enough to realize Lonny was more than a little disturbed. "She's been needing the truck all week. It seems she's always got some errand or another to do. I don't have much use for it myself, and frankly, I don't mind. She puts gas in it. But then yesterday I noticed that she'd been putting one hell of a lot of miles on it. I asked her about it, but she got so defensive and closemouthed we nearly had another fight."

"Did you find out where she's going?"

"Rock Springs," Lonny said shortly. "At least, that's what she claims."

"Why?"

Lonny looked away. "Hell if I know—she never did say exactly, although I told her that if she was using my truck I had a right to know."

"Mommy goes to see a man," Cricket interjected brightly. "He looks like the one on TV with the mustache."

"The one on TV with the mustache," Lonny repeated, sharing a blank look with Chase. "God knows what she means by that."

"He's real nice, too," Cricket went on to explain patiently. "But he doesn't talk to me. He just talks to Mommy. Sometimes they go in a room together and I have to wait outside, but that's all right because I color pictures."

Lonny's face tightened as he looked once more at Chase. "I'm sure that isn't the way it sounds," he murmured.

"Why should I care what she does," Chase lied. "I don't feel a damn thing for her. I haven't in years."

"Right," Lonny returned sarcastically. "The problem is, Chase Brown, you never could lie worth a damn."

Chapter Eight

The arrival of Letty's first welfare check had a curious effect on her. She brought in the mail, sat down at the kitchen table and carefully examined the plain beige envelope. Emotion clogged her throat as tears filled her eyes, then crept silently down the side of her face. Once she had been so proud, so independent, and now she was little more than a charity case, living off the generosity of taxpayers.

The realization settled over her shoulders like a steel-weighted mantle.

Lonny came in the back door and wiped his feet on the braided rug. "Is the mail here?" he asked impatiently.

Her brother had been irritated with her for the past couple of weeks without ever letting her know the exact reason why. Letty was intelligent enough to realize his displeasure with her was tied in with her trips into Rock Springs, but she didn't mention them again and neither did he. Although he hadn't said a word, she could feel the strain of his annoyance every time they were together. More than once, over the past few days, Letty had toyed with the idea of telling Lonny about her heart condition, but every time she thought to approach him, he'd look at her with narrow, disapproving eyes.

Without waiting for her to respond to his question, Lonny walked over to the table and sorted through the bills, flyers and junk mail.

Letty stood and turned away from him. She wiped the moisture off her cheeks, praying that if he did notice her tears he wouldn't comment.

"Mommy, Mommy," Cricket cried, crashing through the back door, her voice elevated with excitement. "Chase is here on Firepower and he's got another horse with him. Hurry, come and look." With that she was out the door with the speed of a roadrunner.

Letty smiled, tucked the government check in her pocket and followed her daughter outside. Sure enough, just as Cricket had claimed, Chase was agilely riding down the hillside atop his gelding. He rode tall and proud in the saddle and was holding on to the reins of a second horse, a brown-and-white pinto that was trotting obediently behind the bay.

"Chase, Chase." Cricket stood on the top step, jumping up and down and frantically waving both arms as if there were a chance he would miss seeing her.

Chase slowed his pace once he reached the yard. Lonny joined his sister, doing his best to hide a smile. Bemused, Letty stared at him. The last time she'd seen him wear a silly grin like that, she'd been ten years old and he was suffering through his first teenage crush.

Unable to wait a second longer, Cricket ran out to greet her friend. Smiling down at the child, Chase lowered his arms and automatically hoisted her into the saddle beside him. Letty had lost count of the times Chase had "just happened" to stop by in the past couple of weeks with Firepower. Cricket got as excited as a game show winner every time he was around. Several times Chase had taken Cricket riding with him. He was so patient with the five-year-old, so tender. The only time Letty could remember Chase truly laughing was when he was with her daughter. Letty was convinced that these special times with Chase and Firepower were the closest thing to heaven the child had ever known. Cricket treasured every moment with her hero.

In contrast, Letty's relationship with Chase had deteriorated to the point where they'd become little more than polite strangers. Chase seemed to go out of his way to avoid talking to her. It was as if their last meeting in the cemetery, several weeks before, had killed whatever love there had ever been between them.

Conversely, Cricket and Chase had become the best of friends.

Letty watched from the porch as Chase eased himself out of the saddle and onto the ground first and then lowered Cricket. He wore the same type of grin as Lonny, looking exceptionally pleased with himself.

"Well, what do you think?" Lonny asked, rocking on his heels, his hands in his pockets. He looked almost as excited as Cricket.

"About what?" Letty felt as if everyone was in on a big secret and she'd been left out.

Lonny glanced at her as if it should be obvious. "Chase bought the pony for Cricket."

"What?" Letty exploded.

"It's a surprise," Lonny whispered back.

"You're telling me! Didn't it cross his mind—or yours—to discuss the matter with me? I'm her mother...I should have some say in this decision, don't you think?"

For the first time, Lonny revealed some sign of uneasiness. "Actually, Chase did bring up the subject with me, and I was the one who told him it was all right. After all, I'll be responsible for feeding it and paying the vet bills for that matter. I assumed you'd be as thrilled as Cricket."

"I am, but I wish one of you would have thought to ask me first. It's only common courtesy."

"You're not going to make a federal case out of this, are you?" Lonny asked, his gaze accusing. "Chase is just doing something nice for her."

"I know," she whispered. But that wasn't the issue.

Chase and Cricket were standing next to the pony by the time Letty joined them in the yard. Apparently Chase had just told her daughter that the pony now belonged to her, because Cricket tossed her arms around Chase's neck, threw back her head and shouted with glee. Laughing, Chase twirled her around, holding on to the little girl by the waist. Cricket's short legs flew out like a tiny top spinning around and around.

Letty felt like an outsider in this touching scene, although she did her best to smile and act pleased. Perhaps Cricket sensed Letty's feelings, because once she was back on the ground, she hurried to her mother's side and hugged her waist so tightly Letty could hardly breathe.

"Mommy, oh, Mommy, did you see Jennybird? That's the name of my very own pony."

Chase walked over and placed his hands on the back of the little girl's shoulders. "You don't object, do you?"

How could she? "Of course not. It's very thoughtful of you, Chase." Her gaze fell and rested on her daughter as she restrained from telling him how she wished he'd consulted her beforehand. "Did you thank him, sweetheart?"

"Oh, yes, a hundred million, zillion times."

Letty turned back to the porch, fearing that if she stood by any longer and watched the two of them, she would start to weep. The emotions that swamped her were almost unidentifiable. As crazy as it seemed, the most prominent one bordered on jealousy. How she longed for Chase to look at her with the same tenderness he did with Cricket. Imagine being envious of her own daughter!

Chase made no effort to hide his affection for the child. In the span of a few weeks, the pair had become bosom buddies.

Letty felt as if she were on the outside looking in and feeling very much like the little match girl in the touching Christmas tale. She couldn't bear to stand there and pretend.

As unobtrusively as possible, Letty turned to leave, and was all the way to the back door when Chase stopped her.

"Letty?"

She turned back to discover him standing at the foot of the stairs, a frown compressing his brow.

"You seemed to have dropped this." He extended the plain envelope to her.

The instant she realized what it was, Letty was mortified to the very roots of her dark, curly hair. Chase was holding her welfare check out to her, his face twisted with shock and what she was sure must be scorn. When she reached for the check, his eyes seemed to leap with stunned surprise and unanswered questions. Before he could ask a single one, she turned and raced into the house.

It shouldn't have been a revelation to Letty that she wasn't able to sleep that night, though she seemed to be the only member of the family with that problem. After all the excitement with Jennybird, Cricket had fallen asleep almost immediately following dinner. Lonny had been snoring softly in his bedroom when Letty had dressed and slipped downstairs.

Now she sat under the stars, her knees bunched under her chin, on a hillside where she'd so often stolen away to meet Chase. She'd been a teenager then, young and naive and filled with impossible dreams. Chase had listened to her talk about all the wonderful things that were in store for her. He'd held her close and kissed her and believed with her.

It was that secure, loved feeling that had driven Letty back to this spot now. There'd been no place else for her to go. She felt more alone than ever before. More isolated—cutoff from those she loved and who loved her. She was facing the most difficult problem of her life and she was doing so utterly alone.

By all rights, Letty should be pleased with the unexpected change in Chase's attitude toward Cricket . . . and she was. It was more than she'd ever expected from him, more than she'd thought to hope. And yet, she longed with everything in her heart for Chase to love her.

But he didn't—that was a fact that he'd made abundantly clear.

It was difficult to be depressed, Letty mused as she studied the spectacular display in the heavens. The stars were like frosty jewels carelessly tossed across a blanket of black velvet. The moon was full and brilliant, a madcap adventurer in a heaven filled with like-minded wanderers.

Despite her low spirits, Letty discovered she was smiling. So long ago, light years in the past, she'd sat under the same yellow moon, utterly confident that nothing but good things would ever come into her life. She realized now that she'd been only partially wrong.

"What are you doing here?"

The crisp voice behind her startled Letty. "Hello, Chase," she said evenly, refusing to turn around. "Are you going to order me off your land?"

Chase had seen Letty approach the hillside from the house. He'd been irritated with her and decided the best thing to do was completely ignore her. She would leave soon enough. Only she hadn't. For more than an hour she'd sat under the stars, barely moving. Unable to resist any longer, he'd marched over to the hill, not knowing what he intended to do or say.

"Do you want me to leave?" she asked.

Part of him was more than ready to show her the way off his property, but some undefined emotion dominated his common sense and refused to let her walk away from him.

"No," he answered gruffly.

His reply appeared to please her and he was aware of the tension that flowed out of her. She relaxed, looped her arms around her bent knees and said, "I can't remember a night any clearer than this." Her voice was low and enticing. "The stars look like diamonds, don't they?"

They did, but Chase obstinately refused to admit as much. Restlessly he shifted his weight and stood stiffly behind her, forcing his gaze toward the heavens.

"I remember the last time I sat on this hill with you, but... but that seems a million years ago now."

"It was," he returned brusquely.

"It was the night you asked me to marry you."

"We were both young and foolish," he said, striving for a flippant air. He would have liked Letty to believe the ridiculous part had been in even *wanting* her for his wife, but if the truth be known, he would have given anything in his world if she'd consented. Despite everything, he felt the same way this very moment.

To his surprise, Letty laughed softly. "Now we're both older and wiser, aren't we?"

"I can't speak for anyone but myself." Before he was conscious of the fact, Chase was on the ground, sitting next to her, his legs stretched out in front of him.

"How I wish I knew then everything I do now," she continued. "If, by some miracle, we were able to wind back the clock of time to that night all those years ago, I'd like you to know that I'd leap at your proposal."

A shocked silence followed her words. Chase would give anything if he could believe her, but he couldn't.

"You were after diamonds, Letty, and all I had to offer you was denim."

"But the diamonds were here all along," she whispered, staring at the stars, discounting his argument.

Chase closed his eyes to a flash of pain that constricted his heart. He hadn't been good enough for her then, and he wasn't now. He didn't doubt for an instant that she was waiting to leave Red Springs. When the time came she would leave so fast it would make his head spin. To be honest, he didn't know what was keeping her here now.

The crux of the problem was that he didn't trust Letty. He couldn't—not anymore, not since he'd learned she was seeing some man in Rock Springs. Unfortunately it wasn't a simple thing to stop caring for her. In all the years he'd cherished Letty, though, the only thing his love had gotten him had been pain and heartache.

When she'd first come back to Wyoming, he'd carefully allowed himself hope. He'd dreamed that together they would find a way to turn back time, just as she was talking about now, and discover a life together. But in the past few weeks she'd gone about proving to him over and over what an impossible dream that was.

Chase's gut twisted with the knowledge. He'd done everything humanly possible to blot her out of his life. In the beginning when he'd realized his feelings for Cricket, he'd thought he would fight for Letty's love, show her how things could change. But could they really? There wasn't anything he could offer her other than a humble life on a cattle ranch—the same thing he'd offered her nine years earlier. Evidently someone else had offered something better. She'd given herself to some bastard in California, someone unworthy of her love, and now, apparently she was doing it all over again, stabbing Chase in the back by blatantly meeting another man. Good riddance then. The guy with the mustache was welcome to her. All Chase wanted was for her to get out of his life, because the pain of having her so close was almost more than he could bear.

"I think Cricket will remember today as long as she lives," Letty said, blithely unaware of his blustery thoughts. "I don't know what changed between you and Cricket, but you've made her the happiest five-year-old in the world."

He responded with a soft snort. He didn't want to discuss Cricket. The little girl made him vulnerable to Letty. Once he'd lowered the guard that surrounded his heart concerning the child, it was as if a damn of love had flowed over him. He didn't know what he would do once Letty moved away and took the little girl with her.

"She thinks you're the sun and the moon now," Letty continued in a way that suggested he need not have done a thing for Cricket to worship him.

"She's a sweet kid." That was the most he was willing to admit, though his emotions ran much deeper.

"Jason reminded me of you." She spoke so softly it was almost impossible to make out her words.

"I beg your pardon?"

"Jason was Cricket's father," she said smoothly.

That man was the last person Chase wanted to hear about, but before he could tell Letty so, she continued in a soft voice filled with pain and remembered humiliation.

"He'd asked me out for weeks before I finally accepted. I'd written you and asked you to join me in California, and time and time again you turned me down."

"You wanted me to be your manager, for God's sake. I'm a rancher. What the hell did I know about the recording business?"

"Nothing...I was asking the impossible," she said, her voice level, her words devoid of any blame. "It was ridiculous—I realize that now. But I was so lonely for you, so lost."

"Apparently you found some comfort."

She let the gibe pass, although he saw her flinch and knew his words had hit their mark. He said things like that to hurt her, and the curious thing was, he was the one who suffered. When he lashed out at Letty, he bled. Apparently he wasn't a fast learner, because he continued to make the same mistake.

"He took me to the best restaurant in town, told me all the things I wanted to hear. I was so desperate to believe him that a few inconsistencies didn't trouble me. He pretended to be my friend, and I needed one so badly. He shared my dream the way you always had. I couldn't come back to Wyoming as a nobody. You can understand that, can't you?"

Chase didn't give her an answer and she continued without waiting for one.

"I was still chasing my dreams, but I was so miserably lonely that they were losing their appeal.

"I never planned to go so far with Jason, but it happened, and for days afterward I reeled with the shock. I was drunk and I started calling him by your name, and he became so angry that he couldn't . . . wouldn't stop."

"He raped you?" Chase didn't need any reason to hate the man more than he already did.

"Not exactly."

"Letty, stop, I don't want to hear this." Chase regretted having asked the question. Her relationship with Cricket's father was a part of her life he wanted to wipe completely out of his mind.

Letty ignored him, her voice shaky, but determined. "Soon afterward I found out I was pregnant. I wanted to crawl into a hole and die, but that wasn't the worst part. When I told Jason, he misunderstood . . . he seemed to think I wanted him to marry me. But I didn't. I told him because, well, because he was Cricket's father. That was when I learned he was married. Married. Oh, God, all that time and he'd had a wife."

"Stop, Letty. I'm the last person you should be telling this to. In fact, I don't want to hear any of it," Chase shouted. His hands bunched into fists as impotent rage filled him. He wanted to strike out and maim the man who had done such a thing to Letty.

"It hurts so much to talk about it, but I feel I have to. I want you to know that—"

"Whatever you have to say doesn't matter anymore."

"But, Chase, it does, because as difficult as you may find this to believe, I've always loved you...as much then as I do now."

"Why the hell didn't you come home when you found out you were pregnant?"

"How could I have? Pregnant and a failure, too. Everyone believed in me. Everyone was looking to me to make a name for Red Springs. I was so ashamed, so unhappy, and there was nowhere to go."

She turned away and Chase saw her wipe the tears from her eyes. He ached to hold and comfort her, his heart heavy with her pain, but he refused to make himself vulnerable to her again. She spoke of loving him, but she didn't mean it. She couldn't, not when there was someone else in her life.

"What changed your mind?" he asked. "What was it that made you decide to come back now?"

Several minutes passed, far longer than what was necessary to answer a simple question. Obviously something had happened that had brought her running back to the Bar E when she'd managed to stay away all those years. Something traumatic.

"I suppose it was a matter of accepting defeat," she answered simply. "In the years following Cricket's birth, the fierce determination to succeed left me. I still dabbled in the industry, but mainly I did temporary secretarial work. As the years passed, I couldn't feel ashamed of Cricket. She's the joy of my life."

"But it took you nine years, Letty. Nine long years."

She turned to look up at him, her eyes round and filled with pain. Whatever she was thinking wasn't apparent in her face, framed in the moonlight.

The anger was still with him. The senselessness of it all—a dream that had ruined their lives. And for what? "I loved you once," he said starkly, "but I don't now, and I doubt if I ever will again. You taught me that the only thing love brings is heartache."

She lowered her head and he saw the tears flow over her cheeks.

"I could hate you for the things you've done," he shouted.

"I think you do," she whispered.

Chase wasn't sure what to expect from her, but it wasn't the calm, almost humble acceptance of his resentment. Not for the first time, he longed to take hold of her and shake some sense into her.

Maybe the proud, confident Letty was gone from him forever, but he couldn't believe that was true. Every once in a while, he saw flashes of the old Letty. Just enough to give him hope.

"I don't hate you, Letty," he murmured, his voice a tormented whisper. "I wish to hell I could, but I can't...I can't."

Chase intended to kiss her once, then release her and send her back to the house. It was late, and they both had to rise early. But their kiss sparked, then caught fire, leaping to sudden brilliance. She sighed, and the sound was so soft, so exciting, that Chase knew he was lost even before he pressed her back against the cool, fragrant grass.

Before he was fully conscious of what he was doing, he was unfastening her blouse, pulling the cotton material free from her waistband and then pressing it open. Her lacy bra was the next to go. The cold air against her breasts must have been something of a surprise, because she whimpered. It wasn't until then that Chase realized that the sigh had been one of sensual excitement and that she was asking him to worship her with his body if he couldn't with his heart.

Chase felt helpless, caught in a maze of love and desire, and it was the very powerlessness of it all that drove him farther than he'd ever planned to go. He tried to slow his breathing, gain control of his senses, but it felt impossible when his body and his heart were fighting against him.

Unable to restrain the heat that poured through him, Chase caught the tip of her breast between his lips, teasing it into an excited peak. He kneaded the pliant flesh, attentive to one and then the other breast, sipping and sucking at each puckered nipple. They seemed to point directly at him, and despite his good intentions, Chase discovered he couldn't ignore their plea.

Letty's hands were in his hair, her fingers digging into his scalp. She tossed her head from side to side and arched her back, until he brought his hand to the juncture of her thighs and began a sensual massage that brought a dazed look to her eyes.

Letty raised her hand and stroked the fabric of his shirt at his rib cage, then glided her fingertips around to his back, shyly investigating the length of his spine. Chase tensed, his breath stopping at his teeth.

When he could no longer endure the heat of her light touch, he closed his mouth over hers, his tongue seeking, dueling with hers in a kiss that demanded and reclaimed everything—her will, her body, her very soul. Chase wanted it all and would be satisfied with nothing less.

He felt engulfed by his love for her, lost, drowning, and it didn't matter, nothing did, except the warm feeling of her beneath him, longing for him as desperately as he longed for her.

Again and again he kissed her, and when he paused to gather his senses, she eased her hand around his neck and gently brought his mouth back to hers.

Their need for each other was urgent. Fierce. Compelling. Chase couldn't get enough of her. He kissed her eyes, her cheeks, her forehead, and tenderly nuzzled her throat.

"Take off your shirt," Letty begged. "Oh, please, I want to feel you . . . please."

Chase's fingers were shaking so much he could barely comply. Only a few moments earlier he'd wanted to punish her, and now he yearned to please her, was willing to do anything in an effort to give her all that she yearned for. She could ask anything of him, demand his heart, his soul, and he would agreeably hand them over. There was no reason he shouldn't. Letty had owned them both for so many years.

When he could, Chase peeled off the long-sleeved shirt, then lay on his back. Letty knelt above him, and their eyes met in the moonlight, her smile tentative, uncertain. He held her narrow waist and brought his head up enough to brush his mouth over hers. Using his strength, he lifted her partially off the grass until he filled his mouth with the heated tip of her breast.

The sound of his name on her lips sent sparks through him.

He released her and she sagged breathlessly against him. The ache to claim her completely clawed at his belly. No other woman affected him the way Letty did. Why her? Of all the women in the world, why did he have to love her so desperately? For years she'd rewarded his loyalty with nothing but pain.

But it wasn't distress he was feeling now. The pleasure she brought him was so intense he wanted to cry out with it. He wanted to forget about Letty, but he couldn't escape her. Everywhere he went, everything he did was dominated by thoughts of her.

He kissed her and as he devoured the sweetness of her mouth her soft, gasping breaths mingled with his own deeper ones. Chase was shaking and he couldn't seem to stop—shaking with anticipation and desire, shaking with resolve not to love her completely, because once he did, he would never be able to let her go. God help him, he wanted her, but he needed her to love him of her own free will.

His jaw tight with restraint, he closed his hands around hers and gently lifted her off him.

"Chase?" she whispered, perplexed.

If she was confused, it was nothing compared to the warring emotions churning inside him. With everything that was in him, he ached to make Letty his own, to claim her body as his. She had belonged to him from the time she was a teenager, and he'd suffered the agonies of the damned knowing another man had tasted the sweet fruit of her innocence.

Yet he was turning her away again, and the agony he experienced in doing so knotted his loins. She wanted him, and she unconsciously let him know that with every soft breath she drew. But he wouldn't make love to her. Not now.

"Letty...no."

She bowed her head and the color mounted high in her cheeks. She bit into her lip and avoided meeting his gaze.

"You . . . don't want to make love to me?" she whispered tremulously.

His heart thundered at the gentle need in her voice. He paused, then reached for her, holding her close against his chest. He felt her draw in a deep breath, then gradually release it.

"Just one time," she murmured.

Her eyes searched his, and what he saw melted and warmed him. Tonight was a moment out of time, she seemed to be saying to him. A night meant to share the future and forget the past. A night to revel in the love they once shared.

"It wouldn't be enough," he told her bluntly.

Her lashes fluttered closed and she nodded in understanding. "I feel so wanton with you."

He stroked her hair and gently kissed her mouth. It hit him then, and he stiffened. She only wanted him to love her *one time*. "You're going away, aren't you, Letty?" He felt her tense in his arms before her startled gaze found his.

"Who told you?"

The knife that sliced through his heart had a serrated edge. He pushed her away from him and stood.

"Chase?"

"No one told me," he said, the love and tenderness he felt evaporating in the heat of her betrayal. "I guessed."

Chapter Nine

"What the hell happened between you and Letty last night?" Lonny demanded of Chase early the following morning. They'd planned on repairing the fence that bordered their property line.

"What's between Letty and me is none of your damn business."

Lonny paused to consider this while impatiently rubbing the side of his jaw. "Normally I'd agree with you, but my sister looked like she'd welcome death this morning. To be honest, I haven't been particularly pleased with her myself lately."

Lonny followed him to the pile of split cedar fence posts, his stride lengthy and restless, as if he found meddling in his friend's affairs as unpleasant to him as it was to Chase.

"When Cricket mentioned Letty meeting some man in Red Springs," he continued, "I was madder than hell.

But after all the fuss I made about her interfering in my life, I didn't think I had the right to start asking her a bunch of questions that weren't any of my damn business."

"Then why start with me now?" Chase did his best to ignore his friend, and loaded the posts into the back of his pickup. His mood hadn't improved much since he'd left Letty.

"I'm sticking my nose in where it doesn't belong because you're the best friend I've got."

"Then let's keep it that way." Chase hesitated long enough to wipe the perspiration off his brow, then went back to heaving posts, doing his best to pretend Lonny hadn't introduced the subject of his sister.

"Damn it all," Lonny shouted. "You're as bad as she is."

"Maybe I am."

Lonny jerked on his gloves and walked toward the pile of wood. He pulled one long section free, loaded it over his shoulder and headed toward the truck.

"I don't think she slept all night," Lonny muttered.

It was difficult for Chase to feel any sympathy when he hadn't, either!

"When I came downstairs this morning, she was sitting in the kitchen, staring into space. I swear there were enough damp tissues on that table to insulate the attic."

"What makes you think I had anything to do with Letty crying?"

"Because she more or less told me so—less if the truth be known," Lonny muttered, slowly shaking his head. "She wouldn't say a word at first, mind you, she's as tight-lipped as you are, but far worse to reason with, Letty being a woman and all."

"Listen, if your sister wants to shed a few tears, that's her business. Not mine. Not yours. Understand?"

Lonny tipped back the rim of his hat and scratched his head. "I can't say that I do. Damn it, Chase, I don't need you to tell me this isn't any of my business. I know you're furious at my butting in, and I can't say that I blame you. But the least you can do is hear me out."

"I'm a busy man, Lonny, and I'd appreciate it if you kept your thoughts to yourself."

Lonny chose to ignore his suggestion. "I don't know what happened between you two, but—"

"It's none of your damn business."

"It is if it's hurting my sister," Lonny countered darkly. "And she's hurting plenty."

"That's her problem." Chase had to take care of himself. Every time he was around Letty, he came away bleeding. It was worse now than it ever had been, and Lonny wasn't helping matters any.

"If you won't listen to me, then the least you can do is talk to her."

"And what do you expect me to say? Are you going to tell me that, too? I respect you, Lonny, but I'm telling you right now to butt out. What's between Letty and me doesn't concern you." The anger was churning inside him like the huge arms of a windmill, stirring up the hot air of his resentments and fears. It would be a shame to ruin a lifetime friendship because of Letty, but Chase wasn't about to let Lonny Ellison dictate his actions toward her.

The two worked together silently for the next few hours. Neither seemed willing to break the icy silence. They were repairing the fence, replacing the rotting posts with new, sturdy ones. Normally, when they worked together, it was a chance to joke and have a little fun. Today, it seemed, they could barely tolerate each other.

"I'm worried about her," Lonny said when they broke for lunch. He stared at his sandwich as if he expected the roast beef to stand up and advise him.

"Are you back to talking about Letty again?" Although she hadn't left his mind for an instant, Chase didn't want to discuss her.

"I can't help it. Damn it," Lonny shouted as he leaped to his feet and tossed the remainder of his lunch against the ground with such force that bits of apple flew in several different directions. "Be mad at me if you want, Chase Brown. Knock me down if it'll make you feel any better. But I can't let you do this to Letty. She's been hurt enough."

"That isn't my fault."

"Like hell. I've never seen her this way—it's like all the life has gone out of her. She sits and stares into space with a look that's so pathetic it rips your heart out. Cricket started talking to her and she barely noticed. You know that isn't anything like Letty."

"She's leaving," Chase shouted, slamming his own lunch against the tree. "Just like she did before—she's walking away. It nearly destroyed me the first time, and I'm not going to let her do it again."

"Leaving?" Lonny cried, and jerked his head to the sky as though to plead for patience. "Did she tell you that herself?"

"Not exactly. I guessed."

"Well, it's news to me. She enrolled Cricket in kindergarten the other day. That doesn't sound like she's planning to move to me."

"But..." Chase's thoughts were in chaos. He'd thought...he'd assumed that Letty would be moving out. She'd certainly given him that impression.

"Would it be so difficult to settle things by finding out yourself what she intends to do?" Lonny asked. "We've repaired all the fence we're going to manage today. Come to the house and ask her yourself—point-blank. Letty may be a lot of things, but I've never known her to lie. If she's planning on leaving Red Springs, she'll admit it."

Chase expelled his breath forcefully. He may as well do what Lonny asked, since it was clear he wasn't going to leave him alone until he did. And yet . . .

"Will you do that, at least?" Lonny urged a second time.

"I..." Indecision tore at Chase. He didn't want to have any contact with Letty; he was still reeling from their last encounter. But he'd never seen Lonny behave like this. Whatever Letty had said and done obviously worried him. It wasn't like Lonny to get involved in another man's business. That fact alone was a more convincing argument than anything he'd said.

"You're driving me back to the house, aren't you?" Lonny asked matter-of-factly.

"What about Destiny?"

"I'll pick him up later."

Lonny said this casually, as if he often left his horse over at Spring Valley. As far as Chase could remember, he'd never done so in all the years they'd been neighbors.

"All right, I'll ask her," Chase agreed, but reluctantly. If for nothing more than to appease Lonny, although Chase wanted this issue with Letty cleared in his mind. From what he remembered from the night before, she'd made her intentions obvious to him. Yet why she enrolled Cricket in kindergarten—which was several months away—was beyond him. As Lonny had said, it didn't make sense.

"Thank God," Lonny muttered, climbing into the cab of the truck.

The first thing Chase noticed when he rolled into the yard at Lonny's place was that his friend's battered pickup was missing. He waited outside while Lonny hurried into the kitchen.

"She's not here," Lonny said when he returned, holding a note.

"Obviously."

"She's gone into town to see Joy Fuller."

Chase frowned. Now that he'd made the decision to confront Letty, he was disappointed about the delay. "I'll ask her another time," he suggested, although he wasn't keen on putting it off.

"No," Lonny said, apparently sensing Chase's frustration. "I mean...I don't think it would do any harm to drive over to Joy's. I've been meaning to talk to her, anyway, and this business with Letty gives me an excuse."

"You told me the woman was a witch. What possible reason could you have to talk to her?"

Lonny had already climbed into the truck, but not before Chase noted the tinge of color that invaded his tanned features. "I may have been a bit hasty in sizing up her character. She might even be a decent enough sort, though that was difficult to tell when I first met her. I mean, she plays the church organ, and the pastor wouldn't let just anyone do that."

"That's Joy Fuller?" Chase couldn't contain his surprise as he started the pickup and headed toward town. The fact was, he'd noticed her himself, but obviously not in the same way Lonny had. "Why, she's downright cute. I didn't know that was the woman you were talking about all this time."

"She teaches second grade over at the elementary school. They're on half days this week."

Chase glanced at his friend a second time, doing his best to disguise his amusement. "How'd you know that?"

Lonny swallowed and glanced out the window, obviously embarrassed. "I must have heard it somewhere. Letty probably. How else would I know something like that?"

"Right," Chase murmured, but a smile twitched at the edges of his mouth. So ol' Lonny was smitten with the church organist. Stranger things had happened.

"Take a right at the next corner," Lonny instructed as they entered town. "Her apartment is the first one on the left."

Chase parked under the row of elms and turned off the engine. "I'll wait here."

Lonny climbed out of the truck and hesitated. "That might not be a good idea."

"Why not?"

"Well, I'm not exactly sure if Joy will talk to me."

Chase was growing impatient with this game of cat and mouse. Personally, now that he'd had time to think about it, running into town to find Letty wasn't that brilliant of an idea, either.

"Why shouldn't Joy want to talk to you, for God's sake?" he barked.

Lonny looked decidedly uncomfortable. "We've had words a few times and . . ."

"Hell, she was the one who ran into you," Chase tossed out, growing more impatient.

"Yes, but—"

"She's not blaming you for the accident, is she?"

Lonny looked all the more uneasy. "Just come with me, would you?"

Chase stepped out of the truck, none too pleased by this unexpected turn of events. This whole idea was nothing short of insane, and Letty was bound to get the wrong impression. She might even assume he cared. A painful bubble caught in his chest. If only he could stop caring.

Chase watched in surprise as Lonny licked his fingertips and smoothed down the sides of his hair before ringing the doorbell. It was all Chase could do not to comment.

To their surprise, it was Cricket who answered. "Hi, Uncle Lonny. Hi, Chase." She twisted around and shouted over her shoulder. "Joy, it's my Uncle Lonny and Chase. You remember Chase, don't you? He's my very bestest friend in the whole world."

A short moment passed before Joy came to the door.

"Yes?" she said stiffly.

Her chin was held at a regal angle, and her feet were braced as if she expected an argument—over what, Chase could only guess. She wore a frilly apron tied around her waist, and traces of flour dusted her nose. She'd obviously been baking, and knowing Cricket, it was probably chocolate chip cookies!

Lonny jerked the hat from his head. "We were wondering...me and Chase, my neighbor here, if it would be convenient to take a moment of your time."

Chase had never heard his friend sound more tongue-tied. Lonny made it seem as though they were salesmen coming to pawn their wares.

"We can't seem to talk to each other without yelling, Mr. Ellison," Joy returned in starched tones. Her fingers were neatly clasped in front of her, and her gaze was focused somewhere in the distance.

"I'd like to talk to Letty," Chase said. The way things were going with Lonny, it could be another half hour before anyone learned the reason for their visit.

"Mommy's gone," Cricket piped in.

"She just left a couple of minutes ago," Joy explained.

"Did she say where she was going?"

"No...but I'm sure you can catch her if it's important."

"Go, man," Lonny said, pointing the bony end of his elbow in Chase's ribs. "I'll stay here—that is, if Miss Fuller has no objections."

"'Ms.' Fuller," Joy corrected, her gaze narrowing.

"Ms. Fuller," Lonny echoed, although he made it sound as if the words were a fish bone stuck in his throat.

"You can stay, but only if you promise you won't insult me in my own home. Because I'm telling you right now, Lonny Ellison, I won't put up with it."

"I'll do my best."

"That may not be good enough."

"Which way did Letty head?" Chase demanded, growing decidedly impatient with the pair.

"Toward town," Joy said, pointing west. "You shouldn't have any trouble finding her. She's driving that piece of junk Mr. Ellison seems to think so highly of."

For a moment Chase thought Lonny had swallowed a grapefruit whole for the way he reacted. His face flamed red and it was obvious he was doing everything within his power not to give a blistering response. His efforts were promptly rewarded with a soft smile from Joy.

"Very good, Mr. Ellison. You've passed the test." She stepped aside in order for him to enter the apartment.

"I won't be long," Chase assured the two.

Lonny twisted the brim of his hat around several times. "Take your time."

"A few minutes may be about as long as we can be civil to each other," Joy inserted. "But do hurry. Otherwise you'll miss her."

"Mommy's not feeling well," Cricket said, looking concerned.

Lonny tossed a searing look at Chase. "Would you kindly hurry!"

Chase didn't need any more incentive. He wanted to talk to Letty.

"West?"

"Toward town." Once more Joy pointed in that direction.

Chase nodded his appreciation and ran toward his pickup. As soon as the engine roared to life, he shifted gears and spun out into the street.

Red Springs's main street was lined with several small businesses with diagonal parking in front. At a single glance, Chase determined Lonny's truck wasn't within sight. He drove the full length of the town and down a couple of side streets, but she wasn't there, either.

Mystified, he parked and stood outside his truck, looking down Main street in both directions. Where could she have possibly gone?

Letty came out of Dr. Faraday's office and sat in Lonny's truck for several moments before she started the engine. After waiting all these weeks, after stringing out the details of her life as though they were laundry on a clothesline for the medical world to examine... after all this, she should feel some sort of release knowing that the surgery was scheduled.

But she didn't.

Instead she was experiencing a chilling sadness that seemed to roll itself around her like the enfolding wrap of a mummy, until she couldn't move, paralyzed by a hundred emotions, many of which she was powerless to identify.

Tears burned in her eyes, yearning to be released, but she held her head proud, shifted the truck gears and headed toward the freeway that would take her back to Red Springs. Now that everything had been cleared with the doctor and the state, Letty felt free to explain what was wrong with her to her brother. She'd leave it to him to tell Chase—if he wanted.

Chase. His name bounced around the dark edges of her mind like a Ping-Pong ball. Quickly she cast all thoughts of him aside, knowing they would only bring pain.

A few miles out of town, Letty noticed another truck in her rearview mirror, several cars back. The first thought that flashed through her brain was that someone drove a model similar to Chase's. The vehicle reminded her of him, but simply because she'd been thinking about him only seconds earlier, she reasoned.

It wasn't until the truck started weaving in and out of traffic in an effort to catch up with her that Letty realized the pickup *did* belong to Chase.

If her heart hadn't already been damaged it would have been, just watching Chase take crazy chances trying to catch up with her. Something terrible must have happened... Cricket... oh, God, it had to be Cricket.

Letty pulled to the side of the road and eased to a stop.

Chase was right behind her.

Shutting off the engine, she climbed out, turned around and saw him leap out of his vehicle and come running toward her.

"Letty, dear God." He wrapped his arms around her, holding her with a tenderness she thought had been lost between them forever.

Wedging her arms between Chase and her, she loosened his grip enough to raise her head. "Is anything wrong with Cricket?"

He frowned and brushed the hair away from her face. "No," he said before he kissed her with a thoroughness that left her weak and clinging.

"Then what are you doing here?"

Chase closed his eyes briefly. "That's a long story. Letty, we've got to talk."

With some effort she was able to break free of his embrace. "I don't know that we can anymore. Every time we're close to each other, the only thing we end up doing is arguing. I realize I hurt you, Chase, but I don't know how much longer I can stand being hurt back. After last night, I decided it was best if we never saw each other again."

"You make us sound as bad as Lonny and Joy."

"We are, only worse."

"It doesn't have to be that way."

"I don't think we're capable of anything else anymore," she whispered, pain tightening her voice.

His eyes burned into hers as he waited several long moments to announce, "Letty, I know."

Chase wasn't making any sense to her. If he knew they were incapable of sustaining a relationship, then why had he been driving like a madman to catch her? Frankly, she wasn't in the mood to listen to his riddles. All she wanted to do was get home.

Chase dropped his arms and paced in front of her, fists at his side. "The day you fainted in the garden, I should have figured it out. For weeks before, Lonny had been telling me how tired you were all the time, how fragile you'd become. At the time I thought it was because you were depressed and California had spoiled you."

"It did. I'm a soft person, unaccustomed to anything resembling hard work."

Chase ignored her sarcasm. "Then that day in the cemetery... you tried to tell me then, didn't you?" But he didn't allow her to answer his question. "You started talking about life and death, and all I could do was be angry with you because I thought you'd lied. I wasn't even listening. If I had been, I would have heard what you were trying to tell me."

Tears blurred her vision as she stood tall and proud before him. Unmoving. Her throat was so thick with emotion she didn't even attempt to reply.

"It's the reason you dragged Mary Brandon over to the house for dinner that night, isn't it?" Once more he didn't wait for her response. "You figured that if Lonny was married and anything happened to you, then Cricket would have a secure home life."

"Not exactly," she managed. In the beginning her thoughts had leaned in that direction. But she wasn't the manipulative type, and it had soon become obvious that Lonny wanted nothing to do with her schemes.

Chase brought his hands to her shoulders. "Letty, I saw Dr. Faraday." A hint of a smile brushed the corners of his mouth. "It took everything in me not to go over to the man and hug him."

"Chase, you're not making any sense."

"I don't suppose I am. Cricket told me that when you came to Rock Springs, you saw a man with a mustache...a man who looked like the one on TV."

"When did she tell you that?"

"Weeks ago. But more damning was that she claimed you went into a room together, but that she had to stay outside and wait for you."

"Oh, dear..."

"You can imagine what Lonny and I thought."

"And you believed it?" It seemed that neither Chase nor her brother knew her. Both seemed willing to condemn her on the flimsiest of evidence. If she were meeting a man, the last person she would take with her was Cricket. But apparently that thought hadn't so much as entered their twisted minds.

"We didn't know what to think," Chase answered.

"But you automatically assumed the worst?"

Chase looked properly chagrined. "I know it sounds bad, but there had been another man in your life before. How was I to know the same thing wasn't happening all over again?"

"How were you to know?" Letty demanded, and slumped against the car, wiping a hand over her face. "How were you to know?" she repeated in a hurt whisper. "What kind of person do you think I am?"

"Letty, believe me, I'm sorry."

She covered her eyes and shook her head.

"From the moment you returned, everything's felt wrong. For a time I thought my whole world had been knocked off its axis. Nothing I did seemed to balance it. Not until today did I realize it wasn't my world that was off kilter, but yours. You were the one spinning so fast and hard and I couldn't help but feel the effects."

"You're talking in riddles and not making a whole lot of sense."

"No, I don't suppose I am." Once more he started pacing in front of her. He stopped and ran his fingers through his hair several times. "Tell me what's wrong. Please. I want to know—I need to know."

"It's my heart," she whispered.

"Dr. Faraday's specialty was the first thing I noticed when I saw you walk into his office."

"You saw me walk into his office?"

His gaze skirted away from hers. "I followed you to Rock Springs." He continued before she could react. "I'm not exactly proud of that, Letty. Lonny convinced me that you and I needed to talk. After last night, we were both hurting so badly...and I guess I wasn't exactly the best company this morning. Lonny and I went back to the ranch and found your note. From there we went to the Fuller woman's place and she said you'd just left and were heading into town. I drove there and couldn't find you anywhere. It was then that I realized you'd probably driven to Rock Springs. If you were meeting a man, then I wanted to find out who. I had no idea what I intended to do—probably nothing—but I had to know."

"So...so you followed me."

"From a safe distance."

"That was certainly wonderful of you."

"Letty, you have every reason in the world to be angry. All I can do is apologize."

She shook her head. "I wanted to tell you. I've kept this secret to myself for so long and there was no one...no one I could tell and I needed—"

"Letty...please, what's wrong with your heart?"

"The doctors discovered a small hole when I was pregnant with Cricket."

"What are they going to do?"

"Surgery."

His face tightened. "When?"

"Dr. Faraday has already scheduled it. I couldn't afford it . . . when you saw my first welfare check I wanted to die. I knew what you thought and there wasn't any way to tell you how much I hated being an object of charity."

Chase shut his eyes. "Dear God, Letty, I failed you . . . you needed me and I failed you."

"Chase, I'm not going to blame you for that. I've failed you, too."

"I've been so blind, so stupid."

"I've suffered from my share of the same afflictions."

"This time I can change things," he said, gripping her shoulders.

"How?"

"Letty." His fingers were gentle, his eyes tender. "We're getting married."

Chapter Ten

Married," Letty said, repeating the word for the twentieth time in the past hour. Chase sat her down, poured her a cup of coffee and delivered it to the kitchen table. Only a few days earlier, he'd thought nothing of her doing a multitude of chores. Now he was treating her as if she were an invalid. If Letty hadn't been so amused by his change in attitude, she would have found his behavior downright irritating. She wasn't exactly on her last leg!

"I'm not willing to argue with you, Letty Ellison. We're getting married."

"Honestly, Chase, you're being unreasonable and just a little dramatic, don't you think?" She loved him all the more for it, but that didn't alter the facts.

"No!" His face was tormented with guilt. "Dear God, why didn't I listen to you? You tried to tell me, and I was so pigheaded, so blind." He knelt in front of her and gripped both her hands in his, his eyes dark and filled with emotion. "You aren't in any condition to fight me on this, Letty, so simply do as I suggest and don't argue."

"I'm in excellent shape." Like her brother, Letty found Chase could be so stubborn that there were times when she found it impossible to reason with him. Knotted in with all her arguments was a deep, abiding love for this man. Yet there existed a multitude of doubts that they hadn't faced or answered.

Chase hadn't admitted he loved her or even that he cared. But, then, Chase always had been a man of few words. When he'd proposed the first time, he'd told her then, simply and profoundly, how much he loved her and wanted to build a life with her. They had been the sweetest, most romantic words she'd ever heard any man whisper. Letty had supposed that that night following her high school graduation was going to be all the poetry Chase would ever give her.

"You're scheduled for heart surgery, for God's sake."

"I'm not on my deathbed yet!"

He went virtually pale with the joke. "Letty, don't even say that."

"What? That I could die? It's been known to happen. But it won't with me. I'm strong, and otherwise healthy. Besides, I'm too persnickety to die in a hospital. I prefer to do it in my own bed with my grandchildren gathered around me, fighting over who will get my many jewels." She said this with a hint of drama, loving the way Chase's eyes flared with outrage.

In response, he wiped a hand over his face.

"I'm not going to buy the farm or kick the bucket, so don't worry."

"I'll feel better once I talk to Dr. Faraday myself. But when I do, I'm telling you right now, Letty Ellison, that I'll do so as your husband."

Letty rolled her eyes. She couldn't believe they were even having this discussion. Yet Chase seemed so adamant, so certain that their marrying now was the right thing to do. Letty loved him more than she thought it possible to love any man, but she wasn't nearly as confident about the importance of linking their lives when the surgery loomed before her—afterward would be soon enough.

Her reaction seemed to infuriate Chase. "All right, if my words won't convince you, then perhaps this will." With that he wove his fingers into her hair and brought his lips to hers. The kiss was sweet and gentle and filled with such tenderness that Letty was left trembling in its aftermath.

Chase appeared equally shaken. His eyes held hers for the longest moment before he kissed her again. This time he used his tongue, bending her will to his. Letty's fingers gripped his shoulders as his mouth played hers like the most delicate, intricate instrument. And the music they made sounded almost angelic.

"Well, this is just peachy."

Lonny's harsh tone broke them apart.

"Lonny," Chase murmured, his voice sounding oddly unlike itself. He cast a glance in the direction of the kitchen clock.

"'It'll only take me a few minutes to find Letty,'" Lonny mimicked, clearly agitated. "It's been nearly four hours, man. Four hours with that...that woman is more than any male should have to endure."

"Where's Cricket?" Letty asked, instantly alarmed.

"With the witch-woman, for all I know. Or care." He turned to Chase, a dark frown creasing his forehead. "Did you know all women stick together, even the little ones? I told Cricket to come with me, and she ran behind Joy's skirts and hid. I couldn't believe my eyes—my own niece!"

Letty sprang to her feet. "I'm going to call Joy and find out what happened to Cricket."

"How'd you get back here?" Chase asked his friend.

"Walked."

Letty paused in the doorway, anxious to hear her brother's reply.

"But it's six miles into town," she reminded him.

"You're telling me?" Lonny moaned and slumped into a chair, looking none too pleased. The first thing he did was remove his left boot, having some difficulty getting it off his swollen foot. He released a long sigh as it fell to the floor. Next he flexed his toes.

"What happened?"

"She kicked me out. What the hell do you think happened? Do I look like the type who would stroll home just for the exercise, for God's sake?" His narrowed gaze accused both Letty and Chase. "I don't suppose you gave me another thought after you dropped me off, did you? Oh, no. You two were so interested in making kissy face that you conveniently forgot about me."

"We're sorry, Lonny," Letty said contritely.

Lonny's gaze shifted between Chase and Letty and back again. "I guess there's no need in asking if the two of you managed to patch things up—that much is obvious." By this time, the second dust-caked boot had hit the floor. Lonny paused long enough to peel off his socks. "Damn it, I've got blisters on my blisters. No thanks to the two of you."

"We're getting married," Chase announced without preamble, his gaze challenging Letty to defy him.

Lonny's head shot up and his foot dropped unnoticed to the floor. "What?"

"Letty and I are getting married," Chase repeated. "And the sooner the better."

Lonny's suspicious gaze narrowed and when he spoke his voice was hardly above a whisper. "You're pregnant again, aren't you?"

Letty burst out laughing. "I wish it were that simple."

"She's got a defective heart," Chase said simply, omitting the details and not giving Letty the opportunity to explain more fully. "If you think about it, it'll hit you square between the eyes the way it did me. She has to have an operation—a delicate one from the sounds of it."

"Your heart?" Shocked, Lonny studied her as if staring at her long enough would enable him to see what was physically wrong. "Is that the reason you fainted that day?"

"Partially."

"Dear God, Letty, why didn't you tell me?"

"I couldn't. Not until I had everything cleared with the government and the surgery was scheduled. You would have worried yourself into a tizzy, and I didn't want to heap my problems on top of all the other responsibility you carry."

"But..." He frowned, apparently displeased by her response. "I could have helped...or at least been a little more sympathetic. When I stop to think about the way you've cleaned up around here... You had no business working so hard planting a silly garden and doing everything else you have lately. I wish you would have said something, Letty. I feel like a jerk."

"No one knew, Lonny. Please understand."

He wiped the back of his hand over his mouth, as though the action would help him accept her explanation. "On second thought, maybe not knowing was for the best, at least in theory. But I hope you won't keep anything like this from me again."

"Believe me, there were a thousand times when I wanted to tell you and couldn't."

"I'm going to arrange for the wedding as soon as possible," Chase cut in. "You don't have any objections, do you, Lonny?" His voice was demanding and inflexible.

"Objections? Me? No... not in the least."

"Honestly, Chase," Letty said, gently patting her brother's shoulder. "This whole conversation is becoming monotonous, don't you think? I haven't agreed to this crazy scheme of yours... The fact is, I don't understand why you're so set on making me your wife now."

"Call Joy and find out what happened to Cricket," he instructed, refusing to address her qualms.

Letty moved toward the phone and quickly dialed Joy's number. Her friend answered on the second ring. "Joy, it's Letty. Is Cricket with you?"

"Yes, of course. I wouldn't let that fool brother of yours take her, and frankly, she wouldn't have gone with him, anyway. I'm sorry, Letty. I really am. You're my friend and I adore Cricket, but your brother is one of the most—" She was speaking ninety miles an hour, and stopped abruptly. "I...I don't think it's necessary to say anything more. Lonny is your brother—you know him probably better than anyone."

In some ways Letty felt as if she didn't know Lonny at all. "Joy, whatever happened, I'm sorry."

"It had nothing to do with you, so don't worry about it. Did Chase ever catch up with you? I didn't think to mention until after he'd gone that you'd said something about a doctor's appointment."

"He found me without too much trouble. That's the reason it's taken me so long to get back to you. I'm home now, but Chase and I've been talking for the past hour or so. I didn't mean to leave Cricket with you so long."

"Cricket has been great, so don't worry about her staying longer than you anticipated. We've had a grand time—at least, we did until your brother decided to visit." She paused and soft regret filled her voice when she spoke again. "I don't know what it is with the two of us. I seem to bring out the worst in Lonny...I know he does in me."

Letty wished she knew what it was, too. Discussing it over the phone made her a little uncomfortable. She needed to see and study Joy; words alone left a lot to be desired. "I'll be over in a few minutes to pick up Cricket."

"Don't bother," Joy said quickly. "I was going out on an errand and I'll be more than happy to drop her off."

"You're sure that isn't any problem?"

"Positive." Once more Joy hesitated. "Lonny made it home all right, didn't he? I mean it *is* a long walk. When I told him I thought he should leave, I didn't mean for him to have to hike the whole way back. I forgot he didn't have the truck with him. By the time I realized it, he'd already started down the sidewalk and he refused to listen to another word."

"He's home no worse for wear, so don't worry about him."

"I'll see you in a few minutes, then," Joy murmured, sounding resigned and miserable. Letty strongly suspected that Joy was bringing Cricket home in an effort to patch things with Lonny. Unfortunately, in her brother's mood, that would be nearly impossible.

Letty replaced the phone, but not before Lonny shouted from the kitchen, "What the hell do you mean, 'no worse for wear'? I've got blisters here that would have brought a lesser man to his knees. Six miles, and you make it sound as if I frolicked through some park."

"What did you want to tell her? That you'd dragged yourself in barely able to move?"

"Letty, I don't think you should raise your voice. It isn't good for your heart." Chase draped his arm around Letty's shoulder, led her back to the table and eased her onto a chair.

"I'm not an invalid," she shouted, regretting it almost immediately. Chase flinched as if she'd attacked him, and in a way she had, only with frustrated words.

"Please, Letty, we have a good deal to discuss. I want the details for this wedding ironed out before I leave." Once more he knelt in front of her, as if he expected her to keel over at any moment and was prepared to catch her.

She sighed and glared at the wall. Nothing she'd said seemed to have reached Chase.

"I'm taking a bath," Lonny announced. He stuffed his socks inside his boots and picked them up on his way into the bathroom.

"Chase, listen to me," Letty pleaded, her hands framing his worried face. "There's no reason for us to marry now. Once the surgery is over and I'm back on my feet again, then we can discuss it, if you still feel the same."

"Are you turning me down a second time, Letty?" His words were fortified with pride.

"Oh, Chase, you know that isn't it. I told you the other night how much I loved you. If my feelings for you didn't change in all the years we were apart, they won't in the next few months."

"Letty, you're not thinking clearly."

"It's my heart that's defective, not my brain."

"I'll arrange for the license right away," he continued as if she hadn't spoken. "If you have your heart set on a church wedding with all the fancy trimmings, we'll arrange for that later." He stopped, as though considering what he'd said. "No pun intended."

"Why not bring Pastor Taylor to the hospital, and while he's there he can administer the last rites," she returned flippantly.

"Don't even think that!"

"If I agree to this crazy scheme of yours—and frankly, I can't see myself doing it—I'll be married in the church the first time."

"You're not thinking."

"Chase, you're the one who's diving into the deep end here—not me. Give me one solid reason why we should get married now."

"Concern for Cricket ought to be enough."

"What's my daughter got to do with this?"

"She loves me and I love her." His mouth turned up in a short, almost chagrined smile. "I didn't think I could love her the way I do. In the beginning, every time I saw her it was like someone had stuck a knife into my heart. One day—" he paused and lowered his gaze to the floor "—I realized that nothing I did was going to keep me from loving that little girl. She's so much a part of you, and I couldn't care about you the way I do and not love her."

It was the closest Chase had come to admitting he loved her. Hearing him talk about his feelings for Cricket and how there were indelibly tied to her greatly lifted Letty's sagging spirits.

"More than that, Letty, if something were to happen to you, I'd be a far better parent than Lonny. Think about that. Can you imagine Cricket being stuck with your brother as a surrogate father? Lonny's simply not equipped to deal with the needs of a child."

"But—"

"I know," he said, stopping her by raising his hand. "You're thinking that you don't have to marry me to make me Cricket's legal guardian, and you're right. But I want you to consider Lonny's fragile pride in all this. If you make me responsible for Cricket, what's that going to say to your brother? He's your only living relative, and it would insult his dignity if he felt you didn't trust him to properly raise your child."

"But nothing's going to happen," Letty argued, knowing she couldn't be completely sure of that.

"But what if the worst *does* happen? If you leave matters as they are now, then Lonny might be left to deal with a grief-stricken five-year-old child. He'd never be able to cope, Letty, and in the end, he'd have to place her in a foster home or find someone else to raise her," he paused to let his words sink in and then added. "I'll tell you right now, the state won't look favorably upon me as a foster parent."

Letty knew he was right about that.

"This situation is much too grave to leave everything to fate," he said, closing his argument. "You've got Cricket's future to consider."

Letty's thoughts were spinning like a child's toy top, careening against the walls of her mind, confusing her all the more. "This surgery is a fairly standard procedure." The doctor had told her so himself. Complicated, yes, but not uncommon.

"All I can do is pray that you're right," Chase murmured.

Letty didn't know what to think. She'd asked Chase to come up with one good argument and he'd outdone himself. There were other areas that Chase hadn't even stopped to consider, however. If they married, he would then become liable for the cost of her medical care.

"Chase this surgery isn't cheap. Dr. Faraday said I could be in the hospital as long as two weeks. The hospital bill alone will run into five figures, and that doesn't include the doctor's fee or the pharmaceutical bills, which will add up to much, much more."

"As my wife, you'll be covered by my health insurance policy."

He said this with such confidence that Letty could almost believe him. She desperately wanted to think it was true, but she knew differently. "I'm afraid that won't be the case. In all likelihood your insurance company would deny the claim since the condition is preexisting."

"That can be learned easily enough. I'll phone my broker right now." He left and returned no more than five minutes later. "It's as I thought. As my wife, you'd automatically be included for all benefits, no matter how long we've known about your heart condition."

It sounded too good to be true. "Chase...I don't know."

"I'm through with listening to all the reasons we can't get married. The fact is, you've rejected one proposal from me, and we both suffered because of it. I won't let you do it a second time. Now will or won't you marry me?"

"You're sure about the insurance...?"

"Positive." He squatted in front of her and took both her hands in his. "You're going to marry me, Letty. No more arguments, no more comments, no more guff! Understand?"

Chase made the question more of a statement. "Yes," she murmured, loving him so much her heart throbbed with it. "But, you're taking such a risk..."

His eyes narrowed. "Why?"

"Well, because..." She paused when Cricket came running through the door, and held her arms out to her daughter, who flew into them.

"I'm home." Cricket hugged Letty once, briefly, then hurriedly moved to Chase and looped her arms around his neck with such enthusiasm it nearly knocked him onto the floor.

Letty watched the pair and realized above anything else how right Chase was to be concerned about Cricket's welfare should something go wrong. She drew in a shaky breath and held it until her lungs ached. She loved Chase, and although he hadn't spelled out his feelings for her, she knew he cared deeply for her and for Cricket.

Joy stood sheepishly just inside the kitchen door, her gaze skirting the area for any signs of Lonny. Letty didn't doubt that if her brother were to make an appearance the church organist would quickly turn a designer shade of red.

"Joy, come in," Letty said, welcoming her friend.

She did, edging a few more feet into the kitchen. "I just wanted to be sure Cricket arrived home safely."

"Thanks so much for watching her for me this afternoon," Letty said, smiling broadly. "I appreciate it more than you know."

"It wasn't any problem."

A soft snicker was heard from the direction of the hallway. Lonny stood there, obviously having just gotten out of the shower. His dark hair glistened with moisture and his shirt had been left unbuttoned over his blue jeans. His feet were bare.

Joy stiffened. "The only difficulty was when unexpected company arrived and—"

"Uncle Lonny was shouting at Joy," Cricket whispered to her mother.

"Don't forget to mention the part where she yelled back," Lonny instructed. "If you're going to tattle on me, kid, get your facts straight."

"I think I'd better go." Joy gripped the doorknob.

"I'm not stopping you," Lonny said sweetly, swaggering into the room as if he were General Patton inspecting the banks of the Rhine.

"I'll be more than happy to leave, Lonny Ellison. The less I see of you the better."

"Lady, those are my feelings exactly."

"Lonny. Joy." Letty threw her hands up at the two of them. They were both so stubborn. Every time they were within close range of each other, sparks ignited.

"I'm sorry, Joy, but I simply cannot tolerate your brother."

Lonny moved closer to Joy and Letty realized why his walk was so unusual. He was doing his utmost not to limp, what with all his blisters. Lonny stopped directly in front of Joy, his arms folded over his bared chest. "The same goes for you—only double the sentiment."

"Goodbye, Letty, Chase. Goodbye, Cricket." Joy completely ignored Lonny, turned and walked out of the house.

The instant she did, Lonny sat down and started to rub his feet. "Fool woman."

"I won't comment on who's acting like a fool here, brother dearest, but the odds are high that you're in the competition."

Chase sat in the hospital waiting room in a molded plastic chair and reached for a *Time* magazine. He didn't so much as notice the date until he'd read three news articles and realized everything he'd covered had happened months ago.

Like the outdated magazine, Chase's life was vastly different, but the transformation had taken place within a few short days and not months.

A week after following Letty into Rock Springs and discovering her secret, he was both a husband and a father. And now he and Letty were facing what could possibly be the most difficult trial of their lives together: her heart surgery.

Setting the magazine aside, Chase wandered outside to the balcony, gripping the railing as he surveyed the lush foliage below.

A line of worry snared him, entangling his thoughts. Even when they'd wheeled Letty into the operating room, she'd been joking with the doctor. A faint smile wobbled over Chase's lips. Letty had dramatically promised to spill her guts and tell them everything they wanted to know.

A vision of the nurse, clad in surgical green from head to foot, who'd wheeled Letty through the double doors and into the operating room, came back to haunt him. They had taken Letty from his side, although he'd held on to her hand for as long as possible. Only Chase had seen the momentary look of stark fear, of panic, in her eyes. But her gaze had found his and her expression was magically transformed into a look of gentle reassurance.

She was the one facing a trauma and she'd wanted to encourage *him*.

Her sweet smile and warmth hadn't fooled him, though. Letty was as frightened as he was, perhaps more; she just wouldn't let anyone know it.

She could die in there, and he was powerless to do anything to stop the hands of fate. To entertain the thought of her death caused his heart and mind to ache with an agony that was beyond description. Letty had been back in Wyoming less than two months and Chase couldn't imagine what his life would be like without her now. The sun was shining, but black clouds formed over his head, blocking out rational arguments. The air on the balcony became stifling. Chase did the only thing he could. He fled.

"Chase." Lonny came running after him. "What's happened? Where's Letty?"

Chase's eyes were wild as he regarded his brother-in-law. "They took her away not more than twenty minutes ago."

"Hey, are you going to be all right?"

The question buzzed around his head like mosquitoes above a stagnant pond.

"Chase." Lonny gripped his shoulders. "I think you should sit down."

"Cricket?" The lone word ushered from his lips, but he was barely aware that he'd spoken.

"She's fine. Joy's watching her."

Chase nodded, sitting on the edge of the hard seat, his elbows braced against his knees while his hands covered his face. Letty had come into his life when he'd least expected her back again. She'd offered him love when he'd never thought to discover it a second time. Long before, he'd given up the dream of her ever being an important part of his life . . . or the dream of her ever being his wife.

They had been married less than twenty-four hours. Only a few hours before Letty had stood before Pastor Taylor and vowed to love him. And here she was, her life on the line, and they had yet to experience a wedding night.

Chase prayed fate wouldn't be so cruel as to rip her from his arms before he'd had the opportunity to share in the joy of loving her, the joy of fulfilling his dreams and building happiness with her and Cricket and whatever more children God saw fit to send into their lives. Ever so fleeting, a picture began to form in his mind. One of two pint-size boys around the ages of five and six. They stood next to each other, the best of friends, each with deep blue eyes so like Letty's that Chase's heart constricted. Their hair was the identical shade of his own when he was about their age.

"She's going to make it just fine," Lonny felt obliged to comment. "Do you think my sister is going to give up on life without a fight? You know Letty better than that. Relax, would you? Everything's going to work out."

His friend's words dispelled the vision. Chase wished he shared some of Lonny's confidence regarding Letty's health. He felt so powerless, so helpless—all he could do was pray.

Chase stood up abruptly. "I'm going down to the chapel," he announced, appreciating it when Lonny chose to stay behind.

The chapel was empty, and Chase was grateful for the privacy. He sat in the back pew and stared straight ahead, not knowing what to say or do that would convince the Almighty to keep Letty safe.

He rotated the rim of his hat between his fingers several times while his mind fumbled for the words to plead for her life. He wanted so much more than for Letty simply to survive the surgery, and then felt selfish for being so greedy. As the minutes ticked past, he sat and silently poured out his heart, talking as he would to a friend.

Chase had never been a man who could speak eloquently—to God or, for that matter, to Letty or anyone else. He knew she'd been looking for the love words women like the day he'd proposed to her. He regretted now that he hadn't said them. He'd felt them deep inside his heart, but something had kept them buried inside. Fear, he suspected. He'd spoken them once and they hadn't meant enough to keep her in Red Springs. He didn't know if they would mean enough this time, either.

An eternity passed and he remained where he was, almost afraid to face whatever would greet him upon his return. Several people came and went, but their presence barely rated a notice from Chase.

The chapel door opened once more and Chase didn't need to turn around to know it was Lonny. The hairs on the back of his neck bristled. Cold fear dampened his brow and he sat immobilized by emotion. The longest seconds of his life dragged past before Lonny joined him in the pew.

"The surgery went without a hitch—Letty's going to be just fine," he whispered. "You can see her, but only for a moment."

Chase closed his eyes as the tension eased from his heart and soul.

"Did you hear me?"

Chase nodded and turned to his lifelong friend. "Thank God."

The two men embraced and Chase's gaze flew to the front of the chapel, his heart and mind filled with overwhelming gratitude.

"Be warned, though," Lonny said on their way back to the surgical floor. "Letty's going to be connected to a bunch of tubes and other stuff, so don't be shaken by it."

Chase nodded.

The same nurse who had wheeled his wife away from him was waiting when Chase returned. She had him dress in sterile surgical garb and instructed him to follow her.

Chase did so into the intensive care unit. Letty was lying perfectly still on a gurney, and Chase stood quietly by her side. Slowly he eased his weight down beside her, and saw that her eyes were closed.

"Letty," he whispered. "It's Chase. You're going to be fine. There wasn't a single problem."

Chase thought he saw her mouth move into something that resembled a smile, but he couldn't be sure.

"I love you," he murmured, his voice tight with emotion. "I didn't say it before, but I do—I never stopped. I've lived my life loving you, and nothing will ever change that."

She was pale, so deathly pale, that he experienced a sudden, sharp fear before he realized that the worst of the ordeal was over. The surgery had etched its passing over her gentle features, yet he saw something else, something he hadn't noticed about Letty before. There was a calm strength, a gentle courage, that lent him confidence. She was his wife and she would stand by his side for the rest of their days and help him meet whatever life threw in his direction.

Chase bent low and kissed her forehead tenderly before turning to leave.

"I'll be back in the morning," he told her, thinking he would share every morning with her for the rest of his life.

On the way out the door, it was all Chase could do not to click his heels for sheer joy.

Chapter Eleven

Here's some tea," Joy said, carrying a tray into the living room, where Letty was supposed to be resting.

"I'm perfectly capable of getting my own tea, for heaven's sake," Letty mumbled, but when Joy approached, she offered her friend a bright smile. It didn't do any good to complain, though having everyone wait on her frustrated Letty more than anything.

She was reluctant to admit that the most difficult aspect of her recovery was this lengthy period of convalescence. She'd been released from the hospital two weeks earlier, but had remained incredibly weak; however, she was gaining back her strength more and more each day. According to Dr. Faraday, this period of debility was to be expected. Overall, he was pleased with her progress, although Letty found herself becoming increasingly impatient. She yearned to go back to the life she'd just begun with Chase. It was as if their marriage had been put on hold.

They slept in the same bed, shared the same house, ate the same meals, but they might as well have been brother and sister, for all the notice Chase paid her. In fact, he seemed to have forgotten the fact that she was a woman!

"You're certainly looking chipper," Joy said as she claimed the overstuffed chair across from Letty. She poured them each a cup of tea and handed the first one to Letty. Then she picked up her own, sat back and relaxed.

"I'm feeling really good." Her eyes ran lovingly over the room with the polished oak floors, the thick braided rug and the old upright piano that had once been her own. The house at Sweet Valley had been built years before the one on the Bar E and Chase had done an excellent job on the upkeep. When she'd been released from the hospital, Chase had brought her to Sweet Valley and dutifully carried her over the threshold. But that had been the only husbandly obligation he had committed himself to the entire time she'd been home.

During her hospital stay, Lonny and Chase had packed up Cricket's and Letty's things and moved them to Sweet Valley as a surprise. Perhaps that had been a mistake, because Letty's frustration level mounted as she hungered to become Chase's wife in every way.

She took a sip of the lemon-scented tea, determined to exhibit more patience with herself and everyone else. "I can't thank you enough for all you've done."

Joy had made a point of coming over each afternoon and staying with Letty. In the early mornings, Chase had hired an extra man so he could be with her until it was nearly noon. By then she'd showered and dressed, and had been deposited on the living room couch, where

Chase and Cricket made a game of serving her breakfast.

"I've hardly done anything," Joy countered, discounting Letty's appreciation. "It's been great getting better acquainted. Cricket is a marvelous little girl, and now that I know you, I understand why. You're a good mother, Letty, but even more important, you're a wonderful person."

"Thank you." Letty smiled softly, touched by Joy's tribute. She'd worked hard to be the right kind of mother, but there were plenty of times when she had her doubts, as any single parent did. Only she wasn't single anymore....

"Speaking of Cricket, where is she?"

"Out visiting her pony," Letty said, and grinned. Her daughter thought that marrying Chase had been a brilliant idea. According to her, there wasn't anyone in the whole world who would make a better daddy. Chase had certainly lived up to the child's expectations. He was patient and gentle and kind to a fault with the little girl. The problem, if it could be termed that, was that Chase was also patient, gentle and kind with Letty, when she yearned to be a wife. A real wife.

"What's that?" Joy asked, pointing toward a huge box that sat on the floor next to the sofa.

Letty's gaze rested on the cardboard carton. "Lonny brought it over to me last night. It's some things that belonged to our mother. He thought I might want to sort through them. When Mom died, he packed her belongings up and stuck them in the back bedroom. They've been there ever since."

Joy's gaze fluttered downward at the mention of Lonny's name. Letty picked up on the telltale action immediately. "Are you two still not getting along?" she asked, regretting it immediately. Neither seemed willing to discuss the other.

"Not exactly. Didn't you ask me to write down the recipe for that meatless lasagna—the one where it isn't necessary to cook the noodles? Well, I brought it along, and stuck it in the kitchen."

From little things Letty had heard Lonny, Chase and Joy drop now and again, apparently her brother had made some effort to patch things up between Joy and him while Letty had been in the hospital. Evidently whatever he'd said or done had worked, because the minute she mentioned Joy's name to Lonny he got flustered and red.

For her part, Joy did everything but stand on her head to change the subject. Letty wished she knew what was happening between the two, but after one miserable attempt to involve herself in her brother's love life, she knew better than to even try.

"Mommy," Cricket cried as she came running into the living room, her pigtails skipping. "Jennybird ate an appple out of my hand. Chase showed me how to hold it so she wouldn't accidentally bite me." She looped her small arms around Letty's neck and squeezed tight. "When can you come and watch me feed Jennybird again?"

"Soon." At least, Letty hoped it would be soon.

"Take your time," Joy said. "There's no reason to push yourself, Letty."

"Oh, honestly, you're beginning to sound like Chase."

Automatically Joy shook her head. "I sincerely doubt that. I've never seen a man more worried about anyone. The first few days after the surgery, I swear he slept at the hospital. Lonny finally dragged him home, sat him down, fed him and insisted he get some decent rest."

Joy wasn't telling Letty something she didn't already know. Chase had been wonderful, more than wonderful, from the moment he'd learned about her heart condition. Now if he would only start treating her like a wife instead of a roommate.

"I want you to come and see my new bedroom," Cricket said, reaching for Joy's hand. "I've got a big new bed with a canopy and a new bedspread to match, and a new pillow and a new everything."

Joy's gaze skirted to Letty. "Chase again?"

Letty nodded. "He spoils her something terrible."

"He loves her."

"He loves me," Cricket echoed, pointing her finger at her chest. "But that's okay, because I like being spoiled."

Letty dropped her gaze. "I know you do, sweetheart, but enough is enough."

Chase had been blunt about Cricket being his main consideration when he'd asked Letty to marry him. His point had been a valid one, but Letty couldn't doubt for an instant that Chase loved them both. Although he hadn't said the words, in her case, they weren't necessary; he'd spelled out his feelings for her in a hundred different ways.

"I'd better go take a gander at Cricket's room, and then I should be thinking about heading back into town," Joy said as she stood. "There's a spaghetti salad in the refrigerator for dinner."

"Joy!" Letty protested. "You've done enough already."

"Shush," Joy countered, waving her index finger under Letty's nose. "It was a new recipe, and two were as easy to make as one."

"You're going to have to come up with a better excuse than that, Joy Fuller! You've been trying out new recipes all week." Although she was chiding her friend, Letty was grateful for all the help Joy had been to her over the past month. Her coming over and sitting with her in the afternoons had given Chase peace of mind so he could work outside without constantly fretting about Letty. The little things Joy contributed for dinner were a help, too.

Chase wouldn't allow Letty to do any of the household chores yet, and insisted upon cooking their meals himself. Never in a thousand years would Letty ever have dreamed that she would miss washing dishes. But there was an unexpected joy in performing menial tasks for the ones she loved that Letty hadn't fully realized until she'd been restricted from them. In the past few weeks, Letty had learned several valuable lessons about life. For example, she'd experienced the nearly overwhelming need to do something for someone else instead of being the recipient of everyone else's goodwill.

The house was decidedly peaceful and still as Joy followed Cricket up the stairs. The pair returned a few minutes later. Cricket was yawning and dragging her blanket behind her.

"I want to sleep with you today, Mommy."

"All right, sweetheart."

Cricket climbed into the chair across from Letty, which Joy had recently vacated, and curled up into a tight ball, piling her blanket around her. From experience, Letty knew her daughter would be asleep within five minutes.

Watching the child, Letty was grateful that Cricket would be in the morning kindergarten class, since she still seemed to need an afternoon nap.

Joy worked in the kitchen for a few moments, then paused in the doorway, smiled at Cricket and waved. Letty heard the back door close as her friend left the house.

Within an hour or two Chase would be in to check her. Letty cherished these serene moments and scooted down to nap herself. A few moments later she realized she wasn't tired, and feeling good about that, she sat up. The extra time was like an unexpected gift and her gaze fell on the carton her brother had brought to her. Carefully Letty pried open the lid.

Sorting through her mother's personal items was bound to be a painful task, Letty realized as she lovingly lifted each neatly packed item from the cardboard container.

The first thing she found was a stack of old pattern books, and cautiously set those aside. How her mother had loved to sew, often whiling away a winter's evening flipping through the pages of those old books. Letty had inherited some of that sewing ability from Maren, although it had been years since she'd sat down at a sewing machine.

Sudden emotion welled in Letty's eyes as her mind was filled with memories of her mother. Happy thoughts of a loving mother who had worked much too hard and died far too young wove their way around Letty's heart. A twinge of resentment struck her. Maren Ellison had given her life's blood to the Bar E ranch. It had been her husband's dream and not hers, and yet her mother had been called upon to make the ultimate sacrifice.

Letty wiped the moisture from her face and felt a swelling surge of sorrow over the unexpected death all those years ago. Her mother had deserved a life so much better than the one she'd lived.

Once Letty's eyes were clear enough to continue the task, she lifted several large strips of brightly colored material in odd shapes and sizes and set them on the end of the sofa. Bits and pieces of projects that had been carefully planned in her mother's eye and now waited endlessly for completion.

Then Letty withdrew what had apparently been her mother's last project. With extreme caution, she unfolded a vividly colored quilt, each stitch done painstakingly by hand.

Examining the patchwork piece produced a sense of awe in Letty. She was astonished by the time and effort invested in the project, and even more surprised that she recognized several swatches of material that made up the quilt. The huge red star in the center had been created from a piece of leftover material from a dress her mother had crafted for Letty the summer Letty had left home. A plaid piece in one corner was from an old Western shirt she'd worn for several years. After recognizing one swatch of material after another, Letty realized that her mother had probably been making the quilt for her for a Christmas or birthday gift.

Lovingly she ran the tips of her fingers over the cloth as her heart lurched with a sadness that came deep from within her soul. With a sudden flood of enthusiasm, it dawned on Letty that without too much effort she might even be able to finish the quilt herself. Everything she needed was right here. The task would be something to look forward to next winter when the days were short and the nights were Arctic cold.

After carefully tucking those items back inside the box, Letty discovered a sketchbook, packed against the side of the container. Her heart soared with excitement as she reverently lifted it from its resting place. Her mother had loved to draw. Her talent had been abundant, her skill undeniable.

The first sketch was of sunset, with a large willow tree dominating the scene against the backdrop of an evening sky. Letty recognized the place immediately. Her mother had sketched it from their front porch years ago. The willow had been cut down when Letty was in her early teens, after lightning had mutilated it.

Letty had often found her mother sketching, but the opportunity to actually complete any full-scale paintings had been rare. The book contained only a handful of sketches, and once more Letty was flooded by a wave of resentment. Maren Ellison had deserved the right to follow her own dreams. She was an artist, a gentle soul who loved with a generosity that touched everyone who came into contact with her.

"Letty." Chase broke into her thoughts as he marched into the house, his pace clipped and impatient. He paused when he saw Cricket asleep in the chair. "I saw Joy leave," he said, his voice reduced to a whisper.

"Chase, there's no need to worry. I can stay by myself for an hour or two."

"No doubt," he murmured. He wiped his forearm over his brow, then awkwardly leaned over and gently brushed his mouth over her cheek. "I thought I'd drop in and make sure everything's under control."

"It is." His chaste kiss only served to frustrate Letty. She wanted to shout at him that the time had come for him to act like a married man, instead of a saint.

"What's all this?" Chase asked, glancing around her. Letty swore the man only slept three hours a night. He never managed to go to bed at the same time as she, and he was always up before she even stirred. On rare occasions, she heard him slip between the sheets, but he stayed so far on his side of the bed that they didn't so much as touch.

"A quilt," Letty said, running her hand over the top.

"Was it in the box that Lonny brought over?"

Letty nodded. "Mom was apparently working on it when she died. She was making it for me." Admitting as much produced a lump of emotion in her throat. Letty turned and pointed to the other things she'd discovered. "There's several pieces of material in here and some pattern books, as well."

"What's this?"

"A sketching pad. Mom was an artist," Letty said proudly.

Chase's frown relaxed as he idly flipped through the pencil sketches. "She was talented, wasn't she."

It hadn't been a question and Letty realized that Chase's praise was sincere. He sounded a little surprised that he hadn't known about her mother's talent with a pencil. "Mom was an incredible woman. I don't think anyone ever appreciated all that she was—I know I didn't."

Chase stepped close and gently massaged Letty's shoulders in an action filled with tender sympathy. "You still miss her, don't you?"

In response Letty nodded. Her throat felt thick, and voicing all that she was feeling, all the emotion rising up inside her, was impossible.

Chase knelt in front of her, his gaze level with hers. He slipped his callused hands around her nape as he tenderly brought her into his arms. Letty rested her head against his solid, muscular shoulder, reveling in the feel of his warm embrace. It had been so long since he'd held her and ages since he'd kissed her... really kissed her.

Raising her head slightly, she ran the moist tip of her tongue along the side of his jaw, loving the salty, masculine taste of him. He filled her senses. Chase tensed, but still Letty continued the sensual exercise, nibbling at his earlobe, taking it into her mouth and sucking gently.

"Letty," he groaned, "no."

"No what?" she asked coyly, already knowing his answer. Her mouth roved where it wanted, while she cupped his face in her hands, mindlessly directing him as she wished. She savored the edge of his mouth, shooting the very tip of her tongue between his lips, teasing him, tantalizing him, until he moaned anew.

"Letty." He lifted his hands to her shoulders, holding them with restrained strength.

Letty was certain he'd meant to push her away, but before he could move, she did by raising her arms and looping them around his neck. As soon as she had, she leaned against him. Chase held her there so that her torso softly brushed his solid chest. Her nipples responded immediately. Chase seemed to stop breathing, then she started to sway restlessly, rubbing himself against her in a gentle agitation that seemed as much a torment for him as her.

"Letty." Her name was a plea in itself.

"Chase, kiss me, please," she whispered timidly in a soft, pleading voice. "I've missed you so much."

Slowly, as if uncertain he was doing the right thing, Chase lowered his mouth to feather her parted lips with his. Letty didn't move, didn't breathe, for fear he would stop. She would have screamed in frustration if he had. His miserly brotherly pecks on the cheeks were driving her insane. Apparently Chase had been feeling equally cheated, because he settled his mouth over hers with a passion and need that demanded her very breath. Exquisite excitement zipped through her as she gripped his shirt collar, needing it to right a world that had unexpectedly started spinning out of control.

"What's taken you so long?" she asked, her voice urgent and needy.

He answered her by closing his mouth deliberately over hers in another fiery kiss that robbed her of what little strength she'd managed to hold on to. Letty heard a faint moan come deep from within his chest. The sound was filled with longing, regret and frustration.

"Letty... this is ridiculous," he murmured, breaking away from her. His shoulders heaved as if he had to pause and gather his shattered will.

"What is?" she demanded.

"My kissing you like this."

He thrust his fingers through his hair with such force that it was a minor miracle he didn't uproot every hair he touched. His features were dark and angry.

"I'm your wife, Chase Brown. Can't a man kiss his own wife?"

"Not like this...not when she's... Good Lord, you're recovering from extremely delicate heart surgery." He moved away from her and briefly closed his eyes, as though needing an extra moment to compose himself. "Besides, Cricket's here."

"I'm your wife," Letty returned, not knowing what else to say.

"You think I need to be reminded of that?" he shot back gruffly. He stood awkwardly and grabbed his hat and gloves. "I've got to get back to work," he announced, slamming his hat on top of his head. "I'll be back in a couple of hours or so."

Letty couldn't have answered him had she tried. Her gaze fell to the lightweight quilt that was spread across the top of her legs. She felt like a fool now.

"Do you need anything before I go?" he asked without looking at her.

"No." Her voice was little more than a soft whisper.

He took three giant steps away from her, stopped abruptly, then turned around. "It's going to be months before we can do—before we can be man and wife in the full sense," he said tightly. "I think it would be best all the way around if we avoided situations like this in the future. Don't you agree?"

It was the only thing Letty could do. "I'm sorry."

"So am I," he returned grimly, and quickly left the house.

"Mommy, I want to learn how to play another song," Cricket demanded from the living room. The five-year-old was sitting at the upright piano, her feet crossed and swinging. Letty had made the mistake of teaching the youngster "Chopsticks" earlier in the day. She'd been amazed at how easily Cricket had picked up the simple piece. Cricket had played it twenty times straight and was eager to master more tunes.

"In a little bit," Letty said, and moaned inwardly. She'd obviously created a tiny monster! Letty sat at the kitchen table, peeling potatoes for dinner and feeling especially proud of herself for this minor accomplishment. Chase would be surprised and probably a little concerned once he realized what she'd done. But the surgery was several weeks behind her and it was time for her to take over the lighter responsibilities.

Eager to have her mother's full attention, Cricket headed into the kitchen and reached for a peeler and a potato. "I'll help you."

"All right, sweetheart."

The chore took only a few minutes, Letty peeling four spuds to Cricket's one. Next the child helped her pick up the peelings and clean off the table before reaching for her hand and leading Letty back into the living room.

"Play something, Mommy," the little girl insisted, sitting on the bench beside Letty.

Lazily Letty's fingers ran up and down the ivory keyboard in a quick exercise. It was astonishing now that she stopped to think about it, but she hadn't so much as touched the piano until after the surgery. Letty supposed there was some deep psychological reason, but she didn't want to analyze it now. Until Cricket's birth, music had dominated her life. But after her daughter's arrival, her life had taken a wide turn in a different direction.

"Play a song for me," Cricket commanded.

Letty did, loving the way the old familiar keys responded to her touch. The piano represented so much love and so many good times. Her mother had recognized Letty's musical gift when she was a child, only a little older than Cricket. Letty had started taking piano lessons by the time she was in first grade. When she'd learned as much as the local music teachers could teach her, her mother had driven her into Rock Springs each week. A two-hour drive for a half-hour lesson.

"Now show me how to do it like you," Cricket instructed, completely serious. "I want to play just as good as you do."

"Sweetheart, I took lessons for seven years."

"That's okay, 'cause I'm only five. I can learn."

Letty laughed. "Here, I'll play 'Mary Had a Little Lamb' and then you can move your fingers the way I do." Slowly she played the first measure, then dropped her hands on her lap while Cricket perfectly mimicked the simple notes.

"This is fun," Cricket said beaming with pride.

Within ten minutes, she'd memorized the entire song. With two musical pieces in her repertoire, Cricket was convinced she was possibly the most gifted musical student in the history of Red Springs.

The minute Chase was in the door, Cricket flew to his side. "Chase, Chase, come listen," she demanded.

"Sweetheart, let him wash up first," Letty said, doing her best to disguise her smile.

"What is it?" Chase asked, his amused gaze shifting from Cricket to Letty, then back to Cricket again.

"It's a surprise," Cricket said, practically jumping up and down with enthusiasm.

"You'd better go listen," Letty told him. "She's been as restless as a newborn filly, waiting for you to come inside."

Chase quickly washed his hands in the kitchen sink, but hesitated when he saw the panful of peeled potatoes. "Who did this?"

"Mommy and me," Cricket told him, obviously impatient for him to hurry.

"Letty?"

"And I lived to tell about it. I'm feeling stronger every day," she pointed out, "and there's no reason why I can't start taking up the slack around here a little more."

"But—"

"Don't argue with me, Chase Brown," she said in what she hoped was a firm voice that brooked no argument.

"It hasn't been a month yet," he countered, frowning.

"I'm as fit as a fiddle!"

It looked as if he wanted to argue the issue, but he apparently decided to bide his time, which was probably for the best, since Cricket was anxiously tugging at his arm, wanting him to sit down in the living room so he could hear her recital.

Letty followed the two and stood back while Cricket pointedly sat Chase down in the overstuffed chair.

"You stay here," Cricket said with all the gravity of a bank president.

Once Chase was seated, she proudly walked over to the piano and scooted onto the bench. Then she tossed a look over her shoulder and ceremoniously raised her hands until her index fingers were pointing at the ceiling. Lowering the two fingers, she put every bit of emotion her five-year-old heart possessed into playing "Chopsticks."

When she'd finished, she slid off the seat, tucked her arm around her middle and bowed. "You're supposed to clap now," she told Chase.

He obliged enthusiastically, and Letty stifled a laugh at how seriously Cricket was taking this whole thing.

"For my next number, I'll play—" she stopped abruptly. "I want you to guess."

Letty sat on the arm chair, slipping her hand around his shoulder. "She's such a ham."

Chase grinned up at her, his eyes twinkling with shared amusement.

"I must have quiet," Cricket grumbled. "You two aren't supposed to talk now... but you can if you want once I've finished."

Once more Cricket gave an Oscar-winning performance.

"Bravo, bravo," Chase shouted when she'd slipped off the piano bench.

Cricket flew to Chase's side and climbed into his lap. "Mommy taught me."

"She seems to have a flair for music," Letty admitted proudly.

"I'm not nearly as good as Mommy, though," Cricket said with a tinge of regret and a potent sigh. "She can play anything...and she sings real pretty, too. She played for me today and we had so much fun."

Letty laughed. "I'm thinking of giving Cricket piano lessons myself," Letty said, knowing Chase would add his wholehearted approval.

To her surprise, Letty felt him tense beneath her fingertips. It was as if all the joy had been mysteriously sucked out of the room by a giant vacuum.

"Chase, what's wrong?" Letty whispered, wondering at his mood.

"Nothing."

"Cricket, go pour Chase a tall glass of iced tea," Letty instructed. "It's in the refrigerator."

"Okay," the child said, as always eager to do anything for Chase.

As soon as the little girl was out of the room, Letty spoke. "Do you object to Cricket taking piano lessons?"

"Why should I?" he asked without revealing any emotion. "As you say, she's obviously got talent."

"Yes, I know, but—"

"We both know where she got it from, don't we," he said with a resigned sigh.

"I would think you'd be pleased." Chase had always loved it when she played; now it seemed that he could barely stand to have her so much as look at the piano.

"I am pleased," he declared. With that, he stood and walked into the kitchen, leaving Letty more perplexed than ever.

For several moments, Letty sat numbly while Chase spoke animatedly to Cricket, praising her efforts.

Letty had thought Chase would be happy, but he obviously wasn't. She just didn't understand it.

"Someday," she heard him tell Cricket, his voice filled with regret, "you'll play as well as your mother."

Chapter Twelve

Astride Firepower at the top of a hill overlooking his herd, Chase stared vacantly into the distance. Letty was leaving; he'd known it from the moment he discovered she'd been playing the piano again. The niggling fear had worked on him for days, gnawing away at his pride and his heart.

Marrying her had been a gamble, a big one, but he'd accepted it, grateful for the opportunity to have her and Cricket in his life, even if it was destined to be for only a short while. From somewhere deep inside, he would find the courage to smile and let her walk away. He'd managed it once, and God help him, he would do it again.

"Chase."

At the sound of his name, carried softly on the wind, Chase twisted in the saddle, causing the leather to creak. A frown crowded his face when he recognized Letty, riding a mare, advancing toward him at a slow pace. Her face was lit up with a bright smile and she waved, happy and elated. Sadly he shared little of her exhilaration. All he could think about was the fact that she would soon be gone.

Letty rode with a natural grace, as if she'd been born to it. Involuntarily Chase's gaze fell to her breasts, which were faintly swaying as she gently bounced in the saddle, and his breath jammed in his throat. He'd never seen them look more full or more seductive.

He swallowed tightly as all sensible thought left his mind and her body captured his full attention. A sense of dread swelled up inside him. The same confusion that being alone with Letty always brought. She was too damn tempting.

"Oh, God," he whispered, his voice husky and raw. Sweat broke out across his upper lip as he forced his gaze away with raw determination. He hadn't touched Letty from the moment he'd learned of her heart condition, not because he hadn't wanted to—but because he couldn't. She needed to recover from the surgery first. It was debatable, however, whether he had the strength to continue to resist her much longer. Each day became more taxing than the one before. Just being close to her sapped his strength. Sleeping with her only inches away had become a living nightmare as his body craved completion with hers.

Chase drew himself up straight when she joined him, and said, "What are you doing here?" He sounded harsher than he'd intended, but that was due to his high level of frustration.

"You didn't come back to the house for lunch," she murmured, casting her gaze downward.

"Did you stop and think that I might not be hungry?" He was tired and impatient and hated the way he found himself speaking to her, but he felt the emotions so powerfully every time he was near her. What little willpower he possessed had been depleted just keeping his eyes off her breasts. Her nipples had pebbled through the material of her blouse and were pouting directly at him, silently asking him to hold and kiss them. He was nearly going out of his mind.

"I brought you lunch," Letty said softly. "I thought we... we might have a picnic."

"A picnic?" he echoed with a short sarcastic laugh.

Letty seemed determined to ignore his bad mood, and smiled up at him, her eyes bright with mischief. "Yes," she said, "a picnic. You work too hard, Chase Brown. It's about time you relaxed a little."

"Where's Cricket?" he asked, his tongue nearly sticking to the roof of his mouth. The inside was so dry it tasted like dust. It was difficult enough keeping his eyes off Letty without having to laze around some grassy knoll and pretend he had an appetite. Oh, he was hungry all right, but it was Letty he needed; only his wife would satisfy his cravings.

"Cricket went into town with Joy," she explained, climbing down off the mare with ease. "She's helping Joy get her classroom ready for her students, although it's debatable about how much help she'll actually be. School's only a couple of weeks away, you know."

While she was speaking, Letty emptied the saddle bags of the picnic items. She didn't look back at him as she spread a blanket across the top of the grass, seeming to accept the fact he would join her without further argument. Next she opened a large brown sack, then knelt and took out sandwiches and a thermos.

"Chase?" she paused and looked up at him.

"I... I'm not really hungry."

"You don't have to eat if you don't want, but at least take a break."

Reluctantly Chase climbed out of the saddle. It was either that or sit where he was and stare down the vee in her blouse. This woman knew tortures an executioner hadn't dreamed up yet. Every time she moved her nipples pointed in his direction, drawing his attention. He hadn't yet figured out how she managed it.

Despite the fact that Letty had spent weeks inside the house, recuperating from the surgery, her skin was glowing and healthy, Chase noted. She'd lost weight and had worked at putting it back on, but he would never guess it, looking at her now. Her jeans fit snugly, and naturally his eyes kept returning to the tight spot at the juncture between her legs. He tore his gaze from her and ground his teeth in silent agony.

"I made fresh lemonade. Would you like some?" She opened the thermos and poured some into a paper cup, ready to hand it to him.

"No... thanks." Chase felt both awkward and out of place. He moved closer to her, drawn by an invisible cord that tugged him at will. He felt defenseless, and what little control he'd managed to hold on to was crafted in the most slender of weaves. His hands ached with the need to feel and taste Letty and, by God, she knew it and was using it against him.

He dropped to his knees simply because standing demanded so much energy.

"The lemonade is sweet and cold," she coaxed. As if to prove her point, she took a sip.

The tip of her tongue came out and wiped off the excess moisture that had gathered at the edges of her mouth. Just watching her was akin of having someone viciously kick him in the stomach.

"I said I didn't want any," he replied gruffly.

They were facing each other, and Letty's gaze found his. Her eyes were wide, hurt and confused. She looked so damn beautiful, so innocent.

It came to him then that he should explain that he knew she was planning to go back to California at the earliest possible moment. But his mouth and tongue refused to cooperate. Letty continued to peer at him, as though trying to identify the source of his anger.

At that instant, Chase realized he was going to kiss her and there wasn't a damn thing he could do to stop himself. The choice had been taken away from him the minute she'd joined him and started jabbering about some silly picnic.

The ache to touch her had consumed him for weeks, tormenting him until he felt like a man in a torture chamber. He reached out for her, gently easing her into his embrace. She came willingly, offering no resistance.

"Letty..."

Intuitively she must have known his intention, because she tilted back her head, anticipating his lips.

At first, as though testing the very limits of his control, Chase merely touched his mouth to hers. His downfall was the way her fingers curled into his chest as though she had been as eager for his touch as he was for hers. He waited, savoring the simple taste and feel of her in his arms, and when he could deny himself no longer, he started to gently rub his lips against hers, back and forth in a slow, hypnotic motion, applying a mild pressure.

Following a soft sigh, Letty brought her arms around his neck. Chase's heart was pounding like a locomotive inside his chest. He paused, taking a moment to breathe in the sweet scent of her. She smelled of wildflowers and honey and the most potent wine.

His tongue touched her upper lip, so lightly it was a new brand of torture—one he was inflicting on himself. He couldn't be sure if the responsive rush of soft, choppy air was Letty's or his own.

He ran his fingers through her hair as he deepened the kiss. He stopped to breathe, then slowly eased them both onto the ground, lying side by side, until his chest gently brushed the tips of her breasts. Her nipples were rigid, and felt so hot against him he swore they were searing holes straight through him. Not taking the time to question what was happening, he sought her mouth once more. He felt consumed with such need, yet he forced himself to go slowly and be as gentle as possible.

Since Letty had returned to Red Springs, Chase had kissed her any number of times. For weeks he had gone to sleep each night remembering how good she'd felt in his arms. He'd treasured the memory, not knowing how long it would be before he could hold her again. Soon, he continued to promise himself; he would make love to her soon. The feel of her body moving against him had stalked him like a bounty hunter for weeks. Every detail of each time he'd touched her was emblazoned on his mind, and he could think of little else.

Now that she was in his arms again, he realized the anticipation hadn't prepared him for how perfect it would be. The reality outdistanced his imagination by light-years. He moaned, wanting her so much he felt ready to explode.

His mouth came down hard on hers as if to punish her for making him desire her so much, releasing all the tension stored inside him these sorry weeks of waiting. Letty's breathing was labored and harsh when he thrust his tongue deep into her mouth. Her fingers curled tighter against the material of his shirt, then gradually began to relax as she gave herself completely over to the kiss.

Chase was drowning, sinking so fast he was certain he'd been weighted down with cement blocks. Guttural moans, his own, filled his ears. Animal sounds emanated from him as he impatiently tore the gloves off his hands so he could work the buttons of her blouse free. He had to feel her breasts. The need in him was so great he felt as if he couldn't breathe again until he touched her there and experienced once more the velvet texture of her filling his hands.

All the while he was working at her blouse, he was rubbing himself against her, mutely letting her know how desperate he was to claim her as his wife. The need was primeval, the instinct to possess, to mate and to protect all jumbled together in one giant wave that swamped him.

At first Chase associated the rumbling in his ears as the thunder of his own heartbeat. It took him a full moment to realize it was the sound of an approaching horse.

Someone was coming.

Chase rolled away from Letty with a groan.

She sat up and looked at him, dazed and confused. Her eyes held his and he looked away.

"Your blouse...button it," he growled. His fingers were shaking so hard he knew he couldn't have helped her had his life depended on it.

"But—"

"Someone's coming."

"Oh."

The lone word bespoke frustration and disappointment and a multitude of other emotions that reflected his own. He retrieved his gloves and stood, using his body to shield Letty from any curious onlooker.

Within a couple of seconds Lonny trotted into view, sitting tall in the saddle.

"It's your brother," Chase warned, then added something low and succulent that wasn't meant for her ears. His friend had one hell of a sense of timing.

Chase saw Letty turn away and busy herself by laying out their lunch.

Lonny approached, pulling on the reins of his gelding. Chase glared at him, having trouble being so much as civil.

Looking more than a little chagrined, Lonny asked, "Am I interrupting anything?"

"Of course not," Letty said, her voice hardly sounding like her own. She kept her back to him, making a task of unfolding napkins and pouring lemonade.

Chase contradicted her words with a dark frown. The last person he wanted to see at the moment was Lonny. To his credit, his brother-in-law looked as if he wanted to find a hole to hide in, but that didn't help matters now.

"Actually, I was looking for Letty," Lonny explained, after clearing his throat. "I wanted to talk to her about...something. I stopped off at the house, but there wasn't anyone around. Mel was working in the barn and he told me she'd come out here. I guess I should have stopped to think things through."

"It would have been appreciated," Chase muttered tightly.

"I brought lunch out to Chase," Letty said.

Chase marveled at that soft sweet voice of hers and that she could recover so quickly.

"There's plenty if you'd care to join us," she added.

"You might as well," Chase said, echoing the invitation. The moment had been ruined and he doubted they would be able to recapture it.

Lonny's gaze traveled from one to the other. "Another time," he said, pulling on the gelding's reigns once more and turning away. "I'll talk to you later, Sis."

Letty nodded, and Lonny rode off.

"You should head back to the house yourself," Chase said gruffly. Letty was driving him crazy, but it seemed his sentence in hell hadn't been fully served. He clenched his jaw in frustration, refusing to look at her.

It wasn't until Letty had repacked the saddlebags and rode after her brother that Chase could breathe normally again.

Lonny was waiting for Letty when she trotted into the yard on Chase's mare. His look was sheepish, she noted, as he helped her down from the saddle, although she was more than capable of getting down on her own.

"I'm sorry, Letty," he muttered. Hot color circled his ears. "Damn, I should have thought before I went traipsing out there looking for you."

"It's all right," she said, offering him a gracious smile. Telling him that he'd interrupted a scene she'd been plotting for days wouldn't help matters any. Actually, her time with Chase told her several things, and all of them pleased and excited her. He was driving himself crazy with need for her. He wanted her as a wife as much as she yearned to be one.

"You may be willing to forgive me, but I don't think Chase's nature is nearly as generous. If looks could kill, I'd need a mortician about now."

"Don't worry about it," she returned absently. Her brother had foiled Plan A, but Plan B would go into action that very evening.

"Come on in the house and I'll pour you a glass of lemonade."

"I could use one," Lonny said, obediently following his sister into the kitchen.

Now that her head had cleared, Letty could see that something was troubling her brother, and whatever it was appeared to be serious. His brow was folded into a thick frown that formed a ledge over his deep blue eyes. Their color seemed clouded and his gaze stubbornly refused to meet hers.

"You wanted to talk to me about something?"

He nodded and took a seat at the round oak table, looking painfully awkward. Removing his hat, he set it on the table beside him. "Do you remember when you first came home how you invited Mary Brandon over to the house?"

Letty wasn't likely to forget it; the entire evening had been a catastrophe. Although her heart had been in the right place, everything else had been sadly off kilter.

"You seemed to think I needed a wife," Lonny continued.

"Yes...mainly because you'd wrapped yourself up in the ranch so completely that all your energies had become channeled in one direction."

He nodded, agreeing with her, which surprised Letty.

"The way I see it, Lonny, you work too damn hard. Over the past several years, you've grown so crusty and impatient. In my arrogant way I saw you as lonely, and decided to do something about it." A good deal of that impression had left her now, although she would still like to see her brother married and with a family. "At the time I was afraid the land was going to suck the life right out of you the way it did Mom."

"Are you still on that kick?"

Her brother's voice had risen with angry defiance the same way it had when she'd mentioned their mother weeks earlier.

"We had a giant fight about this once before, and I swore I wouldn't mention it again, but honestly, Letty, you've got Mom painted as some kind of martyr or something. She loved the ranch...she loved Wyoming."

"I know," Letty answered simply, quietly.

"If you realize that, then why are you arguing with me now?"

Letty ignored the question, deciding that discretion was well advised at the moment. "It came to me after I sorted through the carton of her things that you brought over shortly after the surgery," she said, toying with her glass. "I studied the quilt Mom was making and realized for the first time that her artistic talent was never wasted. She merely transferred it to another form. Quilting became her avocation and she loved it. At first I was surprised that she hadn't used the sewing machine to join the squares. Each stitch in that huge quilt was done by hand, every one of the countless thousands."

"I think she felt there was more of herself in it that way," Lonny suggested softly.

"The blending of colors, the design, each section spells out how much love and skill Mom put into it. When I decided to leave Red Springs after high school, I went because I didn't want to end up like Mom, and now I realize that I couldn't strive toward a finer goal."

Lonny frowned once more. "I don't understand. You left for California because you didn't want to be a rancher's wife, and yet you married Chase..."

"I know. But I love Chase. I always have. It wasn't being a rancher's wife that I objected to so much. Yes, the life is hard. But the rewards are plentiful. I knew that much nine years ago, and I realize it all the more profoundly now. My biggest fear was that I'd end up dedicating my life to ranching the same way Mom did and never achieve my own dreams."

"But Mom was happy. Never once did I hear her complain. I guess that's why I took such offense when you saw things so differently. You made it sound as if Mom had wasted her life, and nothing could be farther from the truth."

"I know that now," Letty murmured. "But I couldn't understand that for a long time. What troubled me most, I suppose, was that she could never paint the way she wanted. There was always something else that needed her attention, some other project that demanded her time. It wasn't until I saw the quilt that I understood so many things. She sketched for her own enjoyment, but the other things she crafted were for those she loved. The quilt she was working on when she died was for me, and it's taught me the most valuable lesson of my adult life."

Lonny's face relaxed into a smile. "I'm pleased, Letty. In the back of my mind I had the feeling that once you'd recuperated from the surgery you were going to get restless. But you won't, will you?"

"You've got to be kidding," she said with a soft laugh. "I'm a married woman, you know." She twisted the diamond wedding band around her finger a couple of times, as if that should be enough to prove her point.

"My place is with Chase—I plan to spend the rest of my life with him."

"I'm glad to hear that."

Lonny did look somewhat relieved, she noted. "We got off the subject, didn't we?" she asked with an apologetic smile. "You said you wanted to talk to me about something."

"Yes... well, it has to do with..." He hesitated, as if saying the church organist's name would somehow conjure up her form.

"Joy?" Letty offered.

Lonny nodded.

"What about her?"

In response, Lonny jerked his fingers through his hair and glared at the ceiling as though the light fixture would give him the words to explain. "I'm telling you, Letty, no one is more surprised by this than me. I've discovered that I like her. I... mean I *really* like her. The fact is, I can't stop thinking about her, but every time I try to talk to her, I do or say something stupid, and before I know what's happening, we're arguing."

Letty nodded to show she understood. She'd been witness to more than one of her brother and Joy's clashes.

"We don't just argue like normal civilized people," Lonny continued. "She can make me so angry that I don't even know who I am anymore."

Letty lowered her gaze to her glass, afraid her smile would irritate her brother, when he'd come to her for help. Only she was suffering through her own problem and didn't feel qualified to offer him any advice.

"I attend church services," Lonny continued, "and all I can see or hear is Joy. I don't think I've caught a single word the pastor's said all summer."

Her poor brother had it bad.

"Yet the minute I'm alone with her, I say some damn fool thing and we're at each other's throats again. The worst part is, I was in town this morning, and I heard that Joy's agreed to go out with Glen Brewster. The thought of her dating another man has me so twisted up inside that I can't think straight anymore."

"Glen Brewster?" The fact Joy would agree to date the other man surprised Letty. "Isn't he the guy who manages the grocery store?"

"One and the same," Lonny confirmed, scowling. "Can you imagined her going out with someone like Glen? Why, he's all wrong for her."

"Have you asked Joy out yourself?"

The way the color sneaked into his face was almost comical. "I don't think I'd better answer that. Everything I do with Joy is a comedy of errors. I want to take her out more than any woman I've known in my entire life, but everyone is working against me."

"Everyone?"

He paused and cleared his throat. "No, not everyone. Mainly I'm my own worst enemy—I know that sounds crazy. All I want you to do is to tell me what it is you women want from a man. If I know that, then maybe I can do something right with Joy. . . for once."

The door slammed in the distance. Lonny's gaze bounced up to meet Letty's. "Joy?"

"Probably."

"Oh, great," he groaned.

"Don't panic."

"Me?" he asked with a short, sarcastic laugh. "Why should I do that? The woman's told me in no uncertain terms that she never wanted to see me again. Her last words to me were—and I quote—'take a flying leap into the nearest cow pile.'"

"What did you say to her, for heaven's sake?"

He shrugged, looking uncomfortable. "I think it would be best if I didn't repeat it."

"Oh, Lord, Lonny! You are such a chauvinist! Maybe if you quit insulting her you'd be able to have a civil conversation."

"I can't seem to stop," he whispered between clenched teeth. "But I've decided something important. I'm going to marry her." The words had no sooner left his lips than the screen door opened.

Letty's gaze was forced from her brother as Cricket came flying into the kitchen, bursting to tell her mother about all her adventures with Joy at the grade school. The five-year-old started speaking so fast that the words ran together. "I-saw-my-classroom-and-I-got-to-meet-Mrs.-Webber...and I sat in a real desk and everything."

Joy followed Cricket inside the kitchen, but stopped abruptly when she saw Lonny. The look she wore suggested that if he said one word to her she would leave.

As if taking his cue, Lonny reached for his hat and stood. "I'd better get back to work. It was good talking to you, Letty," he said stiffly. His gaze skipped from his sister to Joy, and he politely inclined his head. "Hello, *Ms.* Fuller."

"*Mr.* Ellison." Joy dipped her head, too, ever so slightly.

The two gave each other a wide berth as Lonny made his way out of the kitchen. Before he opened the screen door, he sent a pleading glance toward Letty, but she wasn't exactly sure what he expected her to do.

Chase didn't come in for dinner, but that didn't surprise Letty. He'd avoided her so much lately that she rarely saw him in the evenings anymore. Even Cricket had commented on the fact. She obviously missed him, although he continued to make an effort to work with the child and the pony.

The house was dark and Cricket had been asleep for hours, when Letty heard the back door open. From the muffled sounds Chase was making, she knew he was in the kitchen, washing up. Next he would shower.

Some nights he came directly to bed; others he would sit in front of the television, delaying the time before he joined her. In the mornings he'd be gone before she awoke. Letty didn't know any man who worked as physically hard as Chase did on so little rest.

"You're later than usual tonight," she said, standing barefoot in the kitchen doorway.

He didn't turn around when he spoke. "There's lots to do this time of year."

"Yes, I know," she answered, willing to accept his lame excuse. "I didn't get much of a chance to talk to you this afternoon."

"What did Lonny want?"

So he was going to change the subject. Fine, she would let him. "Joy problems," she told him.

Chase nodded, opened the refrigerator and took out a carton of milk. He poured himself a glass, drank it down in one long swallow and then turned back toward the sink.

"Would you like me to run you a bath?"

"I'd rather shower." Reluctantly he turned to face her.

This was the moment Letty had been waiting for. She'd planned it all night. The kitchen remained dark; the only source of light was the moon, which cast flickering shadows over the wall. Letty was leaning against the doorjamb, one foot braced against the side, her hands behind her back. Her nightgown had been selected with care, a frothy see-through piece of chiffon that covered her from head to foot, yet revealed everything.

Letty knew she'd achieved the desired effect when the glass Chase was holding slipped from his hand and dropped to the floor. By some miracle it didn't shatter. Chase bent over to retrieve it, and even from that distance, Letty could see that his fingers were trembling.

"I saw Dr. Faraday this morning," she told him softly, keeping her voice low and seductive. "He gave me a clean bill of health."

"Congratulations."

"I think this calls for a little celebration, don't you?"

"Celebration?"

"I'm your wife, Chase. For the past few weeks you seem to have conveniently forgotten that fact. There isn't any reason why we should wait any longer."

"Wait?" His voice sounded like a tin echo.

Letty prayed for patience.

Before she could say anything more, he added abruptly, "I've been on the range for the past twelve hours. I'm hot and tired and badly in need of a shower."

"I've been patient all this time. A few more minutes isn't going to kill me." She'd never thought it would come to this, but she was literally being forced into seducing her own husband. Then so be it. But she wasn't exactly a sex kitten. Instinct was directing her behavior more than anything.

"Letty, I'm not in the mood. As I said, I'm tired and cranky and—"

"You were in the mood this afternoon," she whispered, moistening her lips with the tip of her tongue in a deliberately slow action.

He ground out her name, his hands knotting into fists at his side. "Perhaps it would be best if you went back to bed."

"Back to bed," she echoed, stunned. She dropped her foot and straightened, her hands on her hips. "You were supposed to take one look at me and be overcome with passion."

"I was?"

He was silently laughing at her, proving that she'd done an excellent job of making a fool of herself. Tears sprang to her eyes. Before the surgery and directly afterward, Chase had been the model husband—loving, gentle, concerned. He couldn't seem to do enough for her or spend enough time with her. Lately just the opposite was true. The man who stood across from her now wasn't the same one she'd married, and she didn't understand what had changed him.

Chase remained where he was, his feet planted apart, as if expecting her to defy him.

Without another word, Letty turned and left. Tears had blinded her vision by the time she walked into their bedroom and sat on the edge of the bed. She covered her face with both hands. She sat there, her thoughts in a whirlwind, gathering momentum, until she lost track of time.

"Letty."

She vaulted to her feet and wiped her hands down her face to remove all traces of moisture. "Don't you 'Letty' me, you...you arrogant cowboy." That was the worst thing she could come up with on such short notice.

He was fresh from the shower with nothing more than a flimsy towel wrapped around his waist.

"I had all these romantic plans for seducing you...and you made me feel I'm about as appealing as an old steer.

So you want to live like brother and sister? Fine. Two can play this game, fellow.'' She pulled the chiffon nightgown from her head and yanked open a drawer for an old flannel one, ceremoniously donning that. When she'd finished, she whirled around to face him, her fists grinding into her hips.

To her chagrin, Chase took one look at her and burst out laughing.

Chapter Thirteen

Don't you dare laugh at me," Letty cried, her voice trembling so badly the words wobbled off her tongue.

"I'm not," he told her softly. The humor had drained from him as fast as if someone had pulled a plug. What he'd told her earlier about being tired and cranky was true. He'd worked himself to the point of exhaustion. But he was a crazy man to reject the very thing he wanted most. Letty had come to him, wiped out every excuse not to hold and kiss her, and like a fool he'd told her to go back to bed. Who the hell did he think he was? Some mighty man of steel? He wasn't kidding anyone, least of all himself. When it came to loving Letty, he was as weak as a newborn kitten, he wanted her so much.

Silently he walked around the end of the bed toward her.

For every step Chase advanced, Letty took one away from him, until the backs of her knees were pressed against the mattress and there was nowhere else to go. Chase met her gaze, holding her captive, needing her love and her warmth so badly he quivered with it.

Ever so gently he brought his hands up to frame her face. He stroked away the moisture from her cheek, wanting to erase each one and beg her forgiveness for having hurt her. Slowly, in a caressing motion, he slid his hands down the sides of her neck until they settled on her shoulders.

"Nothing in my life has been as good as these past few months with you and Cricket," he told her, although the admission cost him dearly. He hadn't wanted to tie her to his side with words and emotional bonds. If she stayed, he wanted it to be of her own free will, not because she felt trapped.

"I can't alter the past," he whispered. "I don't have any control of the future. But we have now... tonight."

"Then why did you... laugh at me."

"Because I'm a fool. I need you, Letty, so much it frightens me." He heard the husky emotion in his voice, but didn't regret exposing his longing to her. "If I can only have you for a little while, I think we should take advantage of that time, don't you?"

He didn't give her an opportunity to respond, but urged her forward and placed his mouth over hers, kissing her several times, applying a gradual increasing pressure until her sweet responsive body was molded against him. He'd dreamed of holding Letty like this, pliable and soft in his arms, but once more reality exceeded his imagination.

"I was beginning to think you must hate me," she whimpered against his mouth. Then she moved her head from side to side, creating the most delicious kind of friction between their moist lips. The action was enough to make Chase's stomach muscles quake, and his breath quickened. He captured her head in his hands and held it still as he slanted his mouth over hers. He pressed his tongue into her mouth, celebrating their love and their need, engaging in a playful foray until she moaned and clung to him.

"Let's take this off," he said, tugging at the flannel gown. With a reluctance that excited him all the more, Letty stepped out of his arm just enough for him to lift the silly gown from her head and discard it. His hands shook with the action as he tried to disguise how eager he was.

"Oh, Letty," he groaned, looking at her, heaving a giant sigh of appreciation. "You're so beautiful." He felt humble just seeing her like this. Her natural beauty was so striking his knees went weak.

"The scar?" Her eyes were lowered.

The red line that ran down the length of her sternum would fade in the years to come, Chase knew. But he viewed it as a badge of courage. Very gently he leaned forward and kissed the long line.

"Oh, Chase, I thought...you found me ugly and that's why...you wouldn't touch me."

"No," he said harshly. "Never that."

"You didn't touch me. For weeks and weeks you stayed on your side of the bed, until I thought I'd go crazy."

"I couldn't be near you and not want you," he admitted hoarsely. "I had to wait until Dr. Faraday gave you a clean bill of health." If those weeks had been difficult for Letty, they had been doubly so for him.

"Do you want to touch me now?"

He nodded, feeling a good deal like a little boy set loose in a candy store with a month's allowance. From the moment they had discarded her gown, Chase hadn't been able to take his eyes off her. Her breasts were full and rose tipped, high and so round that just gazing at them caused a surge of hot blood to fill his manhood to the point of agony.

"Dear God, yes. I want to hold you the rest of my life." He brought his hand up and gently fanned her nipple with the pad of his thumb until it pearled and puckered. He closed his eyes as a wealth of sensations shot up his arms and moved directly to his heart. He'd been starving for the feel of her, a self-inflicted fast that had driven him to the point of lunacy.

He lifted his other hand and caressed the soft globes reverently, elevating them slightly and bunching them together, letting their lushness fill his palms. His tanned skin was dark and hers a soft ivory in comparison. Again and again he rotated his thumbs over her rosy peaks until Letty bit into her bottom lip and sighed his name—saying so much more.

Her low, seductive voice was all the encouragement Chase needed. He eased her onto the mattress, gently securing her there with his torso, fearing that his weight might hurt her. He had to taste her, had to experience anew all the pleasure she'd so unselfishly offered him earlier. He kissed her once, hard and fast, then slid his mouth to her breast, leaving a dewy trail down her neck and over her creamy smooth skin. His tongue rolled over the hard bead of her nipple, bathing it, lapping it, until her hands closed over his head. He sucked lightly. She sighed anew.

Chase couldn't wait a second longer. If he did, he would explode right then. Cautiously he moved over her, kissing her once, twice and again as he moved toward completion with her.

Letty smiled up at him and he inhaled sharply at the way she welcomed him readily, holding back nothing. He pressed forward ever so slightly until his penetration was complete. He felt as though he'd been swallowed whole into her sweet, luscious body. He was lost in her, swept away by her freshness, awed by her generosity, and he never wanted to be found.

He dared not move, but lay perfectly still, his breathing labored as he struggled with his own desire, which clamored for release.

"Oh, Chase," she murmured, reaching up to kiss him, her tongue outlining his lips. "This is so good..." She wrapped her arms around him and smoothed the hard muscles of his back.

Fearing still that he might be too heavy for her, he tried shifting his weight, but she stopped him by looping her feet around his ankles. "I love you," she whispered, and kissed him again, using her mouth in ways he had taught her. She slid her palms down the length of his spine, past the slight indentation at the small of his back, then settled over his buttocks.

Chase bit into his bottom lip and groaned.

"I never knew it could be so wonderful," she said, her voice filled with awe.

Chase was unable to find the words that would convey all the pleasure he was experiencing. Unable to delay any longer, he began to gently pump his hips against hers. He stroked the narrow walls of her womanhood again and again, alternating his rhythm in an effort to hold off his tumult as long as possible.

She fit him so snugly, closed around him so firmly, gloving his manhood with such perfection that he shuddered each time he delved into her. With each stoke, the tips of her breasts brushed his chest, creating a new kind of agony, until he was breathless with anticipation. When his release came, he ground his teeth and moaned her name. They clung to each other, panting, as they were cast into the heavens, then left to gently float back to earth.

Chase rolled onto the mattress beside Letty and gathered her in his arms. He felt the moisture that slid down the side of her face and became instantly alarmed. Although he'd been careful, he must have hurt her in some way—perhaps it had been too soon after the surgery. Regret filled him and he thought to ask her forgiveness, when she folded her arms around his neck and buried her face there, kissing him again and again.

"I hurt you?" he asked, silently cursing himself.

"No...no," she countered adamantly, shaking her head. "It was so beautiful...I didn't know anything could ever be this exquisite." She kissed him, then snuggled close, asleep before he could tell her all the words that had been stored up in his heart all these months.

Perhaps it was better this way. Her sensual nature had haunted him for weeks. Now there was no reason to hold back any longer, and he had every intention of loving her well. Sleep lapped at him, and briefly he wondered, before fatigue claimed him, how he had ever been able to resist her for so long.

Letty awoke at dawn, securely tucked in Chase's arms. She felt utterly content, and excited. Plan B hadn't worked out exactly the way she'd thought it would, but her scheme had certainly produced the desired effect. Happiness gushed over her like a churning waterfall and she hugged her arms close about her. For a moment, in Chase's arms the night before, she'd thought she might be dying. No wonder the French referred to lovemaking as "the little death." She felt like sitting up and throwing her arms into the air and shouting for sheer joy. She was a wife!

"'Morning," Chase whispered, and rubbed his hand down his face.

He didn't look at her, as if he half expected her to be embarrassed by the intimacies they'd shared the night before. Letty's thoughts did a tailspin. Dear heaven, had she said or done something a married woman shouldn't?

She was about to voice her fears, when her husband turned, fastening her to the bed, his arms braced on either side of her head. She met his eyes, unsure of what he was thinking. Slowly he lowered his mouth to hers, kissing her with a hungry need that surprised as much as delighted her.

"How long do we have before Cricket wakes up?" he asked.

He moved slightly and Letty felt his bulging manhood brush against her thigh. A slow smile eased its way across her face as she looped her arms around her husband's neck.

"Long enough," she whispered back.

In the days that followed, Letty was convinced that Chase was insatiable. Not that she minded. In fact, she was delighted that his need to make love to her was so great. Chase touched and held her often and each caress caused her to long for sundown. The nights were theirs.

Cricket went to bed early, often tired out from the long day's activities. As always, Chase was more than patient with her, reading her bedtime stories and making up a few of his own, which he dutifully repeated for Letty.

Cricket taught him the game of blowing out the light that Letty had played with her from the time she was a toddler. The little girl seemed utterly content to have

Chase take over the role of parent. Every time she watched Chase with her daughter, Letty was amazed at how gentle and good he was to Cricket.

Letty couldn't remember a time when she was happier. Chase had never verbally told her he loved her, but she was reassured of his devotion in a hundred different ways. He'd never been a man to freely communicate his feelings, and the years hadn't changed that. But the looks he gave her, the gentle way he reached for her and loved her, told her everything she needed to know.

The first week of September Cricket started kindergarten. On the opening day of school, Letty drove her daughter into town and lingered after class had started to talk to the other mothers for a few minutes. Then, feeling a little melancholy, she returned to the ranch alone. A new world was about to open up for Cricket, and Letty would soon claim a slightly lesser role in her daughter's young life.

Letty pulled into the yard, parked the truck and walked into the kitchen. Chase wasn't due back to the house until lunchtime and Letty's morning was free. She did a little housework, but without a lot of enthusiasm. After putting a load of clothes in the washer, she decided to vacuum.

Once in the living room, she was drawn by all the emotion churning inside her to the old upright piano. She stood over the keys and with one finger played a couple of the songs she'd taught Cricket.

Before she knew it, she'd slipped onto the bench and ran her hands up and down the yellowing keys, playing a few familiar chords. Soon she was singing, and it felt wonderful, truly wonderful, to release some of the emotion she was experiencing in song.

She didn't know how long she'd been sitting there when she looked up and noticed Chase standing there, watching her. His frown was tight, his eyes round and sad.

"Your voice is as beautiful as always."

"Thank you," she said, feeling a little shy. It had been months since she'd sat at the piano like this and sung. Once it had been her life, her dream; now it was a way to celebrate advancing a stage in her life. Cricket had started school and soon, God willing, she would have other children to love and nurture. She had Chase now and her commitment to him exceeded by far any public acclaim her voice would ever bring her.

"It's been a long time since I've heard you."

She scooted off the piano bench and closed the keyboard. It was in her mind to tell him she didn't do this often, knowing how he frowned upon her playing. That saddened Letty—even more so because she didn't understand his feelings.

An awkward silence passed.

"Chase," she said, realizing why he must be in the house. "I'm sorry. I didn't realize it was time for lunch already."

"It isn't," he said.

"Is anything wrong?" she asked, feeling unnerved and not knowing why.

"No." His eyes filled with tenderness and something else she couldn't name. It looked as if it could be fear or pain, but that made no sense to her. Chase had no reason to feel either that she knew.

Not knowing what directed her, she slipped into his arms, hugging him close. He held himself so stiffly, so tense, and she couldn't fathom the problem.

Tilting her head up, Letty studied him, not knowing what to think. He glided his thumb over her lips and she captured it between her teeth. "Kiss me," she said, knowing one sure way of reassuring him.

He complied, kissing her ravenously, running his hands through her short, curly hair. His mouth was both urgent and tender at once. His tongue probed the recess of her mouth as his hand slipped from her shoulder to her breast, covering it, kneading the pliant flesh.

Letty felt him relax against her, and sighed her relief.

"I need you, Letty," he murmured against her mouth. "Feed me. Nourish me."

"Now?" she asked, amazed.

He nodded, almost shy with his request.

Letty could deny him nothing and she answered him with her lips. Chase groaned and kissed her rapaciously, using his mouth and his tongue as if she were unsuspecting prey. He nibbled his way down her throat, while his fingers worked at lifting her sweater and unfastening her bra.

"Chase," she said softly, taken by surprise at the searing heat of his passion. "Let's go in the bedroom."

"I don't know if I can wait that long," he moaned.

They did make it into their room, but just barely. Chase lifted her into his arms, carried her upstairs and then gently deposited her on the bed. He joined her a couple of seconds later, removed her sweater and bra completely, then feasted on her breast, taking as much of it into his mouth as possible. Already he was working on the zipper of her jeans.

Again and again he whispered her name, as though in entreaty. Letty had never seen him like this, so eager, so impatient. Until now their lovemaking had been a slow exercise; they'd striven to prolong the pleasure until the last possible second. It wasn't that way now. Chase couldn't get her clothes off her fast enough. His love words were disjointed, his breathing hard and ragged.

She longed to strip him of his clothing, too, but he wouldn't allow it. Capturing her hands and holding them prisoner above her head, he sheathed himself in her dewy warmth in one fierce stroke.

Letty cried out at the swift flow of pleasure.

Chase's moan joined hers. Only then, she noted, did he pause; only then did he breathe again.

When it was over, Letty was bathed in the golden glow of exhaustion and supreme satisfaction. She ran her hands down his rippling muscles and released a long, slow sigh that sounded something like the purring of a cat.

Chase's face was buried in the hollow of her throat. She burrowed her fingers in his hair, needing to continue to touch him. "I think I've created a monster," she murmured, unable to keep the happy excitement out of her voice.

Chase lifted himself off her and supported his weight with his forearms. He kissed her once more. "I want you as often as I can have you before you go," he whispered, refusing to meet her gaze.

"Before I go?" she repeated. "I don't understand."

Chase climbed off the bed and quickly rearranged his clothing. He didn't stop to look at her as he stuffed his shirttail into the waist of his jeans. "I accepted the fact when I married you that sooner or later you would leave," he said, his voice filled with resignation.

Letty was so stunned, so shocked, that for a second she couldn't believe what she was hearing. She sat up and brushed the hair from her face. "Let me see if I understand you correctly. I married you, but you seem to think that I did that as a lark . . . that I had no intention of remaining in the relationship and that sooner or later I'd fly the coop? Am I understanding you correctly?" It was an effort for her to disguise her sarcasm.

"You were facing a life or death situation. I offered you an alternative because of Cricket."

Chase seemed to think that explained everything. "I love you, Chase Brown. I loved you when I left Red Springs. I loved you when I came back...I love you even more now."

He turned his back to her. "I never said I felt the same way about you."

The world seemed to skid to a halt; everything went perfectly still. Her heart was ramming against her chest like a machine gun that repeatedly misfired.

"True," she said when she could find her voice. "But you show me every day how much you do. I don't need the words, Chase. You can't hide what you feel for me."

He was making his way to the door when he turned back and snorted softly, once. "Don't confuse great sex with love, Letty."

She leaped to her knees atop the bed, unbelievably hurt and fiercely angry. If he'd been looking to destroy her, he'd found the perfect means.

"Do you want me to leave, Chase? Is that what you're saying?"

"I won't ask you to stay."

"In . . . in other words, I'm free to walk out of here anytime?"

He nodded. "You can go now, if that's what you want."

"That's generous of you," she snapped.

He didn't respond.

"I get it," she cried sharply, waving her hand at him as if she were orchestrating some momentous event. "Everything's neatly falling into place now. Every time I sit down at the piano, I can feel your displeasure. Why did you bring it here in the first place if it bothered you so much?"

"It wasn't my bright idea," he returned curtly. "Joy thought it would help you recuperate. If I'd had my way, it would never have left Lonny's place."

"Take it back, then."

"I will once you're gone."

Letty pressed her hand against her forehead. "I can't believe we're having this conversation. I love you, Chase... I don't ever want to leave you."

"Whatever you decide is fine, Letty," he said, and again his voice was filled with resignation. "That decision is yours." With that he walked out of the bedroom and out of the house.

For several minutes, Letty did nothing but sit on the top of the bed, her thoughts churning and boiling, spitting over, scalding her pride. Chase's feigned indifference infuriated her more than anything. Hadn't the past few weeks meant anything to him? Obviously that was what he wanted her to think. He was pretending to be so damn smug...so damn condescending, that it demanded everything in her for her not to haul out her suitcases that instant and walk away from him just to prove him right.

His words made a lie of all the happiness she'd found since marrying him. Furious tears filled her eyes. Chase wanted her to think he was using her, and he might as well; he'd paid a steep price for the privilege—he'd married her.

Letty sank back down onto the bed and covered her face with her hands, feeling wretched to the very marrow of her bones.

All along, like some romantic fool, she'd innocently held on to the belief that everything between her and Chase would be perfect now and forever after. It was a blow to her pride to discover otherwise. She had faced death, stared it down. But her husband's attitude was a far greater challenge.

When she'd first come back to Wyoming, Letty had believed her life was nearly over and the only things that awaited her were pain and regrets. Instead Chase had gifted her with a glimpse of happiness. He had shown her that her life could be filled with every good thing and that the very best part of it lay stretched before them. Then he'd taken her hand in his and lovingly led the way.

With Chase, for the first time in years Letty had experienced an immeasurable sense of inner satisfaction and joy. She'd discovered a peace that comes from inside oneself, and all because of this man and his love for her and Cricket.

Tears rained down her face and she wiped them away with the back of her hand. Nearly blinded by them, she climbed off the bed and reached for her purse. She had to get away to think, put order to her raging thoughts.

Chase was in the yard when she walked out the kitchen door. He paused, and out of the corner of her eye, Letty noted that he advanced two steps toward her, then abruptly stopped. Apparently he'd changed his mind about whatever he was going to say or do. Which was just as well, since Letty wasn't in the mood to talk to him.

His gaze followed her as she moved toward the truck, as if he suspected her of leaving him right then and there. As if he didn't expect her to return.

Perhaps that was exactly what she should do.

Chapter Fourteen

Letty had no idea where she was headed. All she knew was that she had to get away. She toyed with the idea of driving to town and waiting for Cricket. But it was still awhile before the kindergarten class was scheduled to be dismissed. In addition, Cricket was so looking forward to riding the bus home. In her kindergarten-geared mind, taking the school bus was the height of maturity, and she'd been looking forward to it for weeks. Letty didn't want to ruin that for her daughter.

As she drove aimlessly down the winding country road, Letty attempted to put the disturbing events of the morning in perspective. To even consider leaving Chase, if only for a day or two, would be an overreaction on her part, but she didn't know how to deal with this situation. The frustration swamped her senses. One moment she had everything a woman could ever want; the next she was struck to the soul, suffering from emotional poverty. Letty felt isolated and vulnerable in a way she couldn't fully understand or explain. The safe harbor she'd anchored in with her marriage to Chase had been unexpectedly filled with mines. Letty felt as if they were primed and ready to explode in her face with the evening tide.

Without realizing where she'd driven, Letty noticed that the hillside where she'd so often sat with Chase was just over the next ridge. With a chagrined smile, she stopped the truck and parked. Their hillside would give her the peace and inner guidance she sought now.

With the autumn sun warming her, she strolled over to the crest of the hill and sat on a grassy knoll. Her thoughts were warped, confused, jumbled. A few head of cattle rested under the shade of trees near the stream below, and Letty idly watched them while her thoughts churned in her mind. How peaceful the animals seemed, how content. Actually, she was a little surprised to see them grazing there, since she'd heard Chase comment that he was moving his herd in the opposite direction. But where he chose to let his cattle graze was the least of her worries.

A slow thirty minutes passed. What Letty found so frustrating, so disheartening about the confrontation with Chase was his almost blithe acceptance of the fact that she would eventually leave him. He'd gone to great lengths to let her know the choice was completely up to her and that when she did decide to pack up and move, he would accept her going with little more than a sigh and a shrug.

To give up on their love, their marriage and all the happiness that their lives together would bring was trauma enough. But for him to do so with little more than a twinge of regret was almost more than Letty could bear. Chase's almighty pride wouldn't allow him to let her know he loved her enough to ask her to stay. Apparently it was easier to accept the fact that she was leaving and to pretend indifference.

Yet he loved her and he loved Cricket. Despite his heartless words to convince her otherwise, Letty could never doubt either of those things.

Standing, Letty let her arms hang limply at her side. She didn't know what she should do. Perhaps getting away for a day or two wasn't such a bad idea.

The thought started to gather momentum in her mind. It was as she turned to leave that Letty noted the steer that had separated itself from the others. She paused, then glared at the brand, surprised it wasn't Chase's. Before she left Sweet Valley she would let Chase know old man Wilber's cattle were on his property.

Chase was nowhere to be seen when Letty arrived back at the house. That was just as well, since she planned to be in and out of the place within a matter of minutes. She stuck a few things in a suitcase for herself, left it in the hallway while she rushed upstairs and grabbed several items for Cricket. Letty wasn't sure when she was going to tell her daughter about this unexpected vacation, but she would think of something later.

Chase was standing in the kitchen when she reached the bottom of the stairs. His eyes were cold and cruel in a way she hadn't seen since she'd first returned home. He lifted her suitcase and set it by the back door as if eager for her to be on her way.

"I see you decided to leave now," he said, leaning indolently against the kitchen counter.

His arms were folded over his chest as if her coming and going were of no concern to him. If he'd revealed the least amount of regret or indecision, Letty might have considered reasoning with him, but it was painfully apparent he couldn't be more pleased.

"I thought I'd spend a few days with Lonny."

"Lonny," Chase repeated with a short, sarcastic laugh. "I bet he'll love that."

"He won't mind." A half-truth, but the minor transgression was worth the effort if Chase believed her.

"You're sure of that?"

It was obvious from Chase's lack of concern that he wasn't going to invite her to stay at the ranch until they resolved their differences—which was what Letty had hoped he would do. If anything, he looked elated she was leaving.

"If Lonny *does* object, then I'll simply have to find some place in town."

"Do you have enough money?"

"Yes . . ." Letty said, striving to sound casual.

"I'll be more than happy to supply whatever you need."

Chase spoke with such a flippant air that it cut her to the quick. "I won't take any from you."

Chase shrugged. "Fine."

Everything within Letty wanted to shout at him to give her some sign, anything, that would show her how much he wanted her to stay. It was the whole reason she was staging this. His nonchalant response was so painful, that just talking to him and not breaking down and weeping was all Letty could manage.

"Is this what you really want?" she asked, her voice little more than a tight whisper.

"If you're set on leaving, I'm not going to stop you." Chase's voice rang clear with male pride and an overabundant supply of arrogance.

Letty reached down for her suitcase, tightening her fingers around the handle. Standing there discussing the fact wasn't solving anything. "I'll think up some excuse to give Cricket." She made it all the way to the back door before Chase stopped her.

"Letty..."

She whirled around, her heart ringing with happy excitement until she saw the look in his eyes.

"Before you go, there's something I need to know," he said, his face tight and dark. "Is there any possibility you could be pregnant?"

His question bounced off the walls in an eerie echo that rang in her ears.

"Letty?"

Chase may have uttered her name softly, but in reality he was repeating the question. She met his gaze. Some of his arrogance was gone, replaced with a tenderness that had been far too rare these past few hours. "No," she whispered, her voice hardly audible.

Chase's eyes drifted closed, but she didn't know if it was with regret or relief. The way things had been going between them, she didn't want to know.

"I... went to the hillside," she said in a low voice that wavered slightly despite her best effort to control her emotions. She sucked in her breath, squared her shoulders and continued. "There were several head of cattle there. The brand is Wilber's."

Chase clenched his jaw so tightly that the sides of his face went pale under his tan. "So you know," he said, his voice husky and filled with dread. His gaze skirted hers and his fists were balled at his sides as if he would have given his soul for her not to have learned the truth.

Letty was baffled. Chase's first response to the fact she'd seen his neighbor's steers on his property made no sense to her. The truth was, she didn't have a clue why he should react so profoundly.

Then it struck Letty with all the impact of a runaway truck. "You sold those acres to Mr. Wilber, didn't you? Why?" That land had been in Chase's family for over three generations. Letty couldn't fathom what could be important enough for him to relinquish those acres. Not once in all the weeks they'd been married or before had he given her any indication that he was financially strapped.

"I don't understand," she said in a tight whisper, growing more confused than ever. "There wasn't any insurance money for my surgery, was there, Chase?"

She'd been so unsuspecting, so confident when he'd told her that everything had been taken care of. She should have known an insurance company wouldn't cover a preexisting condition without a lengthy waiting period.

"Chase?" She continued to hold him with her eyes. She was incredulous, shocked. She set the suitcase down and advanced one small step toward her husband. "Why did you lie to me about the insurance?"

He tunneled his fingers through his hair.

"Why would you do something like that? It doesn't make any sense." Very little of this day had. "Didn't you realize the state had already agreed to cover all the expenses?"

"You hated being a charity case. I saw the look in your eyes when I found your welfare check. It was killing you to have to accept that money."

"Of course I hated it, but I managed to swallow my pride—it was necessary. But what you did wasn't. Why would you sell your land? I just can't believe you'd do it." The very thought was inconceivable to Letty. Chase loved every square inch of Sweet Valley. Parting with so much as a single acre, especially the prime ones near the creek, would be akin to his cutting off one of his fingers.

Chase turned away from her and walked over to the sink. His shoulders jerked up and down in a hard shrug as he braced his hands against the edge. "All right, if you must know. I did it because I wanted you to marry me."

"But you said the marriage was for Cricket's sake...in case anything happened to me...then you could raise her."

"That was an excuse."

The words were wrenched from him as though she'd had to torture them out of him.

"I love you, Letty. I have from the time you were fifteen years old."

He made it sound as though caring about her was something very wrong. "I love you, too...I always have," she whispered, awed by what he'd done and, more important, the reason behind it. "I told you how I felt about you not more than three hours ago, but you practically threw it back in my face. If you love me so much," she murmured, still having trouble comprehending what was happening, "why couldn't you let me know it? Would that have been so wrong?"

"I didn't want you to feel trapped."

"Trapped?" This conversation was as clear as a Louisiana mist. She didn't know how Chase could possibly view their marriage in such a light. He made it sound as if she'd been forcibly taken hostage and was struggling to find her way back to freedom.

"Sooner or later I realized you'd want to return to California. I knew that when I asked you to marry me. I accepted it."

"That's ridiculous," Letty cried. "I don't ever want to go back. There's nothing for me there. Everything that's ever been good in my life is right here with you."

Chase turned to face her, his features tight. "What about the fight you and Lonny had about your mother? You said—"

"I realized how wrong I was about Mom," she interrupted, gesturing freely with her hands. "My mother was a wonderful woman—but more significant than that, she was fulfilled as a person. I'm not going to say she had an easy life—we both know differently. But she loved the challenge here. She loved her art, too, and found diverse ways of expressing her talent. The problem was that I was just to blind to recognize it. I was so caught up in striving toward my dreams that I failed to realize my happiness was right here in Red Springs with you. The biggest mistake I ever made was leaving you. Do you honestly believe I'd willingly do it again?"

A look of hope crept into Chase's gaze.

"Telling me I'm free to walk away from you is one thing," Letty said softly, tears filling her eyes. "But you made it sound as if you wanted me gone—that you couldn't wait for me to get out of your life. You weren't even willing to give us a chance. That hurt more than anything."

"I was afraid to," he admitted, his voice husky and low. "Over and over again you kept saying that you wouldn't stop me from leaving. It was almost as if you'd been waiting for it to happen, because I'd been such a disappointment to you."

"Letty, no, I swear that isn't true."

"Then why are you standing way over there... and I'm way over here, loving you so much I could weep." She raised her fingertips to her face and chuckled. "In fact, I *am* crying."

"Dear God, Letty." He devoured the space between them in three giant strides, wrapping his arms around her with such force that the air was squeezed from her lungs. But it was a joy-filled kind of pain. When he lifted his head, their eyes melted together. "I love you, Letty, more now than I thought it was possible to care about anyone. I haven't told you that, and I was wrong. You deserve to hear all the words."

"Oh, Chase, you didn't need to say them for me to know how you feel. That was what was so confusing. I couldn't doubt you loved me, yet you made my leaving sound like some long-awaited event."

"I couldn't let you know how much I was hurting."

"But I was hurting, too."

"I know, love, I know." He rained hot, urgent kisses over her face, as if he couldn't get enough of her.

His kiss intensified, and Letty threaded her fingers through his hair, glorying in the closeness they shared. She was humbled by the sacrifice he'd made for her. Awe-struck. He could have given her no greater proof of his love.

"Chase." His name was a broken cry across her lips. Her tears made her cheeks slippery as he rubbed his jaw over her upturned face. "The land... you sold... I can't bear to think of you losing it."

He captured her face and tilted it back. "It's not as bad as it sounds. I have the option of buying it back at a future date, and I will."

"But—"

He silenced her with his mouth, kissing away her objections and her concerns. Then he tore his mouth from hers and buried it in the hollow of her throat, kissing her there. "I would gladly have sold all of Sweet Valley if it'd been necessary." He plunged his tongue recklessly into her mouth and roamed at will.

By the time he was finished Letty was clinging to him, too weak to argue.

"You've given me so much," he whispered, his words husky with need. "My life was an empty shell until you came back and brought Cricket with you. I love her, Letty, as if she were our own. I want to adopt her and give her my name."

Letty nodded through her tears, knowing that Cricket would want that, as well. Her daughter had loved Chase from the moment they'd met. It was as if it had all been by design.

Chase inhaled deeply and exhaled in a long, slow breath. "As much as I wanted you to stay, I couldn't let you know that. When I asked if you might be pregnant, it was a desperate attempt from a desperate man to find a way, any way, I could to keep you here, despite all the claims to the contrary. I think my heart dropped to my feet like a lead ball when you told me you weren't."

Letty wasn't exactly sure she understood.

He gently framed her face with his hands and stared down at her with a tender warmth. "I don't know that I can explain this, but when I mentioned the possibility of you carrying my child, a vision of two little boys filled my mind."

Letty smiled. "Twins?"

"No," Chase said softly. "They were a year or more apart. I saw them so clearly, standing beside each other, and somehow I knew deep down in my soul that those two were going to be our sons. The day you had the surgery...I saw them then, too. I wanted those children so badly that for a moment I couldn't so much as breathe. You were about to walk out the door and I didn't know if you'd ever come back. I knew if you left me, the emptiness would return, and I didn't know if I could bear it. I'd tried to prepare myself for your going, but I didn't know if I could have ever fully accepted it."

"I couldn't have stayed away for long. My heart is here with you. You gave me life, taught me to forgive myself for the past and cherish whatever the future may hold."

His eyes drifted closed. "We have so much, Letty." He was about to say more, when the kitchen door burst open and Cricket came rushing into the room.

Chase broke away from Letty just in time for the five-year-old to vault into his arms. "I have a new friend, and her name's Michelle and she's got a pony, too. I like school a whole bunch, and Mrs. Blake let me hand out some papers and she told me I could be her helper every day."

Chase hugged the little girl. "I'm pleased you like school so well, sweetheart." Then he put his hand on Letty's shoulder, pulling her to him.

Letty leaned into his strength and shut her eyes, savoring the few moments of contentment. She'd found her happiness in Chase. She'd come home, prepared to die, and instead had found life in the most abundant form.

Sweet Valley was their future—here was where they would thrive. Here was where their sons would be born.

Cricket stepped to her mother's side, and Letty drew her daughter close. As she did, she caught a glimpse of the sky through the kitchen window. The Wyoming sky had never appeared bluer. Or filled with greater promise.

* * * * *

COMING NEXT MONTH

#571 RELUCTANT MISTRESS—Brooke Hastings
The prophecy clearly stated that a tall blond *haole* would enter Leilani's Hawaiian paradise, bringing both love and anguish. Was irresistible Paul Lindstrom that man, and was their mutual destiny one of passion or pain?

#572 POWDER RIVER REUNION—Myrna Temte
Their feuding fathers had snuffed out JoAnna and Linc's teenage romance, but a Powder River High reunion relit the fuse. Could their own stubborn wills stem an explosion this time?

#573 MISS LIZ'S PASSION—Sherryl Woods
Locking horns with angry parents was elementary for passionate schoolteacher Elizabeth Gentry—until she confronted single father Todd Lewis, who offered *her* some *very* adult education....

#574 STARGAZER—Jennifer Mikels
With a family scandal to live down, high-principled attorney David Logan knew he should avoid kooky occultist Jillian Mulvane. But her love potion proved extremely potent....

#575 THE LOVE EXPERT—Maggi Charles
Stacy Mackenzie suddenly found herself in uncomfortably close quarters with sex psychologist James Ashley-Sinclair. Could she possibly hold her own with this notorious love expert?

#576 'TIL THERE WAS YOU—Kathleen Eagle
Forest ranger Seth Cantrell had chosen quiet solitude. Skier Mariah Crawford was always in the limelight. One night of passion changed their two lives forever...by making them reckon with a third.

AVAILABLE THIS MONTH:

#565 MISS ROBINSON CRUSOE
Tracy Sinclair

#566 RENEGADE
Christine Flynn

#567 UNFINISHED BUSINESS
Carole Halston

#568 COME GENTLE THE DAWN
Eileen Nauman

#569 TENDER TRAP
Lisa Jackson

#570 DENIM AND DIAMONDS
Debbie Macomber

INDULGE A LITTLE SWEEPSTAKES

OFFICIAL RULES

SWEEPSTAKES RULES AND REGULATIONS. NO PURCHASE NECESSARY.

1. NO PURCHASE NECESSARY. To enter complete the official entry form and return with the invoice in the envelope provided. Or you may enter by printing your name, complete address and your daytime phone number on a 3 x 5 piece of paper. Include with your entry the hand printed words "Indulge A Little Sweepstakes." Mail your entry to: Indulge A Little Sweepstakes, P.O. Box 1397, Buffalo, NY 14269-1397. No mechanically reproduced entries accepted. Not responsible for late, lost, misdirected mail, or printing errors.

2. Three winners, one per month (Sept. 30, 1989, October 31, 1989 and November 30, 1989), will be selected in random drawings. All entries received prior to the drawing date will be eligible for that month's prize. This sweepstakes is under the supervision of MARDEN-KANE, INC. an independent judging organization whose decisions are final and binding. Winners will be notified by telephone and may be required to execute an affidavit of eligibility and release which must be returned within 14 days, or an alternate winner will be selected.

3. Prizes: 1st Grand Prize (1) a trip for two to Disneyworld in Orlando, Florida. Trip includes round trip air transportation, hotel accommodations for seven days and six nights, plus up to $700 expense money (ARV $3,500). 2nd Grand Prize (1) a seven-night Chandris Caribbean Cruise for two includes transportation from nearest major airport, accommodations, meals plus up to $1,000 in expense money (ARV $4,300). 3rd Grand Prize (1) a ten-day Hawaiian holiday for two includes round trip air transportation for two, hotel accommodations, sightseeing, plus up to $1,200 in spending money (ARV $7,700). All trips subject to availability and must be taken as outlined on the entry form.

4. Sweepstakes open to residents of the U.S. and Canada 18 years or older except employees and the families of Torstar Corp., its affiliates, subsidiaries and Marden-Kane, Inc. and all other agencies and persons connected with conducting this sweepstakes. All Federal, State and local laws and regulations apply. Void wherever prohibited or restricted by law. Taxes, if any are the sole responsibility of the prize winners. Canadian winners will be required to answer a skill testing question. Winners consent to the use of their name, photograph and/or likeness for publicity purposes without additional compensation.

5. For a list of prize winners, send a stamped, self-addressed envelope to Indulge A Little Sweepstakes Winners, P.O. Box 701, Sayreville, NJ 08871.

DL-SWPS

INDULGE A LITTLE SWEEPSTAKES

OFFICIAL RULES

SWEEPSTAKES RULES AND REGULATIONS. NO PURCHASE NECESSARY.

1. NO PURCHASE NECESSARY. To enter complete the official entry form and return with the invoice in the envelope provided. Or you may enter by printing your name, complete address and your daytime phone number on a 3 x 5 piece of paper. Include with your entry the hand printed words "Indulge A Little Sweepstakes." Mail your entry to: Indulge A Little Sweepstakes, P.O. Box 1397, Buffalo, NY 14269-1397. No mechanically reproduced entries accepted. Not responsible for late, lost, misdirected mail, or printing errors.

2. Three winners, one per month (Sept. 30, 1989, October 31, 1989 and November 30, 1989), will be selected in random drawings. All entries received prior to the drawing date will be eligible for that month's prize. This sweepstakes is under the supervision of MARDEN-KANE, INC. an independent judging organization whose decisions are final and binding. Winners will be notified by telephone and may be required to execute an affidavit of eligibility and release which must be returned within 14 days, or an alternate winner will be selected.

3. Prizes: 1st Grand Prize (1) a trip for two to Disneyworld in Orlando, Florida. Trip includes round trip air transportation, hotel accommodations for seven days and six nights, plus up to $700 expense money (ARV $3,500). 2nd Grand Prize (1) a seven-night Chandris Caribbean Cruise for two includes transportation from nearest major airport, accommodations, meals plus up to $1,000 in expense money (ARV $4,300). 3rd Grand Prize (1) a ten-day Hawaiian holiday for two includes round trip air transportation for two, hotel accommodations, sightseeing, plus up to $1,200 in spending money (ARV $7,700). All trips subject to availability and must be taken as outlined on the entry form.

4. Sweepstakes open to residents of the U.S. and Canada 18 years or older except employees and the families of Torstar Corp., its affiliates, subsidiaries and Marden-Kane, Inc. and all other agencies and persons connected with conducting this sweepstakes. All Federal, State and local laws and regulations apply. Void wherever prohibited or restricted by law. Taxes, if any are the sole responsibility of the prize winners. Canadian winners will be required to answer a skill testing question. Winners consent to the use of their name, photograph and/or likeness for publicity purposes without additional compensation.

5. For a list of prize winners, send a stamped, self-addressed envelope to Indulge A Little Sweepstakes Winners, P.O. Box 701, Sayreville, NJ 08871.

© 1989 HARLEQUIN ENTERPRISES LTD.

DL-SWPS

INDULGE A LITTLE—WIN A LOT!

Summer of '89 Subscribers-Only Sweepstakes

OFFICIAL ENTRY FORM

This entry must be received by: Nov. 30, 1989
This month's winner will be notified by: Dec. 7, 1989
Trip must be taken between: Jan. 7, 1990–Jan. 7, 1991

YES, I want to win the 3-Island Hawaiian vacation for two! I understand the prize includes round-trip airfare, first-class hotels, and a daily allowance as revealed on the "Wallet" scratch-off card.

Name ______________________________

Address ______________________________

City ____________ State/Prov. ______ Zip/Postal Code ______

Daytime phone number ______________________________
Area code

Return entries with invoice in envelope provided. Each book in this shipment has two entry coupons — and the more coupons you enter, the better your chances of winning!

DINDL-3

INDULGE A LITTLE—WIN A LOT!

Summer of '89 Subscribers-Only Sweepstakes

OFFICIAL ENTRY FORM

This entry must be received by: Nov. 30, 1989
This month's winner will be notified by: Dec. 7, 1989
Trip must be taken between: Jan. 7, 1990–Jan. 7, 1991

YES, I want to win the 3-Island Hawaiian vacation for two! I understand the prize includes round-trip airfare, first-class hotels, and a daily allowance as revealed on the "Wallet" scratch-off card.

Name ______________________________

Address ______________________________

City ____________ State/Prov. ______ Zip/Postal Code ______

Daytime phone number ______________________________
Area code

Return entries with invoice in envelope provided. Each book in this shipment has two entry coupons — and the more coupons you enter, the better your chances of winning!

© 1989 HARLEQUIN ENTERPRISES LTD.

DINDL-3